DETECTIVE LAURIANT INVESTIGATES:

A DEATH IN A DITCH

Saint Sauveur

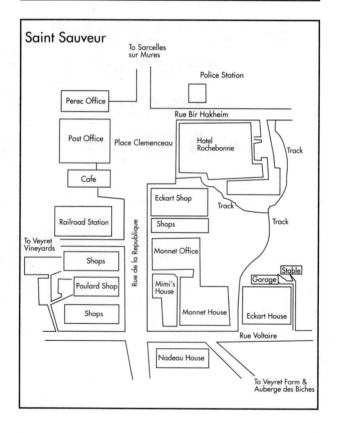

Saint Sauveur

To Sarcelles sur Mures

Police Station

Perec Office

Rue Bir Hakheim

Post Office

Place Clemenceau

Hotel Rochebonne

Track

Cafe

Eckart Shop

Track

Railroad Station

Rue de la Republique

Shops

Track

To Veyret Vineyards

Monnet Office

Shops

Stable

Poulard Shop

Mimi's House

Garage

Shops

Monnet House

Eckart House

Rue Voltaire

Nadeau House

To Veyret Farm & Auberge des Biches

DETECTIVE LAURIANT INVESTIGATES

A WorldKrime Mystery

featuring

A DEATH IN A DITCH

and

THE MURDER IN THE VENDEÉ

by
Graham R. Wood

Philadelphia

ISBN 1-890768-44-8

This book is a work of fiction. Names, characters,
places and incidents are either the product of the
author's imagination or are used fictitiously. Any resem-
blance to actual events or locales or persons, living or
dead, is entirely coincidental.

Library of Congress Cataloging-in-Publication Data

Wood, Graham R., 1945-
    (Death in a ditch)
    Detective Lauriant investigates: A WorldKrime
        mystery / by Graham R. Wood.-- 1st Intrigue Press ed.
        p. cm.
    Contents: Death in a ditch -- Murder in the Vendee.
    ISBN 1-890768-44-8
    I. Police--France--Fiction. 2. France--Fiction.
    I. Wood, Graham R., 1945- Murder in the Vendee.
    II. Title.

PR6123.O525 D43 2002
823'.92--dc21   2001052512

10 9 8 7 6 5 4 3 2 1

For
Lynda, Amelia, Vera and Trissie

A France in Turmoil and Transition

Since the Great Revolution of 1789, when the feudal regime was consigned to the guillotine, France has been governed by three monarchies, two empires, the sham-fascist Vichy political system of Marshal Pétain, and five republics.

The latest of these republics, the Fifth French Republic of General Charles de Gaulle, was born like the first, in violence, war and upheaval, when in May 1958, generals of Algeria threatened to bring revolt to Paris. In the midst of the tumult the call went up for the discarded hero General de Gaulle to return to lead France. Upon his return, the antiquated, threadbare regime of the Fourth Republic committed suicide.

De Gaulle granted Algeria independence in the face of those in the military who had supported his resumption of power in the mistaken belief that he shared their views. So resentment against de Gaulle was rife and attempted assassination and turmoil were its blood-stained bedfellows. De Gaulle was perceived by many as the betrayer of French history and a traitor to France. Thus, in the dying throws of French Algeria, the Organisation Armée Secrete (OAS)—an uneasy, deadly cabal was born, a convergence of soldiers and terrorists, of militant students and idealists with the merely fright-ened and desperate.

So, with bombs and with bullets, the OAS went about its business. The aim was to bring down the new govern-ment which had betrayed French Algeria and France herself. But if the roots of the OAS lay in the common people, the high foliage of the movement was found amongst the generals, the senior civil servants and the ousted politicians including certain ex-prime ministers.

A LADY'S MEMORIES
OF A FEW THINGS PAST

———————————

Mimi, mature and attractive, precisely dressed and perfectly groomed as always on these occasions, took a so delicate sip at her tiny glass of the fierce, raw marc . . . savoring it as it spread its fiery warmth across her pallet.

Her companion for her after dinner drink, an old acquaintance—indeed, she would like to think, an old friend—Superintendent Lauriant had suggested marc and after the richness of their meal, she had been glad of it's cathartic brutality.

It was growing late and the restaurant was gradually emptying as the clients shook hands with each other and with the owner and, one by one or in little melees, slipped out into what remained of the temptingly cool evening that had followed a warm day.

Here in the corner of the bar, Mimi placed her drink gently on the glass-topped table.

The table had wicker legs to match the large comfortable chair in which she sat back with consummate relief. She would have loved to have removed her shoes, but she was of an age where such weakness was unthinkable, and so the seemingly unendurable was endured and she turned her thoughts to other things.

Gently, the drab glow from the discretely shaded table lamp invaded the surrounding darkness, contriving to throw just the right amount of light around the two of them that a self-respecting restaurateur would deem chic.

The superintendent's choice of restaurant had, as always, been excellent.

A waiter emerged from the gloom and refilled her coffee cup—a small, white, thick Apilco, which Mimi thought would have been more at home in Helène's café in Saint Sauveur, than here in the so very fashionable Parisian Restaurante La Langoustine.

Saint Sauveur, she remembered. She and Lauriant had first met there almost six years before. Mimi sadly admitted to herself that she had already been middle-aged then. They had dined together in Paris at least twice a year since. It had become almost a ritual without being the chore that so many rituals so easily become.

As this time, their conversation was never forced. They merely resumed where they had left off—almost as if there had been no months-long interruption in their discussion. It was the ultimate measure of their growing ease in each other's company.

This meeting did have a slightly different air to it, however, in just one respect.

Today it was Superintendent Lauriant, not Mimi, who was the visitor from the provinces.

His work, he explained to Mimi, had taken him there. To the Vendeé.

He was honest enough to use the word banished.

And by contrast, Mimi was currently a Parisienne—at least for the month that she was borrowing her sister's apartment in what she fully realized was a most stylish area of the capital. Adele, her sister, was now marooned in the Mediterranean on some luxury cruise liner with a Russian name. A fate Mimi, had she ever been given the opportunity, would happily have wished to avoid. Nevertheless she had to admit, perhaps with a mental shake of the head, that her brother-in-law had done very well.

As always, in contrast to her sister's no doubt idyllic existence, Mimi worried about Lauriant. But she was more than wise enough not to let this show.

He drank too much and he certainly smoked too many cigarettes and the last few years had seen him become, well . . . sadder. Was that the right word? Mimi considered the problem. Emptier—yes, that was more precise.

She looked hard at him. He was over forty now—a little overweight but still careful of his appearance. A good jacket and smart trousers, she thought, without being expensive. Once, they would have been. Not tall, she saw, but he gave that impression despite being rounder at the shoulders than when she had first met him. The hair was thinner too, but still neatly cut rather short for these days, when hair clear of the collar, even in middle aged men, was a rarity. Deep down inside, she suspected that he was a worrier and that he was, perhaps, a disappointment to himself.

Now he had, it seemed to her, deliberately and almost literally buried himself in an obscure Vendeé village in the

Marais, of which she had never heard: L'Ile Bois Aubrand.

For a time her Lauriant (she sometimes thought of him that way) had been famous. He was the famous detective when he came to Saint Sauveur. That, she knew now, was why Guichard had asked him to come to her hometown. He was still well known and respected in some circles, but the heady days were gone. That, she fully recognized, was the way of the world.

The fashion and the gossip and the spotlight move on. She remembered some of them then and now: the film stars, the singers, the soldiers, the dancers, the sportsmen, the politicians. Now, with the OAS on the rampage in France, she supposed she would have to include the terrorists. There were names: Sartre, Clair, Truffaut, Camus—he had just died in an automobile crash, Malraux, and now the papers talked of people called Genet and Robbe-Grillet, Salan, Vadim, Debre. And there was Pompidou, Françoise Sagan and Brigitte Bardot. This time her shake of the head was not merely mental.

The cafés across the River Seine on the Left Bank now had scooters and motorbikes abandoned outside them. Some were gleaming to show the status and maybe the wealth, or, perhaps, the debt level of their owners, and others were dirty, battered and bent to demonstrate impeccable left wing credentials to a right wing government.

But, the student cafés really were what they had always

been: filled with the smell of pipe tobacco and beer, Galloise and cheap red wine, Disque Bleu and embryonic ideas—talk and, well . . . more talk.

That was both a comfort and a dilemma for a middle-aged devout Catholic lady from Saint Sauveur.

Then there was Algeria and the bombers, the oh-so-thin girls in the oh-so-short skirts—funny new fads for Coca-Cola, for Italian sports cars and fast food.

Which was the real France of the 1960's, she wondered? Perhaps, they all were.

Mimi sighed, as those of a certain age do when contemplating such things, remembering a simpler life in a simpler France. Lauriant looked up to see if she was all right. She smiled fondly at him, but said nothing, letting her unstructured thoughts roll on.

The groups who still highly regarded Lauriant were the only ones that really mattered to him anyway. Mimi understood that and, tired now, she just looked at him.

Through eyes more than half closed, she watched him and she remembered, warmly, the man with a head cold who had come to her home in Saint Sauveur all those years before.

1

RICH LOBSTER, UNPAID ALIMONY & A CHANCE TO ESCAPE

The telephone ripped through the black void startling Lauriant from a disturbed sleep. He reached out his hand to silence the thing and spilled the water jug.

"Merde!" he cursed.

The woman currently sharing his life and his bed groaned, almost growled, as she turned away. Her blonde hair, disheveled and untidy, vanished beneath the covers as she pulled the duvet over her head to shut out the noise.

Lauriant guessed that she had a hangover, as he had, but harshly he wanted to selfishly concentrate on his own headache, and he mentally shrugged her off, found the receiver and reluctantly put it to his ear.

"Lauriant? Is that you?"

The voice came from some other universe.

"What's this? Who the hell is this?"

"I'm sorry to call so early. It's Chief Inspector Guichard from Sarcelles sur Mures."

There was a pause. Lauriant tried hard but . . . Sarcelles sur Mures! The place meant nothing to him.

"Do you remember me?" the voice persisted.

Lauriant, fiddling through his memory, tried harder. In his condition it was a tough struggle. Then, yes!

Guichard—the Gascon—he had been a colleague in Paris years ago when they had joined the police within a few months of each other. They had had something in common . . . what was it? He remembered. They had both been wartime deportees. Until now, Lauriant had had no idea what had happened to him.

"Of course."

Despite this, Lauriant was not being encouraging. His stomach was in revolt against last night's overly rich lobster and overly dry white wine and his head thumped. He tried to find the glass in the dark, hoping that some water remained in it, whilst the rest spread a damp stain across the carpet.

Guichard heard a gulp down the line and wondered whether he was doing himself any good by calling an old colleague. He tried again.

"Like I said, I'm sorry about the time."

Lauriant looked at his watch. There was a first hint of a September day beyond the curtains. He was certain that it was raining. He swung his feet to the floor, failed to miss the wet patch, shivered slightly and found his dressing gown.

"Stop apologizing—what do you want?"

"I've got a corpse down here, murdered. It isn't an easy thing—it may be very complicated. Can you come? I can explain when you get here."

"Don't need a corpse," Lauriant said morosely into the mouthpiece. "I've got enough of them right here. Lately, we've been averaging ten or twenty on some nights."

Lauriant searched his mind trying to remember where Sarcelles sur Mures was. He thought that it was in the southwest. The southwest, where there was sun and warmth even in September. The southwest, where he could avoid the traffic, the woman in the bed and his ex-wife's almost daily calls about last month's unpaid alimony. It sounded good right then revolving around his befuddled brain. The southwest, where he could desert his post for a while.

"The southwest."

He must have breathed the words into the mouthpiece without realizing it, for Guichard, with a little more hope replied, "Yes! That's it . . . the southwest."

Lauriant looked at the shape still in the bed and mused on the reasons why God chose to limit himself when fashioning women. When they looked good, they rarely were good. Why were nearly all the good women plain? This one was not plain. Thinking like that, it suddenly came to him that he was still at least three parts drunk. Still, he thought wryly, I'm sober enough to realize it!

In the distance, across Paris, Lauriant heard a deep crump. It was yet another plastiquage—a terrorist bomb destroying innocent people and their property, planted by one side or the other in the on-going crisis which everyone now just called "Algeria".

This time, he judged it was on the edge of the city, towards the Porte de Lilas, largely a low-income district. So in their madness, he thought, the self appointed alternative leaders of his country had begun to consume their own. He wondered how long this could go on. It was a question that seemed to be without an answer, but the explosion made up his mind for him.

"Okay, Guichard. I'll come."

The sense of relief at the other end of the telephone was almost audible.

"I'll do what I can. Is there a train?"

Guichard had obviously already consulted the timetable.

"Ten o'clock. I can meet you here and then we can go on to Saint Sauveur."

"Where?" asked Lauriant.

"It's a small town about thirty kilometers from here. That's where the murder happened. As I said, I can explain it when you get here."

"I'll see you this afternoon."

Lauriant replaced the receiver and crept to the kitchen for several cups of strong black coffee. No point in going back to bed now.

Lauriant sat back in the seat, a Chesterfield between his lips and his eyes half closed. Had he dozed? The train was old and wheezy and the regular click of wheel on rail was, as the world over, almost hypnotic.

He thought back to his morning meeting with the chief superintendent.

"Is this an official request?"

"It comes from Guichard . . . he's the chief inspector

down there," Lauriant had replied, without really answering the question.

He adopted what he hoped was his most "correct" expression, determined that no one was going to spoil his breakout.

"It's a bad time," the boss, an old hand, said, looking at Lauriant with a knowing shrug. "This place is crawling with government spooks. Last week they even asked me to turn out my desk! Can you believe it? And the bastards broke my emergency bottle of cognac without so much as an apology!"

They both knew that some of their colleagues were, at least, ambivalent towards the new regime of de Gaulle, but the spooks were one of the government's less than inspired methods of keeping them in line.

"Bomb in Lilas this morning—blew out a café front— killed eight of the poor devils who had stopped in for early coffee on their way to work. Some mess, I'll tell you!"

The chief and Lauriant were career policemen, and as such they were subject to orders from their political masters. That was accepted—spooks or no spooks. Pierre Messmer, the armed forces minister, had said that a man could only serve the one who paid him. Perhaps Messmer was right. Just now, nonetheless, the army was hesitant and divided. But how much did obeying orders make them all responsible for what might happen in their country?

How far would they—or could they—go without compromising their conscience?

That would depend on who won the current political

and military battle for the thoughts and hearts of the French people. After all, only the winners write the histories.

"And," the chief continued remorselessly, "We've got the problems with the students at the Sorbonne. We had to mount a baton charge last night. The little bastards actually beat up Pardreux, and he's at least fifty. They put him in hospital, minus a few teeth and nursing broken ribs. Doctor thinks that he's got a punctured lung. When we arrested some of the rioters, one had a father in the assembly and one's mother was a countess!"

The boss shook his head in massive disbelief.

"We live in bloody funny times."

"Any 'ordinary' types arrested?" Lauriant asked.

"Too many for comfort!"

Lauriant, not liking the way the conversation was going, returned to his guns and tried to re-establish control.

"Anyway, is there ever a good time?" he asked, returning to the boss's first point without expecting an answer.

The eventual permission had been grudging, but Lauriant had expected that and now the old train lurched on southwards towards escape and the sun.

His cigarette burned down and without thinking he lit another, deciding at the same time, once again, that he smoked too much.

The Chesterfield habit had been picked up from the Americans in 1945, when Lauriant returned from Germany and the marshalling yards at Munich, where as a young man he had served out his forced labor under a brute of a German sergeant.

Still, everyone was friends now and you were supposed to forgive and forget. This was the Common Market and the politicians had been saying so many kind things to each other for almost twenty years that people were, at last, beginning to buy it. And, the money flowing into France from the CAP was a fine sweetener.

The President of the new Republic had fought the Germans and depended on the Americans and the British for his own survival when Lauriant was being kicked to work by the German sergeant. Now, de Gaulle shook hands with Adenauer and made speeches against his old supporters in Britain and America—he was even nice to the Russians. Lauriant, although Frenchman enough to resent the humiliation of Algeria and to enjoy a little Yankee bating, still wondered if he understood the point of it all.

He took another pull at the Chesterfield.

Lousy habit! At first, back in 1945, he had traded the cigarettes for food and shelter. Then he had started smoking them.

Then, like now, it had been a hard time in France. Meat, bread, flour and butter had all been scarce. Also, it had been a France heady with recrimination—and Frenchmen were thirsty for the blood of other Frenchmen. The Communists had inspired strikes which had sent the tottering economy plunging. It was understandable; at one time the bread ration was actually smaller than it had been during the war.

By the time Lauriant got back from Germany, thank God, the worst of the head shavings and the gory personal reprisals against collaborators—and sometimes against fellow resisters from the wrong outfit—was over.

He was glad of it and, as his father had done, he became a policeman. In those days, with the French economy in chaos, what else was there to do? He needed to make a living.

What would . . . what *could* . . . these new generation kids understand of that?

Pulling himself together, Lauriant pushed open the door of the compartment and went looking for the buffet car. Finding it, he bought a ham sandwich, long and limp, and ordered a biere blonde. He bit into the sandwich and finished the beer in one swallow, hoping to finally drown the wretched lobster. He signed to the barman for a second.

Next to him sat two young girls. Their skirts were hitched high and their legs were very fat. Country girls, Lauriant thought. Their hair—dark and blonde in patches and by turns—was bouffant and lacquered to the point where it refused to move even in the stiff breeze from the open carriage window.

They were drinking coffee and a thin, blue colored liquid in tiny glasses. Lauriant was sure that their immensely long eyelashes were false; stuck on to their eyelids and thickly blackened with mascara. Their makeup was dense and inexpertly applied—they were not used to it—and the colors of their clothes fought each other vio-

lently. They had been to Paris and, probably, a bit frightened of the city, but the more determined for that had set
out to enjoy themselves. Now, it was time to go home to
the farm.

The train lurched over a set of points and one of them,
grabbing out to save her precious blue drink, pitched into
him. This brought on a fit of giggles, which only momentarily stopped the flow of their chatter about pop stars and
cows, shoes and sheep.

This journey was taking an eternity.

2

ESCAPE ACHIEVED
& A DEATH IN A DITCH

It was early evening when the train at last reached
Sarcelles sur Mures.

Lauriant took his suitcase from the rack and stepped
out on to the low platform.

It was raining . . . a fine, persistent rain . . . the kind
that soaked through clothes and chilled the skin.

Other passengers made for the benches—inadequately
covered by awnings designed more for shade than protection—or searched for friends, relatives and taxies.

Wet and feeling more out of sorts than ever, Lauriant
looked around the platform trying to spot a Guichard fif-
teen years on, and found him looking much heavier than
Lauriant recalled, below the shining SNCF sign, near the
station entrance. Behind him the old train wheezed away.
There was a finality about that. No changes of mind, rain
and doubts notwithstanding, allowed now.

Guichard came forward, smiling, hand outstretched.

"You haven't changed much," he said.

"And, you've put on weight," Lauriant replied.

Guichard smiled again.

"A good wife and good cooking."

It was the time-honored reply of every happily married

Frenchman. Lauriant envied him that.

Guichard took Lauriant's case.

"I've brought a car. There's a local train to Saint Sauveur, but I thought you would have had enough of trains for one day. Especially as the local one is even older than that." He jerked a finger of his free hand in the general direction of the departing locomotive.

"Too right!"

Guichard drove the gray Peugeot 403 out of the station and turned south. The wipers lazed across the windscreen coping easily with the continuing drizzle.

"First rain we've had in four weeks."

"Really," sighed Lauriant, not trying to hide his displeasure at the news.

"We'll eat at the Hotel Rochebonne," Guichard said, and, aware of Lauriant's obvious disgust, added: "It's one of only two decent places in Saint Sauveur. You'll be staying there."

The car hit a bump. The lobster gave one ultimate convulsive heave in Lauriant's stomach and was finally laid to rest. Relief, at last. He immediately felt better.

"Who's dead?" he asked.

"A man named Eckart, first name Emile. At least, that's what he called himself. His passport is Argentinean. It's genuine enough, but it was probably bought. I don't speak Spanish, despite being so close to the frontier, so I can't tell you what his Spanish was like, but there was nothing wrong with his German, if you see what I mean. . . ."

Lauriant looked hard at Guichard, but he saw well enough.

"You knew him, then?"

"Yes. I've met him. He is . . . was . . . well known hereabouts. He's even dined occasionally with the sub-prefect."

"Oh God!"

"That's another reason for getting you involved."

"Oh God," Lauriant repeated.

"I'm sorry," Guichard apologized again, as he pulled the car to the left, the steering wheel brushing his bulging stomach, to drift effortlessly past an ancient 2CV, which was loaded with two sheep and their feed. It was barely struggling along close to the curbside. The driver, florid faced, seemed to be urging the vanquished old car on for all he was worth. The Citroen looked cross-eyed—one headlamp had broken free of the string that had held it to its stalk and, suspended, bumped along on the front mudguard, waiting for the most inconvenient moment to fall off.

"Do I take it that Eckart had influence then, friends to call on?"

"That's about it, but it didn't stop him ending up dead, face up in a ditch."

Lauriant grimaced.

"They had trouble finding an examining magistrate who didn't know him to take on the case. Servolin drew the short straw in the end."

This meant nothing to Lauriant.

"That's the one piece of good news," Guichard continued, perhaps a little encouraged.

"Servolin is clever, but he won't play politics, even these days and that is . . ." he hesitated looking for a careful word (no one was really sure of anyone anymore). ". . . rare."

Lauriant's face registered nothing, at least as far as fat Guichard could tell.

"He's about our age. I've told him that I've contacted you. He seemed relieved, which did nothing for my self-respect, I'll tell you. But at least he'll leave you alone. He agreed that he would deal through me."

Lauriant showed a little pleasure for the first time since he had arrived, despite the rain getting heavier, as they drove south. The *parquet*, even when only doing their job, were a burden not often avoided.

"How long had Eckart been in Saint Sauveur?"

"Since the early fifties—say, ten or twelve years. He bought an antique shop in the Place Clemenceau. That's the main square in Saint Sauveur. It's right next to the Hotel Rochebonne, opposite the post office."

"Antiques or junk?" Lauriant asked.

"Truthfully, I'm no expert, but as far as I can tell, both. But he must have had some good stuff, especially the paintings. Dealers came to him from all over France and even some from abroad, but he sold cheaper stuff to the tourists in the summer too."

At last, as they entered Saint Sauveur, Guichard turned left off the main street, the Rue de la République, and onto a side road.

Lauriant read the blue and white sign *Rue Bir Hakheim* and an immediate right turn placed the Peugeot in the car park at the rear of the Hotel Rochebonne.

The car park was surfaced with pebbles and there were, miserable in the rain, sawn off tree trunk tables with complimentary chairs scattered across the open space. The Peugeot bounced to a halt, as Guichard turned off its tired wipers and grateful engine.

The Hotel Rochebonne was redolent of an earlier France, an old hotel with a porch and a servants' staircase at the side.

"Continuity in change," Lauriant found himself quoting, but not sure of its source.

Enamel plaques on the rear entrance porch proclaimed the hotel's august status—according to the Michelin and Les Routiers.

Guichard took the suitcase and Lauriant crunched across the car park at a run and dashed under the porch without avoiding a soaking.

Inside, Guichard took care of the formalities.

"You're in room twelve," he said. "I'll wait for you in the bar."

Lauriant's room overlooked the Place Clemenceau. The room was filled with dark oak and heavy old country furniture—pretty depressing on the surface. One of the new hotel chains would no doubt soon buy the place, rip it all out and replace it with sleek orthopedic chairs and jaunty psychedelic wallpaper, whilst, of course, increasing the prices.

The bed itself was just a little short of massive. A clear oversight, thought Lauriant. In one corner there was a large fireplace with a big old-fashioned solid brass poker and an equally imposing pair of tongs spread across the hearth. Beside the bed was a stout table on which was perched a telephone, which must have been at least thirty years old.

The room smelt vaguely of new paint, and that was unusual in French country hotels.

Once last year, when his marriage was in chaos, Lauriant had stayed, desperate and alone in a hotel in Alsace, where his room still had a hole in the wall produced by a First World War German shell. In more ways than one, the room had been cold.

Now, out of the window, which was running with rain, away to his left, he could see a large shop. Its hoarding, green and gold, proclaiming EMILE ECKART - ANTIQUES. The shop looked smart. The exterior was newly decorated. The windows were dark, but in them, well displayed, there were old tables and chairs, porcelain and paintings on easels.

Across the square, the lights of the post office, surrounded by a soft halo of drizzle, glinted through the rain.

Here and there, a huddled figure trudged through the wetness, staying close to the walls and near to the shop windows. Further down the street a drenched woman struggled forward with an umbrella held in front of her and a grizzling child, miserable and past its bedtime, dragging disconsolately at her free arm.

Lauriant was not impressed.

In the bar, Guichard had shaken the rain from his coat and was holding his second pastis like a faithful, warm old friend.

"Join me?"

Thoughtlessly, Lauriant ordered the same and immediately regretted it (he was not that fond of aniseed.) He felt—and probably looked—fed up. This was not going at all as planned.

They were late and the pre-dinner drinkers had mostly left. Those still around eyed the policemen with suspicion.

"Don't worry," Guichard reassured Lauriant, "they don't like outsiders around here; even those that they know, they begrudge—especially out of the tourist season and . . ." He sounded sad. ". . . that goes for us in particular. Come on, let's eat."

The restaurant too, oaked and carpeted, was quiet. It smelled, so typically, of garlic, cutlets and good cooking, mixed with beeswax polish. No new paint smells here.

They took a table near the window.

The waiter, managing to show lack of interest without being openly surly, put a bottle of Perrier water and a basket of cut bread on their table. He took their order: chicken in the local style for Guichard and, for Lauriant, true to his northern roots, pork with a Calvados sauce.

The waiter also, without being asked, brought more drinks. Pastis again.

Guichard, perhaps ashamed of his neighbors, felt the

need to say something. But he could think of nothing that would fit. Some salesmen on the next table were dwelling with great disappointment on the uses to which other lower, and less worthy workers were putting their excessive holidays and shorter working week, as afforded to them by the new Fifth French Republic.

Guichard raised an eyebrow to Lauriant as one of the salesmen, clearly very drunk, informed the others (and the rest of the room as well) that these unfortunates should be kept steadfastly at their work so that they should not have the time to drink.

"It's no good for them," the speaker concluded with as much grave finality as his condition would allow.

He finished his sermon with a long draft of red wine and refilled his glass—no doubt, Lauriant thought, at the expense of the company which the government had so thoughtlessly burdened with the costs of shortening the working week.

Doing his best to hold back a smile, which, under the influence of the pastis, was threatening a laugh, Guichard nodded towards two other men sitting at a corner table.

They were leaning towards each other and speaking softly. Lauriant had the impression that their dinners remained largely untouched.

"The tall one in the dark suit is Michael Harris, an American."

Lauriant noted the short cut hair and the sallow complexion. The man, who looked no more than thirty-five, removed his iron rimmed spectacles and cleaned them thoroughly in his napkin, before replacing them and openly examining the policemen with undisguised interest.

"The other one is Etienne Perec, the local lawyer . . . accountant too."

Guichard paused as the men acknowledged him, the American with a short wave and the Frenchman with a barely perceptible movement of the head.

"Perec is, or was, rather, Eckart's man of affairs," Guichard added with emphasis. "And the American came here to meet Eckart."

Lauriant registered the information, and the extra meaning which Guichard had given it by his tone of voice.

"The American seems very sure of himself. A buyer, I suppose," said Lauriant, fishing for something to say.

"No. Some sort of valuer of fine arts. He's been here four or five days."

After ten minutes or so, the first course arrived.

"Okay. Tell me about this murder of yours. What have you found out so far?"

3

THE GROCER'S SON

After dinner, Lauriant returned to his room and, thoroughly exhausted, crawled into bed and fell straight to sleep.

Next morning the maid's shout, in a rounded local accent from the other side of the door, announced the arrival of his coffee and brought him back from a dream; a dream he could not quite recall, but which he was sure was unpleasant.

Without looking at him, she placed the tray on the table next to the window and was rewarded for her cheerful good morning with a loud, unfriendly grunt from the bed.

The maid, a pretty enough girl, if a bit skinny and in her early twenties, left to report to the rest of the hotel staff that the policeman from Paris had typical big city manners and, therefore, was best avoided as much as possible.

Outside Lauriant's room the town was gradually waking up, coming to life. Little individual noises were slowly mingling together to make a single continuous sound. The shutters on the café clattered down, making ready for the first drinkers of the day, and the vans from the post office barked into vociferous activity.

Lauriant drank the boiling coffee in short sips and nibbled at the rolls before lighting his first Chesterfield.

And still it rained.

As he dressed, his mind ran over what fat Guichard had revealed over dinner.

"At first," Guichard had explained, "it was thought that he had fallen from his horse and broken his scrawny neck. He kept two horses, you see, in the stable block to the rear of his house on the Rue Voltaire—a spirited stallion and a more docile mare. He rode every morning. The day before yesterday, the day of his death, he took out the stallion, so, naturally. . . ."

The local doctor, Nadeau, had thought so too until he examined the corpse more closely in the local morgue.

"By that time the scene had been trampled over by half the population of the town, so that we could get no useful information from the site," Guichard had admitted.

"Where was it?"

"There is a track, not much more than a footpath, which runs to one side of Eckart's house dividing his place from Monnet's. Jerome Monnet is the local notary," Guichard added by way of explanation, "and Eckart's neighbor. He's a bit of an old woman, but he must have managed it at least once in his life, as he has a daughter who is something of a local beauty. She dresses like one of the models in *Elle*. His wife also, as you will see, is a superb looking woman, still full in her prime. One of those who grows better with age, you know the sort. She must be forty-five now."

Lauriant, noting Guichard's interest in the women, pursued the same line.

"And the girl?"

"Twenty-three."

Guichard looked wistful for a long few seconds, before pulling himself together.

"But, back to the track. It runs into the woods and, just after where the body was found, divides, one leg running on to the Rue Bir Hakheim back there"—Guichard had pointed with his fork—"and the other branching left to the Rue de la République, emerging just south of the Place Clemenceau opposite the café."

At this point Guichard had risen from the table and pointed out the café from the window of the hotel restaurant, before resuming his seat.

"At the morgue, Nadeau noticed an ugly mark on the back of Eckart's neck—straight and blue and surrounded by broken skin. This discovery made him take a closer look at the corpse and he realized that there were no other injuries. A man falling from a horse hard enough to kill himself, well, he'd have at least bruised or broken something! But nothing! No bruising and definitely no breaks."

Guichard looked grim, as if he was personally responsible for this dreadful lapse. He shook his head.

"So, right! There it was! Nadeau says that Eckart was off the horse when he was struck. Had to be . . . it was the only thing that makes any sense. He was hit hard from behind with something heavy and then rolled into the ditch, so that the corpse could not be easily seen."

"What did the doctor do?"

"He called the mayor and then went over to the police station and told Manod, the local constable."

"In that order?"

Guichard looked even more embarrassed and he seemed to feel that another explanation was called for.

"Yes. That's how it is in these small towns. Anyway, Manod isn't of the brightest and so the doctor probably thought it was for the best."

There was a pause whilst Lauriant lit another cigarette.

"What happened to the riderless horse?"

Guichard seemed surprised at the question.

"It found its way back. Went home to the stable."

"And no one saw it?"

Lauriant put on his shoes. They were new and he looked at them ruefully. He knew that they were about to be ruined, but there was no help for it. He pulled on his overcoat and went downstairs.

The hotel receptionist, wearing a regulation white blouse marred by a big, rebellious, and fashionable frill down the middle of the front, took his key almost as if it were tainted. Obviously, she had been warned by the maid.

As soon as his back was turned, Lauriant guessed that the receptionist would dive back into her little office behind the desk to resume her communing with the RTL

pop music radio station, which he could just hear proclaiming its tenuous, but vibrant message of love and
romance from beyond the door.

At the hotel entrance he turned around and sure
enough, there was no sign of the girl. But he could still
feel, more than hear, the thump of the music.

Outside, hands buried deep in his overcoat pockets,
he set off through the rain to find young Marc.

"The body," Guichard had explained, "was found by
Marc, Madame Poulard the grocer's son. He works selling
vegetables in his mother's shop on the Rue de la
République, when he's not out around the local farms
trying to buy them—and probably pinching what they can't
afford."

Guichard clearly had a low opinion of the no doubt
dashing young cavalier Poulard.

Perhaps Marc was cavalier in both senses of the word;
Guichard certainly thought so. Lauriant would have to
find out. Lauriant wondered, irrelevantly, if Guichard
was of the sort that saw no good in anyone (except the
girls) whose affliction it was to be younger than himself.

"They've been hit hard, the Poulards," Guichard continued, "by the new Carrefour hypermarket at Sarcelles."

He felt the need to explain further.

"Of course, there's always been the weekly market here
in the Place Clemenceau to give them some competition,
but the hypermarket is in a different league. It's big and

they organize a free bus service twice a week. People like the ride and the prices are better—and so's the choice. In a few months time there will be a new Leclerc as well and that will start a price war around here. I don't see how the Poulards can last out much longer. I don't think that they've got a chance."

Guichard did not look unhappy about this. He was just stating a fact.

The Poulard shop was small and old fashioned with bleached advertisements across its windows for coffees long gone and for obscure aperitifs. Produce was piled outside on the pavement despite the rain.

Inside, hams—looking delicious beyond the imaginings of Anglo Saxons used to the soggy, the limp and the processed—hung from hooks. There were shelves carrying a display of aging tins with fading, once multi-colored labels and potatoes and cabbages were stored in sacks in front of the counter.

Lauriant liked it. It reminded him of home.

The shop was empty. No one, Lauriant guessed, would want to be out in this weather without good cause. Behind the counter, nevertheless, as she did every day of the year, Madame Poulard waited for her customers.

Lauriant was about to introduce himself.

"I know who you are," she announced, "and everyone around here will recognize you by the lunch hour."

Lauriant was dripping onto her scrubbed wooden

floor and she looked at the spreading puddle with dismay, her bitter expression indicating her belief that this unavoidable circumstance was typical of the male with his inherent complete lack of sense.

Lifting her eyes—which performed the miracle of being tired, aggressive and resigned at one time—from the wet floor to Lauriant's stupidly embarrassed face, she said, "You'll want Marc. He's at the back with the van. It's broken down again."

She led Lauriant through the rear of the shop into a yard. She pointed to the boy's backside, which was all that could be seen emerging from under the bonnet of an old Renault Estafette. With a shake of her head, she vanished back into the shop to await her dwindling number of customers.

Marc emerged; an untidy lad in oil splattered overalls. He had his fair ration of pimples decorating his young face. Behind the seat of the Renault lay a tie of the latest style and cut, the colors of which gatecrashed the eyes and an expensive black leather blouson—no doubt one of the boy's most treasured possessions.

Despite his dismal situation in life and the remoteness of Saint Sauveur, Lauriant recognized that even young Poulard had joined, or attempted to join, the emerging revolution of la jeunesse.

Also, lying on the front seat, much to Lauriant's surprise, was the latest copy of *Le Canard Enchaine.* A satirical magazine that questioned and poked fun at anything and everything French.

It struck Lauriant suddenly just how few of these southerners seemed to be sun-tanned. Immediately, he put that unwelcome thought behind him.

"So, you're the man from Paris?" Marc wiped his oily hands on an equally oily cloth. "Well, I've told Manod and the other policeman, the fat one from Sarcelles all I know."

The boy was not defiant, as so many were at his age; he was merely stating a fact. A mongrel dog, soaking wet, appeared from somewhere and nuzzled at his legs. He looked down, taking pity on the miserable animal. "Come on," he said, "let's get out of the rain."

Followed by the smelly disheveled dog, he walked casually across to an old tin roofed shelter, where, no doubt, the dubiously reliable Renault normally rested between forays. Lauriant trailed behind the oddly well-matched pair.

Lauriant, on impulse, offered the boy a cigarette. He threw down the rag and took the cigarette gratefully, like a smoker with too little access to the source of his addiction.

"I know that you've said it all before, but help me will you?"

Marc inhaled again. The Chesterfield was doing its work.

"All right."

"What time was it when you found the body?"

"About seven-thirty. I almost missed it. If I hadn't seen the horse trotting down the track on its own, well . . . anyway, there's a ditch on one side of the old track. Eckart was in it—on his back, eyes open, staring straight up. He looked, well, surprised."

Marc took a pull at the cigarette, holding it cupped in his palm, like a man used to smoking in the open air.

"And, he wasn't the only one, I can tell you!" His body gave a perceptible shudder.

"Did you see anyone else?"

Marc shrugged.

"No. That's why I go that way. I see Eckart on his horse sometimes, but I step back into the bushes out of sight before he sees me."

Lauriant thought it best to leave following that up for the moment.

"What did you do when you found the body?" he asked instead.

"First off, I was sure that he was dead. Then I ran back down the track to the Rue Voltaire. Dr. Nadeau has his rooms there—where it joins the Rue de la République. I made so much noise that Mimi actually came out of her house. I had to wake Dr. Nadeau up, you see."

"Mimi?"

"Yes, Mimi. Well, that's what everyone calls her. She's the woman who lives on the other corner of the Rue Voltaire next to Monnet. Monnet's place is between Mimi's and the dead man's house. She lives there with her husband. He never gets out of bed."

Lauriant was struck by the woman's absurdly girlish name.

"What's wrong with him?"

"Shot, I think, in Indochina. He can't walk. How old Monnet must hate the woman living next to him! Anyway, with her husband like he is, she hardly ever emerges except for church and particularly for weddings and funerals—then she dresses in all her finery. I deliver her groceries every week and she always gives me that all knowing look . . . you know the sort of look I mean?"

Lauriant nodded.

"Anyway, the damned woman is strategically positioned—she sits by one window or another all day with one ear cocked in case her husband needs her. There's not much goes on around here that she misses, I can tell you."

The boy's second cigarette drew to its end and Lauriant proffered another.

"What were you doing on the track at that hour?"

"Well, not collecting and delivering, that's for sure."

He cast a sideways glance at the entrance to the shop, making sure that his mother was out of earshot.

"Not a word to her?"

Lauriant gave a shrug. "Agreed."

"You have to understand, she's not bad, my mother, just bitter. She can't help herself. She nagged the old man for years until he took off when I was still a kid. No one's heard a word from him since. It was probably the best move he ever made! Now, well, now it's my turn to take it and I can do without more trouble than is inevitable." He drew a deep breath, stubbed out his cigarette with his foot and made his confession.

"Okay. Here goes. Two nights a week, I slip out. I have

a few drinks at the café on the Place Clemenceau, play cards with some of the other lads and just have what generally passes for a good time in this place. And that's not saying much. I use the track to come home—because I might be seen coming down the Rue de la République, you see. Anyway, whichever way I go I have to pass Mimi's place and I'm sure that she spots me every time."

"Doesn't your mother ever notice mud on your shoes from the track when you get home?"

"Of course not. It almost never rains here!"

Somewhere deep down inside himself, Lauriant suppressed a nearly overwhelming desire to hit the boy in the pimples, but, instead, he just said, "Go on."

The boy remained silent for a long time, but something in Lauriant's expression clearly made him uncomfortable. As he still said nothing, Lauriant reluctantly prompted him again.

"Look, try this. You weren't in the café until seven-thirty in the morning," Lauriant said reasonably enough. "It closes before midnight. I can see it from my hotel room and last night its shutters were up by eleven." A little edge invaded Lauriant's voice. "Come on, boy, where the hell were you?"

Marc shuffled his feet, looking increasingly like a naughty schoolboy.

"It's Adrienne," he said, as if that were explanation enough and, probably, for him it was.

"Adrienne?"

"She's the notary's daughter."

There was still no reaction from Lauriant which young Poulard could possibly have considered satisfactory testimony to the reality of the legendary Adrienne. He did not look happy with this, but he went on.

"As I said, twice a week, I slip out. After the café, I use the track to visit her. As I said, it runs between her father's house and Eckart's. I climb over the wall and she lets me in."

Lauriant nodded. So that was how Monnet's pretty daughter spent at least two nights of her week: bedding the grocer's son—a thing, he was well aware from his own experience, not unthinkable ten years ago.

What would have been unthinkable then was admitting to it at all unless you were caught, let alone owning up to it in this casual way.

Lauriant, to his own surprise, found that he was slightly shocked. He was beginning to show his age in a time when the young were becoming the center of the world—at least that was what they believed. Lauriant thought that he knew better, but he had his nagging doubts.

"Monday is one of my nights, you see," Marc continued his explanation without noticing Lauriant's uneasiness, "so Tuesday morning early, before the house is awake, she lets me out and I head back down the track, normal as you like . . . until this Tuesday, that is."

4

THE DOCTOR, THE WOMAN & THE GIFT

The doctor's housekeeper placed the bottle of cognac between them and, showing no inclination to leave them alone together, went to sit across the room. She took out her knitting and began to click away.

The doctor filled the two glasses.

Lauriant drank a little and the doctor, with an over magnanimous gesture, immediately topped up his glass, leaving it fuller than ever.

The small, rather untidy room smelt vaguely of disinfectant that had leached through from the surgery next door.

Lauriant was reminded of the smell at the vet's house, where he had taken his worn out old cat to be put down when he was a boy. Some smells stay with you like memories.

"The weapon—may I use that expression?" Nadeau began ponderously.

Lauriant had known many doctors. Some had been, without doubt, very clever; more had just been competent or plain stupid. Alerted by Guichard's remarks, he recognized this white-haired, red-faced, elderly doctor as being firmly amongst those in the latter category.

Lauriant looked at his soaked new shoes and then at

Nadeau's watery eyes. He was not in the mood for this nonsense and he waved the question aside.

"Just tell me what you've found. And, if you have thought about it at all, your opinion."

The doctor did not fully recover his composure after this. His mouth, already drooped with old age, dropped several levels further. He had prepared himself to deliver a lecture to the non-medical unenlightened and this policeman was having none of it.

Nadeau coughed and looked at the housekeeper. The clicking of the needles had stopped and her face was some way between bewildered, stunned and livid. No one had talked to her good doctor like that ever before.

Nadeau drank a large volume of the brandy, swallowed hard and cleared his throat.

Again, he looked to the housekeeper for guidance and support, but in her state she was doomed to disappoint him. He had to answer the question. He clung to the word weapon as the place to start.

"Well, the weapon must have been at least half a meter long . . . that is my guess; heavy, but narrow and not sharp—blunt, not rounded. Whoever it was who killed him needed to take a good swing at Eckart to do the damage he did."

"And you missed it," Lauriant said dryly. "Would it be true to say that someone was thoroughly professional or exceptionally lucky?"

"According to the postmortem, done by the hospital in Sarcelles sur Mures," he added quickly, as if to give the findings more authority than Lauriant was prepared to concede to him, "the vertebrae and the spinal cord snapped as neatly as you like. Death must have been almost instantaneous."

"You are sure that he was alive when the blow was administered?"

"Undoubtedly."

"Would the blow have needed exceptional strength? Could, for example, a woman have managed it?"

"Oh, yes."

"Was he healthy in general?"

"He was in fairly good condition for a man of his age. There was no life-threatening disease, if that's what you are asking."

"How long had he been dead before you got to him, do you think?"

"Not above a few minutes. The Poulard boy must have passed the spot almost immediately after it happened."

"Who knows that it was Eckart's habit to go riding along the old track each morning?"

"That won't help you," the doctor replied smugly. "I knew and so did practically everybody else in the town, I should think."

He somehow felt he'd scored against the policeman with this.

"Did you strip the corpse?" Lauriant was relentless.

"Me and Josephine." Dr. Nadeau indicated his house-keeper.

"What was in the pockets?"

"Nothing to interest you. I gave it all to Manod. A few

pieces of paper of no importance—bills, that sort of thing. His keys, his wallet containing a few francs . . ."

The doctor's voice drifted away.

Dr. Nadeau was not only incompetent, he was depressing.

Lauriant had one more call to make before meeting Guichard.

But, before he made it, he stopped at a shop in the Rue de la République and emerged with a gaudily wrapped package secured with several turns of gold colored ribbon.

As he waited for Mimi to answer his knock, the curtains moved at an upstairs window in the notary's house next door. They closed quickly, but not quickly enough. Lauriant smiled to himself and, shaking the rain from his coat, knocked on the woman's door again.

This time, a head appeared around the door.

"Good morning, Mimi. I have a small gift for you."

The house was not at all what Lauriant had anticipated. It was clean and bright and the room he was in overlooked the crossroads of the Rue de la République and the Rue Voltaire.

If the sun had been shining, he could imagine the room with its surprisingly light and modern furniture, being bathed in its warmth. It was, he decided, a good room.

There was a faint smell of lavender in the air and a small cross hung on the white painted wall between the two windows—testimony to Mimi's beliefs. Somewhere in the house, a radio was playing softly.

Mimi, dressed in an old, faded housecoat and embarrassed about it, nevertheless bent over her table to unwrap the gift. Lauriant heard her intake of breath as she admired the little porcelain figurine. She held it for a few moments.

"What's this for?" she asked.

The question was put simply and there was none of the peasant-like suspicion in it that he had half expected.

"Shall we call it a gift from a colleague?"

Mimi frowned, not understanding for a moment, and then the frown was followed by a broad smile, which brightened up her face and highlighted the lines on her forehead.

Her violet blue eyes twinkled wickedly, delightfully. She understood him now well enough.

"Excuse me," she said and vanished into the kitchen to turn off the gas under the stew which was to be her lunch. This was going to take some time . . . and she was going to enjoy it!

Seconds later, she was back, still self-conscious.

"Excuse me," she repeated and went out through another door.

This time, she was gone longer and when she returned, she was transformed.

Her dress—in a shade which Lauriant's inadequate vocabulary when faced with such things could only describe as light blue—was obviously, even to him, silk and the brunet hair was coiffured and the face made up.

She looked ten years younger.

"Sorry," she said, "Now where were we?"

Mimi took her knitting from a basket next to her chair, settled back and began clicking industriously with the needles.

Did every woman in this place knit?

After a few seconds Mimi stopped, looking at Lauriant who had taken up an equally comfortable station in the chair opposite the now elegant woman.

"Do you mind?"

Lauriant brushed the possibility aside.

"I find it helps me to think."

"Please, carry on."

She was not, he felt, one of those women who could become easily accustomed to solitude, used to silence . . . maybe even enjoying it. But with her husband in the condition he was, she had still bravely chosen this way or perhaps it had been forced upon her. He did not yet know.

Now, she paused thoughtfully and Lauriant waited for her to speak.

"So! You're the man from Paris come to solve the mystery of our so called Argentinean." She smiled.

"My name is Lauriant. So, you don't think he was an Argentinean either?"

Mimi laughed at the very idea. It was a pleasant laugh, low pitched and slow rolling.

"No of course not! He was no more Argentinean than you or I. The disguise was so thin that I wonder that he thought that it would fool anyone. Or maybe he just didn't care. Anyway, Eckart was as German as Hock—which, like him, is filthy disgusting stuff anyway."

"You didn't like him?"

"Dislike is too harsh. Let's say he was not a man I would enjoy sharing dinner with. Will that do?"

"I think that sums it up pretty well."

An idea occurred to her.

"Have you tried our local red yet? You must before you leave us. It is really very good."

Lauriant said that he would.

"Now, where do I start?"

Once more, she gave him that little frowning smile.

"Yes," she decided, "the German, let's start with him. Anyway, he spoke good French—I'll give him that—but he could never disguise the accent. It was not much, but it was there for anyone who cared to notice. Some of us did and, then, some of us didn't."

Lauriant would, no doubt, learn who in due time.

"Now," Mimi continued, warming to her theme, "he had money when he came here, that's the first thing. But after the first few years he became something of a big spender, not a man careful of his wealth—even more so lately. My first thought was that he had had some inheritance, but, on balance, I think that's wrong. He spent mostly in short, irregular sprees, which is not what one would do with an inheritance. You see, there was no," she searched her mind for the precise word, "no steadiness about it."

"Perhaps he merely made the occasional high profit from a sale at the antique shop," Lauriant tried.

Mimi looked disappointed in him and, stupidly, Lauriant felt embarrassed that she did.

"No! No!" she said impatiently. "The prices in that shop made sure hardly anyone ever bought, apart from a few tourists. Anyway, the German's spending was as likely to go up in the winter, when there are no tourists, as in the summer."

She cocked her head to one side slightly as her ear caught some slight noise outside the window.

"That will be Madame Monnet. On Thursday's she lunches with friends at the Auberge des Biches just outside town."

Mimi went to the window and watched her neighbor's departure. Marc Poulard was right. She did not miss much.

Back once more in her chair, she asked herself, "Where was I? Ah yes! Eckart certainly impressed some people in the town, especially with his visitors from abroad. Veyret, our fool of a mayor, for one. He fawned on him. I knew Veyret when he was a boy. He was asinine then and age hasn't helped his brains any more than his figure."

"You're from here originally?"

"Both of us. Alain, my husband, that is, and me. He was in the army."

Mimi, dignified and comfortable in her chair, continued her knitting for a minute . . . her mind elsewhere.

"I must check on Alain," she said suddenly.

She was gone for some time and Lauriant found himself, for reasons he would have been unable to explain, doing exactly as Mimi would have done. He stood up and stared out of the window down the Rue de la République.

She came back to her chair.

"So he was impressive, this German?"

"Could be . . . particularly when it suited him. But, he never wasted his time on me. He knew that it wouldn't wash and that I saw him for exactly what he was and Alain . . . well, Alain would be no use to him socially or in business any more."

As she spoke, Lauriant began to build up a picture of the victim. A man who, yesterday, he had not known existed and whose name he had learned only the previous evening. A man who had been a barely perceptible profile of a broken body in a ditch—just an untidy piece of refuge in the landscape. Now, thanks to Marc Poulard and mostly to Mimi, the man grew clearer, like a developing photograph. Now he had habits, he spent money, he had friends (well, at least acquaintances) some of whom felt themselves important people, but who were, nevertheless, impressed by Eckart and flattered by his company.

"No," Mimi added with finality, "only Nicole Putet— she's a friend of ours since we were all children—takes time to visit us nowadays."

Lauriant felt deeply sorry for her.

"Putet?" he asked.

"Like Alain, her husband was a soldier. It's a tradition with some families, provincial as well as Parisian. He's dead now. He died at Dien-Bien-Phu."

He understood the massive meaning those few words had for his generation of Frenchmen.

He remembered when French soldiers were surrounded in a green jungle valley. They had been ripped apart by Viet Minh artillery supplied by the Russian and Chinese friends of the Communist defense minister in a government of France, who had remained seated in the National Assembly, whilst his prime minister paid homage to the French soldiers fighting and dying in Indochina.

Lauriant was hesitant. He did not want to ask the question, but . . . there was something in him, and he could not let it pass.

"And, Alain?"

"Not Dien-Bien-Phu. He was on Navarre's staff. You know, the general who went there after the famous General Salan had made a mess of things?"

"Yes."

"Bad luck. Just one of a series of things, you know. One would have not been important, even two or three. But taken together these little things . . . they make a whole. They change or break a life . . . lives."

He was silent, so she explained.

"Alain was sent to inspect some village, somewhere nobody had ever heard of or ever will. There was a French garrison there. It was small, but with everything going on north of them around Hanoi, somebody decided—without too much thought probably—that it needed checking, or maybe just a morale boost from a colonel's visit."

The needles clicked for a very long time. There were

tears, fought back, just behind her eyes.

"Any other day it would have been fine—no attack. There hadn't been one for weeks. If the weather was different . . . if the truck had not broken down . . . if Alain had not decided to stay overnight rather than risk the return journey in the dark. Anyway, it cost him a bullet in the spine and the inability to move from the neck down ever since."

No more needles clicked now.

"It is not that uncommon a story."

There was a silence that was on one level oppressive and, on another, warm. She knew why she had answered, but he did not completely understand why he had asked.

"What about Monnet?" Lauriant said, recovering himself a little, although to her the voice betrayed more than he knew. "Did Monnet and Eckart get along?"

"They could not avoid each other, living next door, so to speak. Also, they moved in somewhat the same circles, attended the same functions at the mairie—that sort of thing. I, myself," Mimi added, showing pride in spite of herself, "have been to one or two of these. Still, Monnet and Eckart did not get on. Their characters were realms apart, you see. I believe Eckart thought of Monnet—if he did at all that is—as a dull provincial old fusspot, with no experience of the world outside of these few streets, Sarcelles sur Mures and an annual two week holiday at Royan."

Lauriant nodded.

"Monnet, in his turn, could not cope with Eckart's brand of man. Eckart, I am sure, made him feel inferior and, as deep down Monnet suspected that he really was inferior, the German had become for him a kind of living, breathing confirmation of his own inadequacy as a man. You see what I mean?"

Again Lauriant gave her his nod.

"Once, Monnet actually openly accused Eckart of making love to his wife!"

"Did he make love to Madame Monnet?"

"There was a hell of a row, but Eckart was too smart for that. Others around here— Etienne Perec for one—might from time to time, shall we say . . . admire Madame Monnet. But the German didn't need that sort of complication. He was too intelligent. He'd have soon decided that such an offer wasn't worth the trouble it would bring. Anyway, Eckart didn't need love as you or I would mean it, just physical gratification once in a while. And, he could— and did—get that in Sarcelles. No doubt, if your fat friend Guichard asked one or two of the usual girls he would soon get confirmation of that. Eckart would take out his car at night, head off for Sarcelles and return at two or three o'clock in the morning, slipping his big Citroen DS into the garage at the back of his house as quietly as he could."

Mimi paused. Lauriant had closed his eyes in order to better imagine this little part of life in the Rue Voltaire.

When Mimi stopped, his lids flicked up. "Go on, please."

"After the argument, relationships were frostily polite between them . . . when, that is, Monnet couldn't avoid Eckart altogether."

"Could Monnet have hated the German enough to kill him, I wonder."

Mimi considered this for some time.

"It's possible, I think. The cowardly blow from behind would be Monnet's style. He's a little man with little habits—the type who would nurse a grudge, cultivate a hatred and await his moment. Yes," Mimi looked even more thoughtful, "it is possible."

Elegantly, she stood up and went over to the cupboard to bring back two glasses and a bottle of wine.

On the cupboard Lauriant noticed several old photographs transferred to modern frames. One, even more faded than the rest, showed a lady in a wide Belle Époque hat and another showed a group of smiling, very young girls in 1930s dresses. The sea was in the background. He wondered which was Mimi.

"Now you must try our red. It's not a great Bordeaux, but it certainly has a character."

She poured two generous measures before continuing.

"Perec the lawyer is, however, more a man of Eckart's kidney. Those two did get on. And, they thoroughly deserved each other! Perec strikes me as being a bit of a liar when it suits him, but he would know more than anyone else about Eckart's affairs. Even then though, I warn you, Perec would only know what Eckart chose to tell him. The German was sharp, almost manipulative and I believe when it came down to it he manipulated Etienne Perec as much as he wished—but I don't think he let Perec see it."

"I saw Perec with the American, Harris, last night. They were having a fine tête-à-tête over dinner."

"Were they now!" Mimi considered this additional

item of information, assessing it and placing it precisely in the scheme of things.

"What would they have to sort out together, I wonder?"

"So do I," Lauriant replied.

"Yes, yes." Mimi was quiet for a moment. "That is interesting." She brought back her thoughts with a little jerk. "The American . . . have you seen his shoes?"

Lauriant shrugged, looking down, ashamed of his own.

"You can tell a lot from a person's shoes. The American's shoes are handcrafted—not bought from a normal shop. Of course most in this town, like everyone else in France, believe all Americans are rich and they would not have thought to look at his shoes. In general, we look at people's suits or dresses or coats and forget about the shoes. I don't forget. Genuinely wealthy people always wear good shoes. Harris has good shoes. He has money, that's a certainty!"

"When did the American arrive in Saint Sauveur?"

"Before or after the murder you mean? He's been here for over a week this time. In short, before the murder. But I saw him first on," she was thinking hard, "Friday . . . in the afternoon . . . four days before Eckart met his, no doubt untimely but deserved, end. The American was going into Eckart's house. And, as the German has no maid, he must have let Harris in himself."

"You said 'this time'. Is Harris a regular visitor to Saint Sauveur?"

Mimi was, as ever, precise.

"This was his twelfth visit."

"On Tuesday, I assume that you saw Eckart set off for his morning ride."

Lauriant said this carefully, not wishing to give the impression that he thought her inquisitive.

"Oh yes. And a few minutes later—five, ten at most—I saw young Marc climbing over the back wall of the Monnets' house."

"I know about that."

Pleased, Mimi warmed even further to a potential confederate.

"The girl, Adrienne, gave him a wave and then he set off up the track, as usual, following behind the German, who was by now, of course, out of sight. As I say, this was all quite usual for a Tuesday morning, so I gave it little thought. What happened next, however, was not normal. First, the horse comes trotting down the track without its rider and seconds later Marc comes flying back as if he has a pack of wolves on his heels. Then he attacks the doctor's door and finally, after a few minutes or so, they go back up the path together. I know that you've met our Doctor Nadeau."

Lauriant could not resist a glance at the appropriate window.

The violet blue eyes, ever lively, brightened even further.

"Don't worry . . . I know my reputation even better than you seem to!"

Lauriant's shrug could only be described as Gallic and Mimi's infectious laugh let him know that she was happy to let it pass.

"I met him and his housekeeper," he said.

"Nadeau's been keeping up that pretence for twenty years to my certain knowledge. It fools nobody now, probably never did. I know that she wouldn't have left him alone with you. It's that sort of relationship."

"Why didn't he marry her?" Lauriant asked.

"Too superior socially. A cut above her, several cuts in reality—those things mattered then. Not a good thing for an up and coming doctor to have a wife he could not show off proudly in the right circles."

Mimi was well aware that such niceties were not supposed to matter now.

"Anyway, by the time the upping and the coming was finished—and that wasn't very long, as Nadeau didn't, and doesn't really have what it takes—he told her that it was too late; not worth it. And he settled into enjoying the produce without actually buying it, if you see what I mean. Nice man our Nadeau. You will have guessed from this that I don't use him. I go into Sarcelles sur Mures."

"Thank you," Lauriant said, finishing his glass and getting up. "You're right. The wine is good."

Mimi looked pleased.

"How long have you been married, Mimi?" he asked as he made for the door.

She smiled as if remembering things long past.

"It's none of your business but . . . shall we say that over time, I've had my moments!"

As she closed the door, Lauriant heard the light little laugh again and it brought an increasingly rare smile to his own lips.

5

THE NOTARY &
THE SCENE OF THE CRIME

Lauriant hitched up his overcoat collar in yet another unsuccessful attempt at keeping the rain from running down between his back and his shirt.

Opposite where he and Guichard stood in communal misery on the muddy track, a small area had been roped off by Manod, the local constable. He was a big man, who, if anything, looked even wetter than the two detectives as he stood beneath the dripping trees. Water ran in a concentrated little rivulet from the peak of his uniform kepi.

Guichard had left the Peugeot in the Place Clemenceau—as close as he could get it to the murder scene—but he was soaked through even before he reached the junction in the track.

Gloomily, Lauriant surveyed the ditch and its surroundings. It all looked so commonplace. The landscape, such as it was, had no particular distinction. It was no place for anyone to die.

Lauriant asked Manod for Eckart's keys and the policeman, after much searching, produced them from the depths of the pockets of his dark blue uniform. Lauriant noticed that the keys were wet too.

The churned up ground, muddy and water logged,

gave ample proof of Guichard's claim that half the town had walked over it since the murder.

"You can remove the ropes. There's no point in them now," Lauriant told Guichard. "Anyway, I have a couple of things for you to do."

They set off down the track, both with hands buried deep in their overcoat pockets, leaving the dripping Manod to coil in the ropes. They could hear him behind them cursing softly. The water from the rope ran up his sleeve as he coiled it around his arm.

"First, get hold of one or two of the street girls in Sarcelles and ask them if Eckart was a customer."

"Do you think that he was?"

"I'm certain of it. They may be able to tell you something, but I'm not hopeful."

Predictably, Lauriant's remark had left Guichard with little enthusiasm for the task.

"Okay," he said reluctantly and paused before adding, "For your information, I have an appointment this afternoon with the examining magistrate. The routine must go on," he grumbled.

Lauriant smiled and Guichard looked even more depressed. Poor old Guichard!

"In that case, ask him to let you bring in an expert on fine arts for me—particularly paintings. I need someone who knows the dealing side of the business, as well as the true arts side, if you see what I mean. You will probably have to get someone down from Paris. Do what you can."

"Leave it with me and I'll get on to the girls later this

afternoon. Some of them sleep through the day."

"Professional habits," Lauriant said. "Also, I want you to get hold of someone in Germany."

"Germany? Oh God!"

"Yes, Germany. Try the police first and if necessary the army records office—there must be one. I want to know what Eckart, if that's his real name, did in the war. Particularly, I want to know if he was stationed in France at any time. Got it?"

"Yes."

"Of course, if Eckart is not his real name you'll be at a dead end. Still, I think he might just have been so sure of himself that he didn't lower himself to bothering with that sort of trick—changing his name. If he didn't," Lauriant added, "that will tell us quite a lot more about him."

"I suppose that it would," Guichard said, looking more discouraged than ever.

They had reached the end of the track. The café was open across the Rue de la République—a bright dry haven in a dull wet world.

"Come on, Guichard. I'll buy you one."

The policeman from Sarcelles brightened up immediately.

As they crossed the street, Lauriant saw the old Renault van, yellow and dented and sounding like it was minus large parts of its exhaust system, emerge from behind the Poulard shop. Marc must have fixed the engine. Lauriant wondered whether the black jacket still lay hidden behind the seat in readiness to impress some local farmer's fleshy daughter.

Lauriant, warmed by drink, found the notary's office on the Rue de la République. It was set back behind a small, old fashioned, black painted, spike topped, iron railing. On the blue door was a brass plate, in much need of polishing, with the words *Jerome Monnet, Notary* etched deeply into it.

Above the plaque, there was a square patch of marginally brighter blue paint, evidence of the spot that had once contained a second plate with another name.

Lauriant's knock was answered immediately.

"You are Jerome Monnet?"

"I am Jerome Monnet, yes."

Lauriant was faced with a man of a most unusual pallor. His face, his whole being somehow, seemed to be colorless.

He was tall, but very thin. His hair was lank and the top of his skull protruded through it where, that morning, he had been unsuccessful in hiding the paucity of it's covering. The man's features were angular, almost chiseled, bony, hollow cheeked and sickly.

Lauriant was reminded of those people you see after they have suffered a long illness. You know that it is them, but they have changed, lost something of their former selves, become in a way less complete. That was Monnet.

The notary's dull eyes hid beneath heavy hairy brows that were of an unattractive faded ginger in color and his lips, in contrast to everything else about him, were overly fleshy and, miraculously, they too had adopted the same repugnant shade of ginger.

His tongue seemed too large for his mouth and pro-truded dankly. It seemed that Monnet made a constant effort to control it by regularly sucking it back in after it had thoroughly moistened the fat lips.

The man wore a jacket and trousers that did not match, but were both faded to the point where it was dif-ficult to guess what their original color could possibly have been. They gave the impression, like him, of always having been old. His clothes hung about his sparse frame making the impression of tawdriness even more pronounced.

"And," he asked, "who are you?"

"My name is Lauriant."

The name seemed to mean nothing to Monnet. His bearing, at least, did not change.

"I am here to investigate the death . . . the murder . . . of Emile Eckart."

The notary's face registered emotion for the first time.

Lauriant would have been hard pushed to describe it. It was not incredulity nor was it indifference. The expres-sion undoubtedly existed but it still managed (with some inevitability with this man) to be somehow neutral. With someone else Lauriant might have felt that the man was trying to understand, but with Monnet, there was no way to be sure.

"I don't see that this has anything to do with me."

He paused as if considering the situation.

"You had better come in," he said eventually. The voice was flat, completely lacking in intonation.

The notary's office was small.

Mostly, the walls were surrounded with decrepit bookcases, some without fronts, which exhibited gaps where the veneer had once clung to their woodwork. Each bookcase contained, as far as Lauriant could tell, old leather bound volumes on the law. These looked as though they had not been opened or consulted for years.

There was no desk as such in the room and it looked as if Monnet worked at the long table, which was pushed into one corner.

The room was, Lauriant thought, unutterably sad. Nowhere was there the least evidence of the world outside this little space. No family photographs, no professional certificate in a frame, no radio, no discarded personal possession, not even a telephone. Indeed the office's single window looked out only on to a crumbling stone wall from which the mortar had peeled and the paint had flaked, leaving telltale patterns of its former glory in a poisonous green.

The whole thing left an impression of solitude, gloom, mustiness and decay.

Lauriant, mentally striving, tried hard to become accustomed to the unfamiliar setting.

Monnet did not ask him to sit down nor did the notary sit down himself.

"You are Emile Eckart's neighbor?" Lauriant began.

"He is my neighbor, yes."

The detective noted the subtle, but significant, change of emphasis.

Monnet's flat eyes were filled with distrust. It was the distrust of those who felt endangered.

"Did your neighbor have any enemies?"

"Not as far as I know. How could I know?"

"You last saw him when?"

"I do not recall."

"Was it, say, on Monday last?"

"As I said, I have no idea."

"Eckart was, I believe, well off? A respected man locally with good connections?"

"I have no idea of his financial position."

"And," Lauriant repeated, "was he a man of standing locally?"

"That depends on one's point of view."

"Has Eckart ever been in this," Lauriant looked about him, ". . . office?"

Monnet's big eyes betrayed no hesitation or uneasiness.

"No, not to my knowledge."

Lauriant walked across to the window and seemed to be inspecting the peeling paint on the opposite wall. He lit a cigarette.

"What do you know of Eckart's habits? For example, did you know that he was in the habit of taking a morning horse ride?"

"Yes, I did. However, the man's activities were of no concern to me."

"Then, you did not meet him socially?"

"Now and then."

There was something in Monnet's demeanor which might have been described as abdication. He sighed, but added nothing more. He was not exactly wearied, but appeared resigned to something inevitable. He gave the impression that the German's death was just another unnecessary burden for him.

"Can I assume, then, that you did not have business with him?"

"I had not . . . nor would I choose to do so."

"Where were you at the time of Eckart's murder?"

"I was with my daughter, Adrienne, at home."

"You are not sorry that Eckart is dead?"

"I have no feelings about it at all."

6

WALKING THE CORRIDORS OF POWER

Lauriant found the mayor in Etienne Perec's slick looking office.

Veyret, red haired and beaming, came forward with his hand outstretched. He shook Lauriant's hand vigorously whilst his smile, far from wilting, grew, if possible, even broader.

If there had been a baby available, Lauriant was sure Veyret would have kissed it.

The mayor was about thirty-five, ruddy featured and clad in a countryman's jacket with too many pockets. He was one of those people who looked five or ten centimeters too short for their girth. He simply seemed out of proportion; too close to the ground.

And, now, withdrawing his hand and clearly considering his civic duty to a visiting non-voter well and truly done, Veyret looked around him for a place to sit down.

Perec was perhaps five or six years older than the mayor. Dark, urbane, smooth and relaxed, he shook Lauriant's hand as soon as the mayor finally let it go.

"Please, please come in," he said.

"We have been expecting you. Indeed, Monsieur le Maire," Perec made a vague deprecating gesture towards the squat bulk that was Veyret, "was just telling me that you have been questioning some of the lesser members of our small community this morning."

Lauriant recognized in the lawyer's manner just the sort of self-satisfied smugness he hated.

"I question those who I think can give me answers," said Lauriant—suddenly angry with himself and irritated by his own childish attitude, which the lawyer's suave condescension had triggered.

"Of course, of course. Please, do sit down." There was no hint that Lauriant's anger had been noticed at all.

Perec went to take up what must have been his usual station behind a large, light modern desk. In the front of the desk were purposeless compartments covered with roller shutters. It must, Lauriant thought, be from the very latest range to grace the retailer's brochure. The chair was equally large with arms that matched the beige coloring in the desk top, on which rested that day's copy of *Le Monde*, its gothic style banner uppermost. Lauriant was sure that it had been placed there quite so perfectly for his own benefit, as so little else filled the off white expanse.

Lauriant pulled out one of his Chesterfield cigarettes and, without asking permission, lit it, blowing the smoke deliberately towards the man of affairs, who barely restrained a cough.

Veyret sat heavily in a corner armchair, his duty done, placidly awaiting developments.

"Tell me, why did Eckart claim to be Argentinean?"

"He did not claim to be an Argentinean!"

Perec looked surprised and affronted that any such suggestion could possibly have been made.

"Eckart was a citizen of that country."

Lauriant sighed audibly.

"Very well. When and why, do you know, did Eckart adopt this new nationality?"

Perec showed some hesitation in answering. Putting his elbows on the desk and squeezing the finger tips of his well manicured hands together to make a kind of tent, he said, "It was certainly before he came here."

The lawyer considered whether or not it was in his best interests to elaborate. He decided that appearing to be open with the detective offered more potential.

"He once told me that following the end of the war he changed his nationality, as Germans were far from popular then and subject, amongst other things, to tiresome, narrow-minded controls by the occupying Allied powers."

Perec's face registered his irritation with all such inferior mortals.

"You believed that?"

"As he needed to travel with as little hindrance and inconvenience as possible, it must, for Emile, have seemed a logical thing to do. Like . . ." Perec searched for the right expression, ". . . exchanging one's overcoat for a mackintosh, when it rains."

"But he did not hide his German origins."

"Not from me, at least. Nor from Veyret"—the polite "Monsieur le Maire" had slipped—"and nor from some others of us."

Lauriant wondered who "us" might indicate.

"Does 'us' include, say, Jerome Monnet?"

"Yes. Also, of course, others—including some of your colleagues in Sarcelles and the Sub Prefect."

"So it was not a well kept secret?"

"As far as I am concerned, it was not a secret at all. For Emile, you see, the change was just a . . . mechanism . . . simply a matter of convenience for a cultured man of the world, so to speak."

Lauriant registered this and changed his approach.

"In that case, why did this cultured man of the world find a remote small town like this to live in? It couldn't be that he was hiding, otherwise he'd have taken much more care to disguise his origins."

"I never asked him, so I have no idea."

"You were his bookkeeper?" Lauriant asked insultingly.

"I was his lawyer and his accountant! I handled all, almost all, his business affairs. And you will find everything in order, you may be sure of that."

Lauriant was sure of it. Perec was far too clever to let it be any other way.

"And where did Eckart bank?"

"In Sarcelles—Credit Lyonnais. I have the details here for you." Perec opened a drawer and pushed some papers across the desk to Lauriant. "You will see that the balance was substantial and, of course, that will be increased further when his insurances are paid."

"Is there a will?" Lauriant asked.

"Yes. I have it."

"Who benefits from the will? Do you know?"

For the first time, Perec looked a little uncomfortable.

"I do, for one. Small amounts are left to me and also to Madame Monnet."

"Madame Monnet?"

"Yes."

Again there was that slight hesitation.

"My inheritance is for the sake of friendship and for my services to Emile over the years. The bequest to Madame Monnet is . . . well . . . for another reason."

Lauriant looked surprised.

"Now, let's get this clear. Are you telling me that there was some sort of relationship between Eckart and Madame Monnet?"

Veyret let out a sound which was something between a snort and a laugh. Perec ignored him.

"No! No! Nothing like that!"

So, Lauriant thought, Mimi was right, after all.

"Emile disliked Jerome Monnet intensely. He used to bait him once in a while. It was almost a hobby with him. The legacy was part of this—designed only to infuriate Monnet. Also, of course, it insured that Monnet would be haunted for the rest of his days by the thought that Emile had slept with his wife. If not, from Monnet's point of view, why would he have left her the money? The harder she denied it, the more convinced no doubt Monnet would be that his suspicions about Eckart were correct. Emile would enjoy the thought that he was able to torment his neighbor even from beyond the grave. He was like that."

Lauriant realized that he had been shown another facet of the German's character—one that he did not like.

"You said small amounts were left to the two of you. Who was the remainder of this money," Lauriant lifted up the bank statements, "almost all of it, to go to?"

Perec paused for a moment and took a deep breath.

"To Marc Poulard."

Veyret jumped from his chair. "Poulard? Young Poulard? That thieving little scoundrel!"

The mayor was clearly hearing this for the first time. He spluttered, managing to say through clenched lips, "He must have been mad—Eckart must have been mad!"

"Yes, the Poulard boy," Perec repeated, ignoring the mayor's outburst, "will receive the great majority of Emile's fortune."

"I don't believe it!" Veyret flopped back into his chair. His bulk seemed to have deflated. "Poulard," he said softly, almost to himself. "Why the devil would Eckart have done such a thing?"

The lawyer turned from Lauriant and answered Veyret.

"I have no idea."

Perec seemed part way between irritated with Veyret and puzzled by the German's decision on the disposal of his estate.

"I only know this because Emile showed it to me before he lodged it with me for safekeeping. I think he only told me to give me a nasty shock. If that was his intention, it worked."

Lauriant thought that Perec may have understood his deceased client better than Mimi had realized.

"Anyway," Perec continued, "I would be surprised if he changed the will without my knowing. He only had it drawn up last year."

"You realize," Lauriant said, "the full implications of what you have just admitted to me?"

The other two clearly did not.

"Marc Poulard was at the scene of the crime. He had, therefore, the opportunity and now you have given him a motive too."

Perec looked amazed at the thought.

"No. That can't be. Poulard didn't know—doesn't know even now—that, for whatever bizarre reason, Emile had chosen to leave money to him. I was the only other one who knew about it. And I have no idea why Emile did it. He never explained it, he just told me about the will and gave it to me to keep in the safe."

"You didn't ask him why?"

"He wouldn't have told me, so what was the point?"

"The notary must have known," Lauriant said. "Who drew it up?"

"Not me, clearly—and not Monnet. Emile had the will drawn up on one of his visits to Paris. The lawyer there would have seen nothing extraordinary in it, not knowing the people involved."

Perec, it seemed, had suddenly run out of words and explanation. He raised his hands and stretched them out in exasperation.

"On the subject of opportunity," Lauriant pressed on, pursuing the advantage, "where were you, Monsieur Perec, at the time of the murder."

"Here in my office. I am an early starter."

"Can you prove that?"

"Not until after nine o'clock when my assistant arrives. She, if need be, can vouch for me after that." Perec laughed quietly. "You'll just have to take my word for it, won't you?"

"Oh, you may laugh, Monsieur Perec, but no alibi is still no alibi!"

Lauriant turned to the mayor. "And you, Monsieur le Maire, where were you at the time of the murder?"

Veyret's already florid complexion had turned puce at the very idea that he could be questioned. Suspected.

"I supervised the milking as I do every morning and then went to inspect some of my vines."

"Alone?"

This time, pink chased red followed by purple across the angry mayor's complexion.

"Not in the milking sheds."

"And inspecting the vines?"

"Alone. Yes."

"And at the exact time of the murder, where were you?"

"Driving through the town, I suppose. My vineyards are on the south facing slopes to the west of the town and my farm is south of here."

As there was nothing more to be had there for the

moment, Lauriant changed the subject.

"Tell me, did Eckart have help in the antique shop? Did he go to the shop every day, as other men would go to their office?"

Perec seemed to be searching for the correct answer, whilst Lauriant wondered why the question might be difficult.

"Yes, every day, when he was here. Only in the summer did he have help and, even then, not always. He would prefer to manage alone when he could. He knew that whoever he employed would know nothing of antiques. Once, one of the women he paid to keep an eye on the place sold an item for a fraction of its true value. After that, he would lock up the shop when he could not be there or was out of town. It never worried him."

Lauriant looked around for an ashtray and, not finding one, dropped his cigarette into the waste paper basket.

"How often was Eckart, as you said, out of town?"

"It varied. Two, sometimes three times in any year I suppose, if you count only the longer absences, say . . . of over a week."

"Do you know where he went?"

"No."

This time there was no hesitation in answering the question.

"He went to America once. I know that."

Both men turned to Veyret, who had spoken for the first time since the shock of being questioned. Perec, Lauriant noticed, was annoyed by the mayor's interruption. Perec did not like to volunteer information unless it was strictly necessary. Or strictly advantageous.

"That," said Lauriant, "will perhaps in some way account for Mr. Harris's presence in Saint Sauveur."

The lawyer, smooth again, clearly felt himself once more on safer ground.

"Yes, a fine fellow, Harris, and very well known in his field. He was one of Emile's closest associates. I have met him several times over the years and, as you know, we had dinner together last night."

"What was the purpose of that meal?"

"Purpose? Purpose? To commiserate with each other on the loss of Emile, of course."

7

THE CAFÉ & LOOKING AT ANTIQUES WITH LITTLE KNOWLEDGE

The interior of Eckart's shop was impressive.

Lauriant stood in the middle of the room, turning slowly, trying to absorb the atmosphere.

The first impression which came to him was one of tranquillity, the second, one of order, the third, one of hollowness.

Eyes half closed, he tried to imagine Emile Eckart in his shop. How had he behaved here, this man whose life had suddenly ended in a ditch with a broken neck, produced by a cruel blow from behind?

How had he worked here? Had he sat for hours simply waiting for a passing customer to come in or had he spent his time on the telephone that stood on the corner of his desk? Lauriant doubted that. Had the telephone rung without reply since Tuesday morning? If it had, who would have called?

Lauriant shook his head slowly.

Clearly, the shop was not crowded with bric a brac. Wherever the junk that Guichard had referred to was kept, it was not exhibited in this room.

Instead, the statues and sculptures were displayed on pedestals carefully chosen to compliment their size and

appeal and the paintings were thoughtfully hung to benefit best from the shaded electric lights above them and the
natural light from the large windows across the front and
side of the shop. The old tables and chairs glinted with the
results of long use and thorough polishing, reinforcing
Lauriant's first impression of tranquillity.

Nowhere, could Lauriant find a price tag.

Did the German adjust the price according to his
assessment of the wealth of the potential purchaser, or was
this an affectation to convey the idea that if you had to ask
the price you could not afford the item? No doubt, the
results had been the same.

Likewise, there was hardly a speck of dust in the place—
even after the shop had been locked up for nearly three days.

Lauriant found it hard to imagine Eckart himself cleaning up his workplace, but apparently, as he had no help in
the shop, this was what he did, and did thoroughly. Very
German.

Lauriant examined the glass display cases that lined the
back wall. They too were lit by hidden fittings. Inside, the
china and porcelain shone under the glare with a luster
designed to encourage interest and expenditure. Blues
and pinks, oranges and golds, greens and yellows, and
combinations of these and other colors came through in
many designs, patterns and shapes.

Almost accidentally, he found a small door masked by the
display cases and pushed through it into a completely different room, a room hardly bigger than a walk-in cupboard.

This room was stacked with broken pieces, old farmhouse fittings, unframed paintings and cheap antiques, which, Lauriant guessed, Eckart would have had no interest in selling.

It was probably from this room that he produced some quickly polished item that his tourist clients could afford and, Lauriant assumed, promptly overcharged them, whilst convincing them of the intelligence of their choice.

Back in the main part of the shop, Lauriant removed his coat and sat behind Eckart's desk. For a moment he wondered what he would do if a customer arrived.

Reluctantly, he opened the first draw of the desk and tipped out the contents. There were bills, a checkbook, a few unimportant notes, a broken pen and a surprisingly feminine cigarette holder, but no cigarettes. The second drawer followed, with much the same results, but including this time two invitations to dinner with the Sub Prefect—one from the previous month and one for a week hence—an appointment which Eckart would no longer keep. There were no books to be found, not even an antiques catalogue or a price guide.

Emile Eckart was clearly not the man to leave anything important lying around for casual inspection. The contents of the desk gave no solid indication of his way of life.

Disappointed but not surprised, Lauriant shrugged. He had more than half expected it. He knew the German would not be that kind of man. Also, he guessed that a search of the man's house would produce similarly sterile results. He decided that he would leave that task to Guichard.

Looking around in the back room once more, Lauriant found an old heater. He plugged it in behind the desk and turned it on, spreading his damp overcoat and his jacket in front of it. After just seconds, steam began to rise from them. He was sure that he was developing a cold.

Sitting back, his eyes rose to the chandelier that hung from the ceiling in the center of the room. Its light reflected into the window and accentuated the angles and curves of the sculptures on their pedestals.

Eckart had sat here for hours looking at the same view with little or no thought of selling antiques, unless by chance, and yet periodically acquiring sums of money which, according to Mimi and his bank account, were substantial.

He had then spent lavishly in what Mimi had called sprees.

Lauriant fancied that the rain might just be easing (but it might have been his imagination) as he paid his second visit of the day to the café.

"On your own this time." The barman—bald, plump and round—had stated the obvious. "Do you want the same again?"

"No, make me a hot toddy with plenty of rum, will you. I think that I'm getting a cold."

The café was bright and modern; no sign of an old metal topped bar to be found here. Like most of the businesses in the town, it probably divided its custom between the tourists in the summer and the locals all year round.

Lauriant looked around at the tables. There were only a few people occupying those in the window. The other customers were hardly speaking to each other. Perhaps the weather was getting to them too.

He decided to stand at the bar, which was backed with shelves supporting bottles, ordered ranks of sparkling clean glasses and little piles of tiny, white Apilco coffee cups.

Behind the shelves was a big wall mirror. Lauriant studied his reflection. Pale and swollen under the eyes, he thought that he looked appalling.

Professionally, the café owner had obviously decided not to notice.

"It's my quiet time," he explained, as he passed Lauriant his toddy. He served it with the glass on a saucer and the remaining half of the squeezed lemon beside it. In the glass was a spoon to stop it shattering under the impact of the hot water. After a second or two and a good look at Lauriant's puffy face, he overcame professionalism and poured in extra rum.

"On the house," he said.

Getting comfortable, he rolled up the sleeves of his shirt and settled his big, bare elbows on the counter, supporting his chin with one hand. He had decided that it was always worth trying your luck.

"We only offer a single dish at lunchtimes and at dinner this time of year," he said. "Tonight it's chicken with my wife's own special sauce. The customers like it." He took another long look at Lauriant. He was plainly not hopeful, but he tried anyway. "Better than the hotel and half the price! Will you be joining us?"

Lauriant considered it, but gave a vague reply. He felt rotten.

"Another?"

"Please."

The café owner's equally hefty wife appeared from the kitchen behind the bar, wiping her hands on her apron. Her appearance immediately transformed the place. Bubbly and bouncy, she greeted the regulars with a cheerful call to each by name. Several of them smiled back at her, mostly exhibiting an array of gaps where teeth had once resided. One even waved.

"Here, Jean-Pierre, give old Paul a red on the house! He looks like he needs cheering up! Not surprised, with this weather!" She looked around her. "And one for that old misery Beliares in the corner as well!"

Another of the regulars, an old man with the kind of bent back only a lifetime of manual labor can produce, cheered up noticeably.

"Who's this then?" she asked, looking at Lauriant. "Bit late to be on holiday!"

"This is the policeman from Paris, Helène," her husband explained.

Her attitude appeared to change not one bit, but a hardness crept into her tone.

"So, you're going to find out who bumped off the German are you? I wouldn't bother, personally."

"My wife's family . . ." her husband shrugged, ". . . in

the Occupation. She's certain all Germans are bastards. Who knows, she may be right. Anyway, not many of us liked Eckart. I wonder sometimes why he ever came here."

"Did you know Emile Eckart?"

"Eckart? No fear. Not personally, anyway. Those people would not be seen dead in here—beneath their dignity, if you see what I mean."

"Those people?"

"Well, Eckart for one. Perec for another and, of course, Monnet the notary—he's a queer one, I can tell you. And, before you ask, we only see the mayor when elections are coming around. Not that that makes any difference. Between them, one way and another, they've got everything pretty much sown up around here anyway."

"No opposition?"

"What do you mean? Political or otherwise?"

"Both, I suppose."

"Not to speak of, politically at least. Not much of a hunting ground for Marchais and the Reds down here—Poujade did all right for a bit. Still, he's gone now. Plenty of mostly silent discontent from the rest of us, mind you. If Delguedre wanted to plant one of his bombs in the town, there'd be more than a few to suggest a worthwhile target or two!"

Jean-Pierre paused.

"Sorry. I forgot who you are."

"Everyone's still entitled to his opinion, as far as I know," Lauriant said. "Even café owners and policemen."

The barman sighed.

"But, we're grumblers and grouchers, not organizers. You know our sort well enough, I dare say. It's probably the same in Paris and everywhere else for that matter. Most of us are too busy trying to make a living to go around picking fights with the powerful. Here, it would be a fight that couldn't be won anyway."

He looked resigned to the inevitable.

The barman's wife came back from serving the customers their wine.

"What old rubbish has he been giving you?" she asked Lauriant cheerfully, with a warm wink and a lively, fleshy nudge at her husband's fat paunch.

"Not much, but I was going to ask him about his customers last Monday night."

She saw the point straight away.

"Waste of time. You're barking up the wrong tree with Marc. He's a good enough sort—there's no real harm in him."

"That's not what some of my colleagues seem to think."

"Ah, policemen." She adopted a look that appeared to give her the wisdom of the years. "So in Sarcelles they still hold that little bit of pinching against him, do they? Manod—and he's not too bright—gave up on that as soon as he saw it was going nowhere easily. Too much like hard work! Not a man to stretch himself unnecessarily, our Manod."

"Yes, so?"

"Anyway, nothing was ever proved."

"On this Monday night, at least, Marc Poulard was here." Lauriant stated a fact.

"Yes, that's right."

The husband and wife looked at each other, silently deciding who would take the lead. No decision resulted from this noiseless debate as they both spoke at once. It took Lauriant to solve the problem.

"Ladies first," he said.

"Well, he was here, of course, as always. Poor devil was hiding out from that old swine of a mother of his. If she had her way, the poor lad would have no life."

"Go on."

"As usual, he played cards with some of the other younger ones and, at some stage—I can't tell you the time—he slipped out into the back room on his own," she nodded towards a closed door, "and played billiards for a while."

"That's a strange game to play alone."

This time the café owner replied.

"Marc—I don't know why, maybe it was his father, who showed good sense when he cleared off—is a lot brighter than most of the boys around here. Mind, his father wasn't so bright when he married the woman!"

He was thinking hard to put his thoughts into the right words.

"He sees things clearer, Marc does," he began again, "you know, understands more—bit clever. He reads the papers for more than the sports or the local scandals and the agricultural prices. He tried to discuss politics with me once—something about the new constitution, or was it a thing called trade liberalization? Anyway, he was wasting his time there. I've no head for de Gaulle and the rest, right or wrong. I run a café and leave the Glory of the French Republic to take care of itself. As I said, all that's none of my business."

Another idea came to him.

"A couple of weeks ago, I even caught him reading a newspaper in English over there in the corner," Jean-Pierre nodded his head to the right, "where that idiot Beliares is drinking his free wine. God knows where Marc got it from. When he knew that I'd seen him, he went red—got all embarrassed like youngsters do and went out, taking his paper with him."

The woman considered that it was now her turn once more.

"What my husband is trying to say is that Marc would get bored with the others once in a while. He needed to get away for a half-hour, be on his own. As none of the others plays billiards—in fact, on Mondays and Thursdays," she looked searchingly at Lauriant, "nobody else uses the back room, so it was a good place for him to go."

Lauriant tried to look as if all this meant nothing to him.

"What time did he go into the billiard room on Monday do you think? How long was he in there?"

There was an exchange of glances.

"I don't know," she replied. "I might have been in the kitchen. Do you know, Jean-Pierre?"

"I can't say."

"Did you hear the billiard balls hitting each other,

perhaps, or dropping into the pockets? Look, did Marc come out of the room at any point and, say, order another drink? Talk to someone? Ask for chalk? Anything?"

"The chalk is in the room. Still, I don't remember."

"Is there a way out of the café from the back room?"

"Yes," the café owner said, "but it is always locked. Either my wife or I keep the only key. A couple of times, people slipped out that way without paying, so we lock it."

Lauriant pondered this.

"All right," he said, "Who had the key on Monday?"

"I did," the wife answered.

"So, you remember that. And, the door was definitely locked?"

"As he said—locked." Helène sounded very sure.

"And you didn't hear Marc, alone and playing billiards in the back room on Monday night?"

"As I said, no."

"Has Marc a particular friend?"

"Not really. If at all, Beppo, I suppose. He's closer to him than most."

"Where can I find Beppo?"

"Tonight?"

Jean-Pierre thought for a moment.

"Tonight, he'll be on the road to La Rochelle, I guess. He drives a truck for Veyret. He will be delivering produce for the morning market."

"And tomorrow?"

"In bed till lunchtime. That's normal. Then, he will come here to eat or, on Friday, he has a day off. Then he will be here all day, getting well and truly drunk—to which I have absolutely no objection."

"And, he enjoys your cooking, I'm sure," said Lauriant to Helène.

She looked pleased.

"If not, he would be the only one who doesn't!"

As he recrossed the Place Clemenceau, Lauriant let out a violent kick at the air. It was raining heavily again and he had sneezed hard.

8

THE LADY REMEMBERS &
THE GIRL WITH LONG LEGS

Lauriant recalled that tinkling laugh from behind her front door at their first parting in Saint Sauveur . . . every time he met Mimi in the years that followed.

Now six whole years later, in the gloom of the Restaurante La Langoustine, he remembered his own rare smile too. Had Mimi but known it, for him it was the beginning of a long way back.

Things were still adrift in his life even now, but she had begun a process of repair that day, which she had, consciously or not, continued ever since. He put his hand lightly on hers.

She placed her little glass of marc on the table, freeing her hand as she did so.

"When *did* you first suspect that Perec was being untruthful about withholding the contents of the will?" she asked Lauriant.

He shrugged.

"Well was it before or after your bedroom meeting with Adrienne?"

Lauriant did not like the implications of that question.

"Before," he said.

"So it was me who put you onto him!"

She sounded relieved.

"I disliked him from the first, but you certainly alerted me to him. Later, of course, I needed him to play his part in the final little subterfuge."

"And Genevieve Monnet? And what about Harris, the American?"

"Slow down!"

He leaned towards her and patted her hand again. This time, she removed it more slowly.

"I had not met Madame Monnet then, remember? And I had only seen Harris at the hotel."

"She was beautiful."

"Who? The mother or the daughter?"

"Don't be mischievous! The mother, of course."

"She was beautiful, I thought, and Guichard was very taken with her. Also, I felt sorry for her."

This time, it was Mimi who was not pleased.

"Now, what else has been happening in Saint Sauveur over the last few months?" he asked.

"Dr. Nadeau has died. As you know he fell ill last year."

"And Josephine?"

"She's sold the house and the practice to a very nice young doctor and taken the money off with her to a nursing home in Saint Jean d'Angely. By all accounts, she is very happy there playing the rich widow! Everybody calls her 'Madame' and she revels in that."

She finished her marc and, over protests which were largely feigned, Lauriant ordered more.

"Now, stop avoiding the issue and tell me exactly

what happened back then, when the girl came to your bedroom. . . ."

Relations with the skinny hotel maid had improved remarkably since Lauriant took to his bed with the flu.

Françoise was, he decided, obviously the kind of girl who drew comfort from being a comfort to others. Like his own mother, she completely reveled in it.

Pandering to her, Lauriant had even allowed her to comb his hair and shave him this morning with almost a complete lack of protest, beyond what was merely polite. If he had been honest with himself (which he was not) he would have admitted that he had enjoyed it.

Taking his cue from the maid, Bertrand, one of the porters, had even taken time out to light a fire in the bedroom's big grate. After a struggle, it had finally sputtered into life.

"That'll do you some good," he said, "Do you want Françoise to sort out your bedclothes?"

The fire took a long time, Lauriant thought, to warm the big room, but that may have just been the result of his temperature.

He alternated in great swings between too hot and too cold—never anything comfortably in between. Frequently, this background misery was punctuated and intensified by prolonged fits of sneezing or coughing.

Now and then, Françoise or the porter came back into the room to check up on him.

"You okay?" Bertrand asked.

"I'm surviving. When will the sun come out?"

"Oh. Any time now."

The maid gave him some pills and some medicine. All medicines, in Lauriant's experience, tasted foul, but this one was in a class by itself. He hated being ill and normally was a bad tempered patient, but it was difficult to be nasty to Françoise.

So, it had taken an illness to break down suspicions along with, had he but known it, a friendly reassessment of him from Helène and Jean-Pierre, the owner of the café. Word, it seemed, had got around.

It was past eleven o'clock when Françoise made another of her appearances.

"Not more medicine already?"

"You've got a visitor," she said.

"Send him in."

"It's not a him, it's a her."

Françoise instinctively came to the bed and tidied it and its occupant as best she could.

"You'll have to do," she said, but did not look that convinced.

"Who is it?"

The maid stood aside with a look of admiration and of jealousy combined with a strong tinge of dislike, to allow the visitor to squeeze by her into the bedroom.

Lauriant saw a tall, dark, overly slim girl, perfectly made up and dressed in the height of fashion (as far as Lauriant understood those things). However, he knew when he liked what he saw. His thoughts went back to the plump farmers' daughters on the train. The contrast could not have been greater.

The girl's clothes were expensive, no doubt bought in Paris. No circulating catalogue could have offered anything like this.

Moreover, the visitor carried her clothes well. She unquestionably had a presence—hard to define, but she would have turned heads anywhere. In short, she looked spectacular. The envy, and the object of loathing, for any woman the world over.

Next to her, poor Françoise in her worn black uniform and white apron looked very shabby indeed.

The girl was wearing a short, light coat, very much in vogue, which she removed immediately to reveal an even shorter and therefore—no doubt to her—even more fashionable pale pink skirt. It was all topped off with an almost transparent pink blouse. Her long, beautiful legs were encased in nylon; the shade perfectly matched her skirt. The color of the shoes—little heals and open, strappy backs—mirrored and complemented the coat.

This, without any argument, was style.

Off guard, Lauriant, the cold momentarily forgotten, made a slight face in pleasure and appreciation. Françoise, from behind the girl's back, misinterpreting his motives, thought that she responded in kind in poking her tongue out. Perhaps combining this with a fresh recognition of her own relative shortcomings, she then chose to put distance between the visitor and herself and left the room.

Lauriant noticed over his visitor's shoulder that the maid kept the door ajar. Perhaps she did not trust the newcomer with her prize patient. Perhaps, he thought, she might even be listening. He would bet that she was.

The girl, very elegantly, shook the raindrops from her coat and placed it carefully across the foot of the bed. She contrived to make even this simple movement appear lissome and graceful.

"I thought I had better come to see you," she said simply.

She took her time and, without a sign of embarrassment, openly inspected what she could see of him above the sheets.

Apparently satisfied, she took a packet of cigarettes from her bag.

"Do you mind?"

She held up the packet and Lauriant registered the long fingernails, painted a delicate rose-color. She lit the cigarette without waiting for him to reply and, affectedly, blew a long stream of blue smoke towards the ceiling.

"I'm Adrienne Monnet," she declared.

"I guessed."

She gave a little laugh. Compared with Mimi's delightful laugh, Lauriant thought hers was, like her, perhaps a little too thin.

"This is my week for collecting policemen."

She let herself down smoothly into the chair, carefully disposing of her long legs to reveal as much of them as possible to the detective without vulgarity.

"I'm not here just because I'm curious. Although, I

confess, that I am. I thought that by now you would have come to question me . . . my family, that is."

Lauriant decided that it was best just to listen. Anyway, what was the point in trying to stop her? Her father had obviously not told her of his meeting with the detective and there was nothing to be gained by Lauriant telling her now.

"Well, I waited for you most of yesterday . . . didn't go out. When you didn't come, I gave it some thought—I *do* think, you know, contrary to some people's opinions—and decided that it was time that I should come to see you."

There was no mistaking it: The girl, used to being the center of attraction, had clearly been put out.

"Thank you for coming. As you see, it would have been difficult for me to come to you, as I planned to do this morning. By the way, was it you who spied on me yesterday when I visited Mimi?"

Adrienne looked genuinely surprised. She threw her head back and did her best to adopt an attitude that conveyed complete disinterest. It almost succeeded.

"Why on earth should I do that?" she asked.

Lauriant smiled at her deliberately sophisticated air.

"Well," he said, "what have you come to tell me?"

"First, I like to get to know people. It's something of a hobby of mine. I add them to my collection."

"So I am now being collected, is that it?"

She shrugged as if he had stated the obvious. Her little shoulders rose and dropped gorgeously.

"What about Marc Poulard? Is he part of your collection?"

She recrossed her legs, a mirage of diaphanous pink.

"So, you do know about that. I thought so. From Mimi, I suppose. That is one of the reasons I came. I would prefer to explain about him without my parents being around and I think that, in a way, I have done that for you."

Lauriant was surprised that she cared about her parents' views.

"I understand," he said. "You collected him."

"Correct. He visits me at home, so to speak. Two nights a week."

"One of which is Monday."

"Yes. Mondays and Thursdays. Of course, he didn't come last night."

"Will you marry the Poulard boy?"

"I don't know. Maybe. Actually, thinking about it . . . no, whatever for?"

"Are there other guests on other nights?"

"Sometimes. Not recently."

"So. Is your collecting currently on hold?"

"Something like that. Shall we say that there is just no one else of interest currently."

"You mean no one worthy of collecting?"

"Yes."

She changed the subject.

"Also, I came to tell you that I disliked Emile Eckart."

Lauriant was sure that her aversion to the German resulted from his lack of interest in her.

"And, your parents? Did they dislike Eckart too?"

"My father did."

"And your mother?"

She pouted. Lauriant caught a glimpse of a petulant overgrown child through her elegant, exquisite exterior. Did the girl really see her mother as a rival?

"Yes, she disliked him too. But only because he wouldn't go to bed with her."

Lauriant felt strongly that the missing last word in Adrienne's statement should have been "either".

"And your father disliked him too, you say."

"Hated him would be nearer the fact—but my father couldn't have killed him."

Well, at least she was blunt.

"Are you so sure?"

"He wouldn't have the guts. He's too weak a man. Eckart once told him to his face that he wasn't a real man at all and he just turned away. After that, of course, they barely spoke to each other."

"Was that when they argued over your mother?"

Adrienne sighed. "So Mimi told you about that too. It wasn't really important . . . except to my father."

"You were with your father at the time that Eckart was killed?"

"How did you know that? I was with him that morning, yes, before he went to his office. But as to the time, I can't be sure. His office connects with our house through a corridor and he uses it all the time going in and out."

Françoise, her face showing concern, looked around the door. Lauriant waved her back out with an encouraging smile.

She was being very truly upstaged and she did not like it.

"We won't be long now," he said to her.

"She," Adrienne indicated the space which Françoise had just vacated, "doesn't like me either . . . because of Marc."

"She'll make someone a good wife one day, that one."

"But *I* won't!"

Adrienne was very certain of that.

"Does Françoise have an interest in young Poulard?" Lauriant asked.

His question was answered with another dazzling shrug.

"She did. But not now. She did . . . before I spoiled things for her."

Adrienne's lovely head came up as if challenging him to disapprove of her. Whatever reaction she had expected to produce, she was disappointed. Defiantly, alluringly, she crossed her legs once more.

"Well, that's all I came to say."

She rose and put on her coat. Lauriant offered her his hand and she shook it with surprising warmth.

"When will you be seeing my parents?"

"Soon, I suppose."

Despite feeling rotten and over prolonged protests from Françoise, Lauriant got up in the mid afternoon. The little maid had lost her patient for now, but she insisted on stuffing his coat pockets with pills and handkerchiefs as mementos.

In reception, Bertrand could not hide his surprise at seeing him up. His first stop was the hotel bar, where he had two hot toddies. They were not as good as the ones in the café the night before. Another plus for Helène and Jean-Pierre.

He had not finished his second drink when Guichard telephoned. Lauriant, closing the door behind him, took the call in the booth near reception. Through the glass, he could see Bertrand carrying out one of the salesmen's cases. The man was following him, waving his arms and protesting. From his complete lack of reaction, the porter, it seemed, had suddenly gone deaf.

"You were right about the street girls," Guichard said. "Three of them knew Eckart. He was a regular but not a frequent customer. He paid well and he gave them no trouble."

"No he wouldn't. Anything from Germany?"

"Not yet. I'll let you know when I get something back."

"Have you seen the examining magistrate?"

"Yes. He is still happy to leave things to you."

"I imagine that you searched Eckart's house?"

"Of course. And, also his stables and his garage."

"Anything?"

"Nothing."

"What about the art expert?"

"He's on his way. You were right, we had to get him down from Paris. His name is Charles Lazareff. He has a shop—a gallery, I mean—in a very smart district. He knows his job, they say. You sound like you've got a cold."

"Something like that."

"Oh well, you must have brought it with you from Paris."

9

THE AMERICAN

On his return to the hotel bar, Lauriant saw Michael Harris seated in a corner. He had slipped in no doubt thinking that Lauriant had left. The American was drinking coffee. Lauriant, resigned, decided that he could put this confrontation off no longer. He picked up a cup from the sideboard.

"May I?"

Lauriant pulled out a chair and planted himself opposite Harris, who made no effort to hide his displeasure.

"I can't object, I suppose."

To Lauriant's relief, the man's French was good.

"There has been a murder, Mr. Harris, so I think any objections you may have would carry little weight."

Lauriant lit a Chesterfield, inhaled once and immediately put it out. In his condition, it tasted bad.

"Okay. What do you want to know?"

The American was, at least, direct.

Lauriant helped himself to some of the coffee.

"You have known Emile Eckart for some years. What was the nature of your relationship?"

"I valued paintings for him and, when possible, located buyers for them."

"Okay. And where and how did you find these buyers for Eckart's paintings?"

"I am not unknown in the art world."

"You are then, I take it, a dealer of some sort?" Lauriant sipped gingerly at the coffee. It was almost cold.

"If you like . . . but as I said, I am really a valuer. My clients are mostly private collectors. Also, once or twice, I arranged a sale to a small gallery or museum for one of Emile's paintings. That, you may not know, is a normal arrangement in the art world. Collectors do not often wish to advertise their interest in certain pictures. As a result, they appoint someone to act for them and, in my case, I can not only represent them, but value their proposed purchase for them as well."

Harris paused like a teacher checking that his class was following a difficult lesson. Satisfied, it seemed, he continued.

"Also, I collect a little myself, but I have never kept one of Emile's pictures for more than a short time in my own collection."

Harris appeared to think that it was time for a confession.

"You see, I not only make my living from paintings, but I build my life around them. It is an abiding passion for me . . . almost my only interest."

"Were these pictures of Eckart's great masters?"

"Oh, by no means. But they were very valuable nevertheless . . . well worthy of their places in museums and collections."

The schoolteacher manner was enhanced, as the American

drank his coffee and adjusted his glasses with his free hand.

"You see it is not every collector who can afford the most expensive and the most rare. However, although their resources mean they must be satisfied only with what they can afford, they, like me, still must pay considerable amounts of money to satisfy their passion. Still, they should not be disappointed."

Again, the American paused to make sure that Lauriant was following what he said.

"Also, of course, some collectors specialize in certain periods or certain artists and will pursue that interest as far as their money will take them."

Lauriant considered this.

"Were these pictures of Eckart's genuine?"

"If you mean were they forgeries, most certainly not."

"And where did Eckart obtain these paintings?"

"I have no idea," the American stated flatly.

Lauriant's disbelief must have shown, as Harris looked bored with such unforgivable ignorance.

"That too is quite normal in our world," he explained, a note of suppressed exasperation in his voice, "even when one has doubts, one rarely asks a seller where he obtained a painting in which one is interested. That would question the integrity of the seller and, worse, risk losing the painting."

There was a pause before Harris chose to explain further.

"However, as Emile's paintings had no provenance— that's our word for no proven history of ownership—their values were perhaps less than they might otherwise have been. Therefore, my expertise and reputation were even more important to Emile in maximizing the prices of the paintings that he wanted sold. If I said they were right, this was accepted and the price paid was correspondingly greater."

There was now a note of pride in his voice.

"Are you a rich man, Mr. Harris?"

Lauriant remembered Mimi's ideas and, despite himself, looked at the American's beautifully crafted shoes.

"That is a matter of definition. I take my commissions, of course, and my profession allows me to make profits, sometimes substantial profits, on my dealings in my own and others' paintings. After all, if a painting has been in my own collection for some time, others look on that as a confirmation of its being genuine."

There was still a strong hint of pride in his voice and, as he had done in the restaurant two nights before, Harris removed his spectacles, wiped them and returned them to his nose. The gesture was unpleasantly self-assured.

"If you want my view," he added, "Emile was killed for some sordid mundane reason. Passion, perhaps, or plain revenge for some slight—imagined or not. Anyway, for some squalid, petty thing. Despite the gloss, this is still a peasant society. They nurse grudges, you know. Still, I suppose that I don't need to tell you that, you're an outsider too. Anyway, I would hardly have murdered him, as it wouldn't have paid me to do so."

Lauriant moved the conversation on.

"The pictures in Eckart's shop, what about them?"

"You've seen them?"

Lauriant nodded.

"Then clearly you know nothing of art. They are adequate enough, no doubt, to decorate some provincial drawing room wall and impress the ignorant neighbors, but not anywhere near being of the same quality as those which we were discussing."

"If these good paintings of Eckart's are not in the shop—and they are certainly not in his house—where are they?"

"I have absolutely no idea. It is, of course, entirely possible that Emile acquired them when he could and currently he just did not have any good painting in his possession."

"In that case, with nothing to value and, therefore, no sale to arrange, Mr. Harris, why are you here?"

"Because Emile asked me to come."

"For what?" Lauriant persisted.

"I have no idea," the American repeated. "He did not have time to tell me before . . ."

"You were here for three or four whole days before the murder. You saw him at least once—I know that. Are you telling me that you did not talk to Eckart about why he sent for you? I don't believe it!"

Harris was completely unmoved.

"Even so. That's how it is."

"Where were you early on Tuesday morning, Mr. Harris?" Lauriant suddenly sounded more official.

"Here in the hotel. In my room."

"No witnesses?"

"No, of course not. None."

"I must ask you not to leave Saint Sauveur without my permission, Mr. Harris."

"But I planned to return to the United States tomorrow."

"I am afraid that that will not be possible."

The American, drinking down his cold coffee in a single gulp, looked very unhappy, as Lauriant left the bar.

Lauriant had put the idea that Eckart was killed in some sort of random attack out of his mind.

He did not, however, exclude Harris's suggestion that the motive itself, whatever it was, might have been simply petty to everyone except, of course, the murderer. That was always possible.

Nor, could he exclude Marc Poulard from his thoughts.

The lad had opportunity and perhaps motive. Somehow, he may have learned about the contents of Eckart's will.

After all, murders are not committed without a motive. Even madmen have motives for their actions in their muddled minds.

Was the motive money? Or, perhaps, it was a crime of passion involving two middle-aged men squabbling over a woman.

According to Mimi, the lady who saw everything, Perec, the man without an alibi, had some relationship with the Monnet woman and Monnet himself had accused the German of making love to his wife.

That left the mayor. Had he been involved with Madame Monnet too? It was possible.

Lauriant gave an involuntary shake of the head.

In either case, the attack was likely to have been pre-meditated. It was hard to conceive of a suitable weapon being accidentally at hand on the track when the attack was made. No, Lauriant concluded that the murderer had planned the thing, that he or she had taken the weapon, whatever it was, to the spot with the sole intention of using it on Eckart. And that intention had been carried out.

Lauriant paused in his walk down the Rue de la République. He was opposite the Poulard shop.

There were no customers. Madame Poulard came out to look at him across the road. She crossed her arms, cradling her big, slack breasts. Lauriant snorted to himself and walked on.

Why, he wondered, had the murder been committed when it had?

It seemed everyone who mattered was aware that the German took a lone ride along the track each morning. Apart from Mimi, who knew about Marc Poulard's twice weekly visits to Adrienne Monnet's bedroom, everyone else would believe that the track would be deserted at that time of the morning—a good place for settling accounts once and for all.

But why had the murderer chosen to, or been forced to act on that particular morning and on no other? Why not a day or a week earlier or later? What had been the trigger which made action possible and maybe even inevitable on that singular morning?

10

THE NOTARY'S WIFE

Lauriant turned the corner into the Rue Voltaire. As he passed Mimi's house, he caught a glimpse of her well-groomed head behind the window.

He knocked on her neighbors' door.

"Is Madame Monnet at home?"

The maid, who must have been well past fifty and a little uncertain on her legs, vanished into the house without replying, leaving Lauriant standing in the rain outside the front door.

After a moment or two, she returned.

"Madame will see you," she announced grandly, as if an audience had been granted with the president of the republic. Was there a slight smell of whisky on the old maid's breath?

Lauriant followed the maid down the hall and was shown into a large, rich sitting room.

If Harris really thought of these people as peasants under the gloss, well, this veneer was very thick indeed.

The furniture was exquisite: a mixture of Louis Seize and First Empire. Everything—the chairs, the tables, the enormous patterned carpet and the deep red curtains at the three tall windows which lined one long wall—blended together to form an extremely pleasing whole.

Outside, trees were visible in a well-tended garden. Equally neat flower borders, in the English fashion, edged green lawns. The garden, as far as he could tell, was empty. It gave the impression of never being used, merely maintained.

Turning back to the room Lauriant was reminded forcefully of monochrome photographs he had seen as a child of rooms in old chateaux. This room was almost as large and it must have stretched the full width of the house.

"Please wait. Madame will be here shortly." The maid tottered out without taking his overcoat.

A very beautiful house. However, unlike Mimi's home, there was no feeling of warmth about the room. Lauriant looked around. People, it seemed, came and went here leaving little trace. He was sure that the items of furniture had been in the same positions for years, polished regularly, by the maid he had seen probably, but hardly used.

Lauriant decided not to sit on one of the fragile looking chairs. He thought about a cigarette and abandoned that idea too. It seemed out of place somehow.

"I am Genevieve Monnet. Please, let me take your coat."

The voice came from behind him. When he turned, he saw a very handsome woman indeed framed in the doorway, the light behind her playing upon her neatly trimmed dark hair which was cut fashionably into the nape of her neck. He could see immediately that her daughter had inherited her color and, no doubt, when she was younger, Madame Monnet had been as slim as Adrienne. Now, she was more rounded and, if anything, even more striking.

"You wished to see me? I'm sorry, but my husband is at his office."

She walked into the room, the skirts of her pale tan colored dress accentuating her plump bottom and the feminine, provocative swing of her hips.

"It's you I want to see, Madame," Lauriant said, "I have already talked with your husband."

"I imagine that you have come about Emile Eckart's murder."

She had the same direct manner as her daughter.

She did not sit down.

"Are you thirsty?"

He shrugged.

She went back to the door—again with that deliberately so provocative move of the hips—and called the maid.

"Bring me a whisky, Marie, and," She turned to Lauriant. "A beer?"

It was the last thing Lauriant felt like, but he nodded dumbly.

She pointed to a chair and he took it. She sat down herself, perched on the edge of the seat.

"I can't think what I can tell you about the murder."

"Frankly, neither can I," he admitted. "First, tell me about your husband and his relationship with Emile Eckart."

"Relationship?" Genevieve Monnet clearly thought the word preposterous. "You could hardly call it that."

"Your daughter tells me that your husband hated the German."

"Ah! So, you have seen Adrienne already."

Madame Monnet nodded absently to herself as if her estimation of her daughter had risen somewhat.

"Well, there is little point in lying to you," she began.

She looked towards the door hoping for the maid's return.

"It was common knowledge anyway. My daughter was right. Eckart was almost the complete opposite of Jerome. He was traveled, carefree, unworried—a man who easily impressed others, including men my husband would have liked to impress, but was manifestly unable to do so. People dealt with Jerome because they had to. They sought out Eckart because they *wanted* to. The difference is enormous."

Another look towards the door and still no sign of Marie.

"Is your husband older than you, Madame?"

"A little, not much. About eight years. However, he is not a man who has aged well, if you see what I mean. He looks, acts and sounds a good deal older than he is."

She thought for a moment and then made up her mind to commit herself.

"It's his disposition I suppose. He spends too much time in his office with all those dusty old records." She laughed suddenly—bitterly. "He has himself become, so to speak, almost as dusty as them."

The maid, at last, brought in the drinks on a silver tray. Lauriant looked at the cut glasses and the tall, elegant decanter. He would have expected it no other way in this house.

Madame Monnet ignored the water jug and drank half of her whisky, which nearly filled the glass, immediately. She touched her hand to her chest, grateful for the drink. She took a deep breath and kept hold of the glass.

"My husband has few friends and no interests," she continued, sipping the whisky more cautiously now. "For some reason which I have never discovered or been able to explain, he is very bitter with life. Deep inside, I believe, he wants to be everything that he is not and despises himself for what he is. Can you understand that?"

A thought seemed to come to her and she moved more comfortably in her chair.

"Do you know that I cannot recall ever hearing him laugh."

She studied this in isolation, ignoring the policeman for a moment as if he had ceased to exist for her. She pulled herself together and took another sip at her glass.

Lauriant, for form's sake, drank a little of his beer.

"My husband treats the world as a place full of threats, a place where suspicion and watchfulness are necessary every minute, if one's not to be discomforted by scoundrels. Somehow, he's convinced himself that without constant vigilance, the world will single him out for . . ." A pause. "For . . . I don't know what. But in his mind whatever it is will be uniquely unpleasant. You see, he's like a small and timid animal in a jungle surrounded by predators—constantly listening, constantly on edge and constantly afraid, even, sometimes, of shadows."

Lauriant really began to appreciate for the first time the impact that the terms of Emile Eckart's will was going to have on this family.

"Was he like this when you married him?"

"I suppose that he was, but it wasn't so . . . developed. As the years progressed, he became worse. He became more suspicious, grayer. Truthfully, I have often thought of leaving him as what he does is, I think, little short of cruel to us—Adrienne and me . . . and poor Marie too."

She poured herself more whisky.

"Have you ever had the feeling that you are constantly watched, day and night, even when you know that there is no one there?" she asked.

Lauriant shook his head.

"Well, it's like that. Each day I wait for some minor misfortune to occur which will be turned into further evidence that the world is against him and that his enemies—whoever they might be—will have scored a major new success in their efforts to make his life ever more miserable. In turn then, of course, he will take his spite out on us."

Genevieve Monnet looked closely at Lauriant as if willing him to understand.

"Also, he comes and goes so silently. You can turn around and find him behind you and you will not have heard a thing. Or, he simply appears where he wasn't the moment before."

"And your daughter?"

"My husband believes that he has both of us totally at his mercy. That, I think, is one of the few pleasures that he takes out of life. But he is not wholly correct. In my case, he's right, but Adrienne is of an age and a generation which can ignore such things."

Madame Monnet seemed sad that she too did not belong to this younger generation of free spirits.

"And," she added quietly, "after all, Adrienne will leave us soon, no doubt."

"Do you expect your daughter to marry shortly?"

"Either that or just move away. That's often how it's done now."

Lauriant thought that marriage might be much further from Adrienne's mind than her mother might wish.

"And your husband's attitude to your daughter? Would he strike her . . . or you?"

"No. No. He's no need to do that. He gets his pleasure more subtlety than that. He inflicts a different sort of pain. Besides, unless he was very greatly provoked, I don't think he would hit either of us."

"Why haven't you left your husband?"

"Look around you. I have great comfort here and some social standing in the town. What would I do and where would I go? I'm not educated to anything. I would end up working in a dress shop . . . or worse."

Lauriant was beginning to think that Genevieve Monnet was one of the saddest people he had ever met.

"You married for money?"

"In short, yes. But I have since earned every franc of it and deserved every last ounce of comfort it has given me."

Lauriant had no doubt that she had.

"Did your husband marry for love?"

"I don't know. I don't think so."

"Then why?"

"I imagine he married because his father told him to. To preserve the family line. Jerome has always been very disappointed that Adrienne is a girl and he has made no effort to hide his feelings on that score from either of us."

Lauriant felt embarrassed at having to ask the next question.

"You have, however, taken some lovers?"

Genevieve Monnet was not offended.

"Frankly, it was a way of staying sane—and, I will admit it to you, also a way of getting a little revenge on him. There have been several over the years."

"Was Eckart one of your lovers?"

"No."

It was the familiar bluntness, but there was, Lauriant thought, a note of regret in her voice.

"And, Perec?"

"Yes."

"What was your husband's reaction to this? Did he know?"

"No. At least, I don't think so. He would have been angry, had he known—you know of his reaction to even the suggestion that Eckart might have . . ."

She paused, sorting out her ideas before continuing.

"He'd have been jealous in his own way, that's true. Felt further diminished rather, I suppose. That more than anything else. Meantime, I'll continue to make the most of things whilst I still can."

"Did you know that your daughter let men into the house at night . . . into her bedroom?"

"Yes."

"And you didn't object or at least talk to her about it?"

"Why should I? It was none of my business. As far as I'm concerned, she can find her own pleasures where she can and in her own way."

"Like you?" Lauriant prompted.

"I suppose so. Yes, like me. After all, I of all people should understand her motives!"

"Where were you on Tuesday morning, at the time of the murder?"

"In bed, of course. Marie always brings my coffee at ten o'clock. She's done it for years. I never rise before eleven."

"Forgive me, but were you alone?"

"In bed?"

"Yes. In bed."

"Of course."

"I just thought that your husband might . . ."

"Hardly!"

"What about Veyret, the mayor . . . was he also one of your lovers?"

Genevieve Monnet seemed taken back at first and, then, she laughed again, more loudly this time.

"The mayor? The mayor, Monsieur Lauriant, is my brother!"

"You . . . you were Genevieve Veyret?"

Lauriant could not keep the astonishment out of his voice or his face.

"Yes, of course. Has nobody told you?"

"No."

"Well! I'm not really surprised. Very few people around here will tell you anything unless they have to."

"So I've learned."

"I was fortunate enough, you see," she added, "to take after my mother in looks, whilst my brother, poor devil, now looks exactly as my father did at his age."

"But if you were a Veyret, why did you need to marry Monnet for his money? Your brother has his farms and his vineyards—"

"Yes," she interrupted him, "and I had nothing. As with old man Monnet, so it was with my father. Everything was for the son and nothing for the daughter."

The empty glass was refilled again.

"My sister-in-law—Jerome's sister—was in the same position as myself. She was left poor after her father's death. She didn't marry and my husband would give her nothing. Jerome used to say that had his own father intended that his sister inherit anything he would have arranged it that way himself. My husband felt in no way responsible for her."

She thought again for a moment or two and then did her best to explain further.

"Jerome did not consider his sister's plight any of his business, you see?"

Lauriant nodded.

"Oh, he was polite enough if they met in the street, but that was all. When I came here, he told her to leave even though she had kept house for old Monnet and Jerome ever since she was old enough to do so. That was now my responsibility and she was cast out as surplus."

Now, Lauriant felt that he needed his beer.

"I don't think that Jerome ever visited her in the tiny apartment she rented on the Rue Bir Hakheim, although, as you know, it's very close to us here. After I married, she would come to me now and then and, when I could, I'd give her money from the amounts I was allowed to keep the house. Marie the maid," there was a nod towards the door, "loyal soul, would cover this up for me. Still, I don't think my husband knows about it to this day."

Another long drink of the whisky followed this.

"I look on it as retribution that my husband has no choice but to leave his money to a daughter."

The satisfaction came through in her manner and Lauriant imagined the lady of the house and the maid, much younger then, taking secret pleasure from outwitting Monnet and pilfering at least a little of his money. Was it then, perhaps, that they started toasting their success together in Jerome Monnet's whisky?

"Do you still help out your sister-in-law in this way?"

"No. She died about four years ago. She had a cancer and she died as she had lived—in poverty. There was no money for the funeral. Jerome arranged things—as cheaply as he could, naturally—and as far as I can tell he has given his sister no further thought ever since. If he does think about it, which I don't think is the case, it will only be to regret spending the money on her funeral."

Lauriant winced inside and changed the subject abruptly.

"Do you think that your husband is capable of Eckart's murder?" he asked directly.

"Frankly, I have no idea of what my husband is capable."

She finished the whisky and Lauriant had become even more grateful for the beer. He finished it in a single swallow.

"Have another?"

"I will."

"Come on. Let's go down and join Marie. She could probably do with a drink."

Genevieve Monnet picked up the tray and glasses and waited.

"Of course," Lauriant said, and it seemed the most natural thing in the world. "Then, if you will excuse me, I must go."

11

DINNER WITH THE TRUCK DRIVER

Lauriant realized that he felt relieved to be back amongst ordinary people with ordinary lives.

Friday, as Jean-Pierre had said, was Beppo's day off and he was almost drunk when Lauriant had found him, exactly as expected, in the café.

The owner had pointed him out at one of the corner tables.

He was a large man, very big indeed, not yet quite thirty, with strong arms and grimed hands, in need of a shave and hair untidy.

He was the very image of the working man. The man whom the students in Paris—how far away that seemed from here!—believed they were representing and leading when they were rioting and beating up middle-aged policemen and putting them in hospitals with a punctured lung.

Lauriant felt, somehow, that Madame Pardreux and her sons would not see things quite that way. And, that symbolized more trouble being stored up for the future.

"You won't get much from him, I don't think, but I've had a word with him all the same. That might help."

Jean-Pierre had clearly done his best.

"Do you want a drink?"

"No. Not just now."

Madame Monnet's beer seemed stale in his stomach now that he was out of that house.

Lauriant joined the truck driver at his table. Beppo had a pronounced sense of loyalty to his friends. He was giving nothing away. Mind firmly made up, he adopted an attitude that combined defiance and distrust. None of the policeman's questions got much of a response.

After ten minutes of this Lauriant said, "Look, Beppo, all I want to do is get at the truth. I've nothing for or against Marc Poulard—neither one way or the other, but if you keep on avoiding answering my questions, even if there is no good reason for it, what am I supposed to think? Can't you see that you'll only make it look bad for Marc?"

Lauriant saw a pair of bleary, bloodshot eyes looking at him. They took their time to focus, whilst Beppo's brain struggled to deal with the implications of the words.

"Marc is a decent bloke," he said firmly, his giant palm hitting the table powerfully, as if that could be the only and the final consideration.

The bar man looked across, ready to intervene, but Lauriant signaled him to stay away,

The detective did his best to appear encouraging.

"True—I'm sure he is a decent bloke," he said.

"Everything was going all right until the Monnet girl got on to him," Beppo added.

"Going all right?"

"Yes all right for him and Françoise, the maid at the hotel. You know her?"

"Yes."

"Oh, Marc got a bit drunk when he could and even played around with one or two," he paused to laugh, "well, four or five of the girls out on the farms. Nothing serious in that. All in the line of duty, so to speak. But, Françoise understood that. She knew him and his ways. It was not a problem for them. Anyway, like me, he would have grown out of it."

He stared into his wine.

"She's not stupid, Françoise. She understood," he repeated.

Having lined up his glass, Beppo reached for it and drank down his wine. Helène appeared, winked at Lauriant and refilled the driver's glass without being asked. Experience had taught her that this was the way to keep him talking.

"But the Monnet girl was different," Lauriant prompted.

"Yes . . . different. She was one of them."

Beppo's nose, red from the wine, wrinkled as if something which smelled bad had been placed under it.

"She had money, you see. It broke the rules, so to speak. Farm girls are one thing, but Adrienne Monnet!" He shook his great head. "That worried Françoise and they—she and Marc—began to argue. The arguments got worse recently."

Beppo checked to see where Jean-Pierre was. There was no sign of him. The driver leaned forward and lowered his voice.

"So last Monday night, Françoise slipped out of the hotel when no one was looking and met Marc in the back room. There was some arguing and more tears."

"You were in the back room with them?"

"Only for a moment . . . just to calm them down. I'd borrowed the key to the back door, you see."

Beppo took another drink of his wine and fumbled for a cigarette.

"You've met Marc's mother?" he asked.

Lauriant pulled a face.

"I see that you have. In that case, you may understand better. The back room was the only place left that the two of them could meet privately. I stood guard at the door to make sure no one else went in."

The smoke and the smell of Beppo's Disque Bleu enveloped them.

"Even then if she'd known," Beppo indicated the café owner's wife, "that there would be trouble and a row, she would not have lent the key to me. But, she's got a good heart, Helene. She thought that she was doing them a favor."

"But they argued and Marc went to the Monnet girl nevertheless?"

"That's right. You've got it. What a bloody mess!"

Lauriant lit a Chesterfield and offered one to Beppo.

"Prefer these," he said.

For the first time that day, through the haze of Lauriant's cold, the cigarette actually tasted good.

"Thank you, Beppo. You're a decent bloke too."

Leaning back in his chair for a moment and thinking over what the truck driver had said, it hit Lauriant that in this case Harris could be right—the gloss on this peasant just did not exist.

But, Beppo was honest and uncomplicated and Lauriant liked him just for that.

Here he was in the middle of an explosion in society, in art, in music, in politics and in what would become known as pop culture—on the streets there was youth optimism and protest, ideals and violence—and Beppo, well, he merely placed importance on a glass or two of wine, good food and loyalty to his friend.

The detective sighed. He was having trouble enough coping mentally with this new reality himself. The genie was out of the bottle and from now on nothing would be the same ever again.

It was impossible to see where it would all end. The jeans clad philosophers thought that the journey was an end in itself. But, journeys are pointless without destinations. They still had to learn that.

In these times what chance had the millions of Beppos in France? Their best hope was to stay out of it all, to survive as their forefathers and mothers had done for generations.

It was getting dark outside and the rain still ran down the café windows in long streaks. Lauriant was finding it hard to imagine it any other way.

"What's on the menu, tonight?" Lauriant asked.

"Beef with a Béarnaise sauce."

"Sounds good to me."

"You want some?" the proprietor's wife asked, looking pleased.

"Why ever not?"

"But, your cold . . ."

She gave her husband a puzzled glance.

"We can't let illness get to us, can we?"

He turned to the truck driver.

"Will you join me, Beppo? Yes? Good! Now, patron, do you have a bottle of the local red? I drank some somewhere and it was pretty good."

The dinner with Beppo led Lauriant to thinking more about Marc and Françoise.

Next morning he went to the Poulard shop. It was empty—as always it seemed—when he pushed open the door.

Madame Poulard appeared from the back.

"Marc's not here," she said, as unfriendly as ever. She turned to go back into the far room.

"That's okay. It's you I want to see."

"Me! Whatever for?"

She was genuinely surprised.

"Tell me about your husband."

"That useless waste of space? Gladly!"

12

THE ART EXPERT

After an unhappy hour with Madame Poulard, it was time to meet Guichard's art expert.

"Harris? Yes, of course. Michael Harris. I don't know him personally, but I know of him, of course."

Lauriant's throat was still fuzzy with the aftertaste of Madame Poulard and of last night's dinner and the wine. Beppo had insisted on buying another bottle. Even after Françoise had brought him extra coffee in his room just now, he still felt dry and thirsty. He sneezed.

"Excuse me . . ."

"Bad cold? I'm not surprised. The weather's been terrible in Paris. It'll do you good down here, as soon as these showers blow over."

Lauriant, lips tightening, ignored this.

More and more he felt the need for a base; an office of his own, somewhere he could concentrate and think things through. There were facts and opinions that needed putting in order and he was not getting the chance to think!

He felt out of sorts at having to receive the art expert in his hotel bedroom, which, despite the window open to the rain, he felt sure, was still malodorous from his occupation and from stale cigarettes.

"Harris is very well respected. I should tell you that he is most definitely not one of the shady, disreputable types who inhabit the fringes of our business."

"Okay."

"In fact, he's quite the opposite. He is, I suppose, at the top of his tree. I myself would have no hesitation in dealing with him."

Charles Lazareff got the impression that he was telling Lauriant something that the detective did not want to hear.

"I see that you had formed a different opinion of Harris," he observed shrewdly.

"I confess that I don't like him."

"I thought that you were supposed to keep an open mind on these things—you know, sift through the evidence and so on."

"That's the theory, of course, but I've never quite succeeded in practicing it myself."

Lazareff accepted this admission without comment.

"Harris," he continued, "I know, has a certain arrogance about him. That is a part of his reputation too. But, he probably considers that he is good at what he does and that his arrogance comes of right."

"If he is, as you say, amongst the very best, the most sort after, why would he be here in this small town doing business with a man like Eckart?"

"Have you asked him?"

"All he will tell me is that in the past he has organized

the sale of paintings which were, if not exactly from Eckart's collection, at least owned or provided by him."

The expert thought this over.

"Unfortunately for your skullduggery theory, that stands up . . . it would make sense," he said at last. "Harris has been involved in some very major art transactions all over the world. That's how he's built his reputation. But those transactions, as you can readily imagine, do not take place every day. He would take, maybe even need, I suppose, smaller commissions meantime, if he could get them. Also, he would probably not be too particular about the source of the commissions as long as he were certain that the paintings involved were not stolen or, at a minimum, did not appear on any missing list."

Lauriant found this strange world difficult to understand.

"That would be the sort of bottom level, then? You say it's okay and I, without trying too hard, can't find grounds to dispute what you say, then everything's all right?"

Charles Lazareff, still unruffled, said, "That's one unfortunate way of putting it that's not exactly inaccurate."

"Then, from what you say, his income under these circumstances would be somewhat irregular."

"Yes."

"I should add that it seems that Emile Eckart's income was similarly erratic."

"The same reasoning could apply, of course," observed Lazareff.

The expert pursed his lips.

"But back to the American," he said. "Irregular income, yes, that's true. But over any period it would be more than sufficient. I'm sure that Mr. Harris enjoys a more than comfortable style of life. The sort of lifestyle that would enable him to travel where he needed—worldwide. He would have to fund that himself, of course, as often his dealings would be purely speculative. Anyway, the costs would, ultimately, be built into his substantial commission level."

He looked at Lauriant.

"His commission levels *are* said to be substantial," he added with emphasis.

The telephone rang and Lauriant, disgruntled, picked it up.

"It's Guichard," said the voice at the other end, "I've got the information you wanted from Germany."

"About time!"

Lauriant excused himself to Charles Lazareff.

"Go ahead," he said to Guichard. He sounded resigned, as if he expected only to hear more bad news.

"Well, first his name really was Emile Eckart."

"That's something."

"But second, if you were expecting some sort of SS or Prussian type, you can put the idea behind you."

"Oh."

Lauriant was disappointed. Subconsciously, he had expected just that.

"Eckart was a Bavarian. He came from Zellingen, near Wurzeburg. And also, I'm sorry," Lauriant braced himself for worse news, "but he never served in France. Before the war, he was a teacher. His father died when he was just a boy and his mother apparently had a pretty hard time of it."

Lazareff watched Lauriant's shoulders sag.

"His rank was that of . . . major," Guichard continued, "but he wasn't in the army. That slowed us down a bit, as you can imagine."

"Yes."

"He was in the air force."

"Eckart, a pilot?"

"No—not aircrew at all."

Lauriant waited as Guichard read through the reports.

"In fact, for most of the war," Guichard was elongating his words to give himself time to read ahead and absorb the information in the papers himself, "from 1940 onwards anyway, it appears that he served on Marshal Hermann Goering's personal staff and spent his time between fatso's mansion, Berlin and Italy. He had, it seems, a soft war."

"Do you know what his duties were?" Lauriant asked.

Guichard had been waiting for the question.

"Yes, I do now. You'll like this bit. After a little time, the Germans admitted to me that he was involved in procuring art treasures for Goering's private collection."

"Good God! So that's it!"

"Looks like it," agreed Guichard. "And of course he got them any way he wanted. No one in those days would have dared question his activities. The Germans thought at first that I might be trying to get some of the stuff back for our government, as Goering did a fair bit of 'collecting' in Paris too, so it took them a time to get even a little bit helpful."

"I can imagine! Thanks anyway, Guichard."

"A pleasure."

Lauriant hung up and turned to Charles Lazareff, who sat patiently awaiting the outcome of the conversation.

"This is a day of broken theories. First, Harris is not by any means shady—thank you for that—and second Eckart was no SS sort. Looks like I'll have to start thinking again! Still, according to my colleague, during the war Eckart collected art. Stole, I suppose would be the better word—for Hermann Goering."

"Really!"

"He probably helped himself to some of the Marshal's little treasures and, when he thought it was safe, began selling them on—using Harris."

Lazareff seemed to consider this possibility.

"No. No. I doubt it," he said at last, "not unless he was both very brave and, at the same time, very foolish."

Lazareff pulled a pipe from his pocket. "I smoke," he said lifting up the pipe, "I hope that you don't mind?"

"Not at all! Please."

The expert spent a moment or so concentrating on filling his meerschaum with light colored Dutch tobacco and lighting it. The tobacco smelt sweet.

"I don't think," he resumed, "that this man Eckart

would have dared to double-cross a murderous scoundrel like Goering. Apart from Hitler, you will recall, Goering was the most powerful man in Germany. He was above the law, such as it was, and his revenge would have been deadly and uncontrolled."

There was another pause.

"Did you know that Goering founded the Gestapo?" Lazareff asked.

"Yes, I did. And I can, of course, see what you mean."

"If Eckart did that—double-crossed Goering, I mean— he would almost unquestionably have been executed, and maybe not too painlessly at that. It would have meant a lingering death in a concentration camp at best."

"So that can't have been it, then?"

"It really is most unlikely."

The expert took a long puff at his pipe.

"You see Goering's agents were jealous of each other as well as smart. Eckart's chances of getting away with stealing from him were so small that . . ."

A thought struck the expert.

"You do think Eckart was intelligent, calculating, don't you?"

"In my estimation, very intelligent."

"He won't have done it, then. For sure, one of the others would have informed on Eckart to curry favor."

Lauriant blew out his cheeks. On top of everything else there went Guichard's hypothesis. He was dishonest enough with himself to disown the thesis and load it on to his fat colleague.

"As an example," Lazareff went on, "these people were adept at evading customs duties between Italy and Germany. They underdeclared the values of shipments to the Marshal and no one dared question it, even though it was, in some circles, common knowledge. Mussolini knew about it, but even he did not dare to challenge Goering. So, I can't see Eckart doing it, can you?"

Reluctantly, Lauriant felt that he had to agree.

"Once," Lazareff continued, warming to his theme, "a consignment for Goering was shown on the manifest as being worth just some few hundred thousand lire— peanuts— when, in fact, the crates involved contained two Canalettos and works by Spanish, Florentine and Venetian masters, plus furniture and a marble relief of the Madonna and Child. And this, I can tell you, was not an isolated occurrence by any means."

"Could Eckart have set up on his own behalf, then?"

"It is more likely than stealing from Goering, but I don't see how. Anything worthwhile would have been logged. If it went missing, there would be a hell of a row and the axe would fall—quite literally, as that was the legal method of execution in Germany in those days."

Lazareff's hand went unconsciously to his neck.

"Nevertheless," Lauriant said, "we know that these paintings do exist. They must have come from somewhere . . . and we know that Harris arranged their sale."

Charles Lazareff puffed hard at his pipe and seemed to consider this.

"Yes, but that is a reason for Harris to keep Eckart

alive—not a reason for him to kill him. Without Emile Eckart, there would have been no more commissions, after all."

"Unless, as we have not found any of the paintings still in Eckart's possession, the source had now dried up," Lauriant tried.

"It's possible, naturally. But, even so, why should Harris have killed the German?"

Lauriant took out a Chesterfield and for a while the two men smoked in silence.

"I assume," Lazareff asked, "that the paintings were genuine?"

"Harris swears so."

"Then I don't see a motive, do you?"

"I suppose not."

13

SOLITUDE WITH FRANCOISE

For the rest of the day, Lauriant stayed in his room.
Françoise was the only person who saw him at all.

Later, she told anyone who would listen (and there were many around Saint Sauveur) that the detective from Paris divided his time between lying on the massive bed, smoking cigarette after cigarette, and pacing the floor.

He looked depressed and withdrawn.

"Fed up. Honestly . . . fed up—that's how he looked," she said.

At one point, he sent her out to the café for even more cigarettes.

When Helène could only provide Galloise, still not completely sure of him, Françoise had worried. But, he accepted them without the least sign of complaint. She was not even certain that he had noticed.

Also, bleary-eyed, he swallowed his medicine and half smiled his thanks at her. She did not like that. No grimace and definitely no outburst.

"He really must have been feeling proper ill," she told everyone, describing and relishing every small detail.

Once or twice, Françoise caught Lauriant talking to himself, as though he were rehearsing a speech.

Then, she would catch him fidgeting with the ornaments in the room. He moved little items into precise positions like pieces on a chessboard. She thought (wrongly) his mind was not registering what he was doing.

"Funny business this. Whispering to himself like that," she said to Bertrand, "He's not himself—really he's not. D'you think we ought to get Dr. Nadeau?"

"Leave it. You go and check his fire instead. Don't want him burning the place down."

Leaving Françoise where she stood, the porter wandered off to contemplate further the mysterious ways life has of sending people, who are not fortunate enough to be hotel porters, mad.

"It keeps coming down to the same thing," Lauriant mumbled when Françoise came back into the room to check the fire. "Always, the same thing."

"What thing?" Françoise asked bravely, but she gave up without receiving a reply.

He moved a small jug to a spot between a mirror and a gaudily painted plate so that it lined up perfectly with the lamp. Bent over with his hands on his knees, he stared at the objects for a moment, almost satisfied that he had fitted another fact precisely in its proper place.

"Good!"

The maid, poker in hand, turned from the fire.

"Good!" she repeated and smiled, without really knowing why.

Lauriant smiled back.

Then, he realized that Françoise had changed something in his thinking.

Françoise had smiled! Françoise had properly smiled—not one of those polite, lukewarm, halfhearted, unconscious smiles. This was a real smile!

Several times during those hours, Françoise emptied the full ashtray into the fire and, having wiped it out, replaced it on the table under the window.

"Thank you, Françoise," he said once, but mostly he did not seem to have heard her or seen her. Perhaps, most of the time, he was not even aware that she was there.

Lauriant, hands to aching temples and sitting on the end of the bed, digested his new fact.

"Well done, Françoise!" he said quietly to himself. "Very well done!"

So, he thought, Perec was right. Marc Poulard knew nothing about the contents of Eckart's will . . . but someone else somehow must have known what was in it. If they did not, either nobody would have killed the German— clearly not right—or Perec himself was the culprit. That was open to question.

But, what had Etienne Perec to gain?

He positively was not in need of the small inheritance Eckart's death had brought to him. He probably received more than that each year for looking after the German's business and legal affairs. Was he protecting someone? Yes, he was! Did he have an alibi? No, he did not!

Lauriant pushed his ornaments to new positions, placing "Perec" with "Monnet", possibly with "Harris" and certainly with "Veyret". The real Perec and Harris had met for dinner and all of them formed a coterie around Eckart—each for their own reasons, Monnet's unquestionably negative. What of the others—positive or negative?

The mayor. Yes, the mayor. Then, there was the mayor. . . .

Not—with his farms and vineyards—in need of money either. Could he have been made angry enough to kill for some reason? It was not unlikely. Maybe the bluff exterior hid some deeper hatreds within Veyret. It was like that in small towns. Lauriant tried to picture how Veyret and Eckart behaved with each other. What could perhaps have driven Veyret to murder? Was Perec involved in that too? They were thick, those two.

Harris and Veyret, however, seemed a very unlikely combination.

So, Lauriant was sure that, whatever it was, the motive was complex. Not just simple greed.

If it was simple greed, all logic led back to Marc Poulard and the circle (another plate completed the pattern) would be complete. The detective removed the plate almost at once. Now, after the maid's smile, he could not bring himself to believe that it was that obvious.

Lauriant thought about the boy. Rascal, yes . . . thief, probably . . . but, murderer? Did he have that in him?

Later, Françoise found Lauriant lying on the bed. He had taken off his shoes and his toes, she saw, were constantly on the move. Both of his eyes were open but this time again, he gave no sign of recognition. His brow was furrowed like a man thinking hard and finding no quick solution to his problems. He was breathing regularly almost as if he were at least half-asleep.

Gently, she covered him with the spare blanket from the wardrobe.

"You're asking to make that cold even worse."

If the motive was not purely money, Lauriant's thoughts turned inevitably to the Monnets. That was a family of complexes—a family in affluent and comfortable tumult, in sheltered and well-bred turmoil.

The wife beautiful, physical, disillusioned, unfaithful . . . that was one side of her; and on the other: the woman settling for cozy cruelty and snug drinking sessions with Marie the maid, who was, probably, her only true friend. The sexual relationship with Perec, readily admitted by Genevieve at least was, Lauriant knew instinctively, important. But, how had it helped to create the climate for murder? Was it her that Perec was protecting?

The husband harsh, even heartless, inadequate in his own eyes and, according to his wife, frightened. Mimi thought he was also a coward. But cowards do kill . . . often.

Was he at last able to avenge himself on the world in general by killing the man whom he thought of as the living embodiment of his own failings? Worse, Eckart was capable of showing contempt for Jerome Monnet in public. Would Eckart's sleeping with his wife or refusing to sleep with his wife been more galling to Monnet?

Adrienne, the daughter, what was he to make of her? Striking she certainly was, but she was deep too. Lauriant knew that he could meet ten thousand girls and not find another like her.

He understood now Marc Poulard's reactions to the notary's daughter when they had first stood together in the rain discussing Eckart's death.

Adrienne certainly had an impact. Impact enough for Perec to wish to protect her? Ruefully, Lauriant admitted that Adrienne had enough impact for anything. Alibi? Yes. She was with her father. Wait a minute! Was she? Lauriant searched his memory. He moved the little painted cream jug, thought for a long time and, then, put a plate next to it.

He knew the problem. Deep down, Lauriant was finding it hard to have the smallest bit of sympathy for anyone implicated in this business, except perhaps for the Poulard boy and Françoise herself. Rarely had he met such an unlovely bunch. And this realization—his dislike for the people involved—was making it difficult for him to work through all the possibilities.

He did not think that he had been at fault professionally, except perhaps in turning his back on his pressing duties, along with his other responsibilities in Paris. But he had paid for that with his cold and by involving himself in a case that was really none of his concern. Also, he realized, he had been influenced by his dislike of narrow-minded local intrigue and by his aversion to self-important people who controlled others' lives without a thought of the consequences of their actions and of the miseries they would bring.

When some of these people had come along, he had taken them almost entirely at their word, at face value. Others he had distrusted from the start. That, he knew went against the grain (good, solid Beppo would have said that it broke the rules) but, ultimately, it had changed nothing.

In the end, it would not influence his judgment or his actions.

Françoise came in once more. She watched him closely, but she could not decide if there was any real change in him.

Seriously worried now, she pulled the curtains together blotting out his view of the lights of the café through the rain.

He regretted not being there in the café, not enjoying a good hot toddy, not eating Helène's food, not enjoying a joke with drunken Beppo and not drinking the local wine.

Irrelevantly, Lauriant guessed that somehow Mayor Veyret probably even had the local wine market sewn up in his pocket. He was sure that he was right.

The maid fished around for the table lamp, finding it where he had left it in a revised line of ornaments. Replacing it on the bedside table, she flicked it on.

Françoise looked at Lauriant. His cold showed in his face, ugly and red now. She was not sure that she did not also see bad temper and frustration in his features.

She thought about offering to get him some more pills, but in the end—her nerves getting the better of her—she decided that she should leave him to himself for a while.

Back downstairs Bertrand had gone home. His day's work was over. She would get no help from the replacement porter. He was, she decided, with all the wisdom of her twenty odd years, just a kid.

She felt very alone.

Lauriant was angry with himself, but he would have found it difficult to explain why.

He was absolutely sure that he had hit upon the truth of the matter at one point, but it had slipped away from him, as one loses the thread of a story or of a television program when it is interrupted by advertisements for toothpastes and cleaning fluids.

Outside, he could hear footsteps as people doing ordinary things on an ordinary night walked quickly through the rain to get to where they were going.

He held back the curtains with one hand and watched the street for a while.

Dropping the curtain impatiently, he started to think again, trying to put each item in its place. Once more positioning each fact as he knew it in relation to the others . . . once more.

He was certain that he did not have all the information he needed to complete the picture, but what he knew was enough for him to construct the alternative possibilities.

But still, the picture stubbornly refused to become clear. The facts still resisted his attempts to fit them together into a coherent whole. He was close, but not yet finished.

It was as though he was trying to stop time and visualize each person in their place. Then he would attempt to wind time on and analyze where they were then, what had changed, what each person knew or could have known, who had spoken to whom in the interim.

This process brought him, next, to the American, Michael Harris.

Harris was different. Harris was the outsider.

He was only here in Saint Sauveur because the German had asked him to come. It was just another business trip. Where was he at the time of the murder? In his hotel room. Any witnesses? Of course not! It was that sort of case.

Harris, Lazareff the expert had said, had no motive to kill. Harris, on the contrary, it seemed had every reason to keep Eckart alive. Just another business trip!

Or was it?

Where was the merchandise? There were no paintings to be found! Where the hell did these paintings fit in? Where had they come from? Lauriant suspected strongly that the paintings were the beginning of the chain. In his mind, he went over his conversation with the art expert again.

True, Harris was well known, very respectable, but murder is sometimes a genteel pastime. Lauriant, anyway, still found it hard to believe that Harris and Eckart had not talked together about the reason for Harris's presence in Saint Sauveur over the days before the murder.

What other reason could the American have for being in Saint Sauveur . . . he knew no one but the German. . . .

Lauriant's hand hit his forehead! In the seconds that it took his headache to recover from the blow he said, "Mimi! Mimi!" He moved the little jug and the plate right next to each other.

Mimi had given him the clue all along!

His colleagues, without doubt, in time would say that for him the solution had been child's play. That was a mistake. But he appreciated when that time came that he would be vain enough not to contradict them.

He rang down for Françoise and she was up the stairs immediately.

"What are you doing up?" she asked.

It was not boldness that made her speak. It was surprise.

"Go down to the bar and get me a bottle of cognac," he ordered.

Her smile went. "Are you sure?"

His look silenced her and, as she left, he called after her, "And don't forget the glass!"

Twenty minutes later Françoise was sitting with him. She was uncomfortable. Normally, she would not dared to have sat down in a guest's room—even when they were not there. After a few minutes, she could take it no longer.

"I must go."

He was on the bed again, enjoying the brandy. He consoled himself, without much conviction, that it was good for his cold.

Lauriant, in his turn, was now playing with peoples' lives. He was, like Harris, the outsider. When this was all over, he would leave it behind him and return to his own world, to his own problems and to his own troubles.

It was a strange feeling—this playing God.

Whatever happened, these people would be the ones picking up the pieces of the existence he left behind him. Would they succeed? Some would and, then, some would not. The notary and his daughter; Marc Poulard and

Françoise; the mayor and his sister; the valuer and the lawyer and man of affairs.

There was no way now, of course, for him to tactfully withdraw into some corner and pretend to himself that he had made no difference, no matter how much he regretted getting involved.

He felt a grudge against Guichard—against them all for involving him in their world and worse, he hated himself for his weakness in allowing himself to be involved.

He looked hesitantly at the telephone on the bedside table, but decided that he was not quite yet ready to use it.

He stood up, irked with himself. Irked by everything around him.

He went over to the door, opened it and called Françoise once more. She must have been waiting, because she was there instantly.

This time, he sent her for coffee.

"Hey, Françoise! Whilst you're downstairs find out for me who was on duty early on Tuesday morning."

"All right."

He drank the coffee in great gulps, as Françoise watched. She felt nervous, but she also felt important . . . maybe for the first time in her life.

"Listen, Françoise, I want you to go around to see Mimi for me," he said between swallows.

"Mimi?"

"Tell her I sent you and ask her if she has seen anyone else," Lauriant chose his words carefully not wanting to use Marc's name. "Apart from the person she mentioned to me visiting the notary's house—his house, mind you, not his office—in the last week. I don't care if it's by the front door or," he paused, there was no avoiding it, "or by the back wall."

The smile vanished from her face. Françoise looked glum. She knew what he meant.

"Also, and this is the most important thing, Françoise, has she not seen anyone she would normally have expected to see. Got that?"

"Yes."

She hesitated.

"But what about the hotel manager? I'm supposed to be working. If he finds out . . ."

"If he gives you any trouble, refer him to me. I'll sort him out for you. Off you go, my girl!"

Françoise, the friend of the powerful, the ally of the man who could intimidate hotel managers, smiled at him again.

"Okay! I'll get my coat."

When she had gone, Lauriant reoriented his thoughts afresh. His luck had improved, but not his mood. He was sure that he had it worked out, but ultimately everything would depend on the information Françoise brought back from Mimi.

He looked at his table, satisfied. He was very tired. He did not want to have to move the ornaments again.

Later, when asked, he would find it difficult to explain his feelings, almost his reluctance to bring the case to its close. But that was not enough . . . not the whole story.

He hated what he had to do and hated more the inevitability of having to do it.

He picked up the telephone.

"Can you get me Monsieur Etienne Perec? . . . Yes, at his home . . . Then Chief Inspector Guichard at Sarcelles sur Mures?" he said to the young porter, who was doubling as switchboard operator for the night.

After a few seconds Perec came on the line.

"This is unexpected," he said.

"I want you to read Emile Eckart's will tomorrow."

"But, it's the weekend."

"I know."

"If you insist. I will invite the beneficiaries to my office."

"No. We'll meet here at the hotel. I'll arrange it."

"I see no point in that, but very well. What time?"

"Say, tomorrow morning—oh, and not too early, eleven will be fine."

"Very well," Perec repeated.

"Also, there will be a few others there besides the beneficiaries. Do you object?"

"No. Not under these circumstances. Emile was murdered, after all."

Lauriant hung up and the telephone rang again almost

immediately. It was Guichard.

"You're working late. Can you arrange for us to meet with the suspects tomorrow?"

"What—all together?"

"Yes, but not at the local police station. If we do that, there is a fine chance that our culprit will run. Tell them we're meeting to read Eckart's will. I've already had a word with Perec. If anyone doubts you, tell them you are acting for him, not me, and because there's a murder involved. That should be good enough."

"Right."

"Also, ask the hotel manager to let us have a room here at eleven. He's not on duty, so you'll have to dig him out at home."

"Tell me who you want and I'll arrange it," Guichard said efficiently.

Lauriant listed the names into the mouthpiece.

"Don't let them give you the run around because it's the weekend."

"No fear of that."

Guichard paused, wondering whether to ask . . .

"You know who did it then?"

"Yes, I know," Lauriant replied, but there was no triumph in his voice.

14

TOO MANY LIES & TOO FEW ALIBIS

———————

Lauriant had only reluctantly decided to see them all together.

He felt uneasy about this, as it was not his usual method of working. Had he been in Paris, in his own environment, he would have interviewed them separately in his office, which would give him maximum advantage in the struggles that were to follow. He would have smoked cigarette after cigarette and he would even pass some of the suspects on for his subordinates to continue the exhausting process of interrogation.

This would go on (sometimes for days) until one or another of them gave up and confessed or until Lauriant could come to the truth by comparing statements, identifying a lie here and a contradiction there. Then he would present his findings to the suspect and the wearisome game would be finished.

Now, as he entered the large dining room of the hotel he saw that fat Guichard had assembled them all—apart, that is, from Mimi, who had hastily arranged for Madame Putet to sit with Alain, and Françoise, who were waiting together in his bedroom.

He wondered, idly, what those two would find to say to each other.

Mostly, the people assembled in the dining room tried to avoid speaking to each other; even exchanging glances seemed too dangerous.

As if by some mutual unspoken agreement, they had spread out about the room under the watchful eye of Guichard and the somewhat less alert gaze of Manod, who stood at the door, stiff in his uniform, his kepi pulled straight and low.

Marc, the leather blouson for once in evidence in his mother's presence (an act of bravery, as Lauriant entirely understood) and Madame Poulard sat at one table. It was the one Lauriant and Guichard had used on their first evening together in Saint Sauveur. That seemed a lifetime ago now.

As far from them as possible—it seemed by design—was another gloomy little gathering of Perec, Veyret and Harris. Perec held a large brown envelope . . . the will.

The Monnet family sat at another table. For once united, they made up a third group hovering somehow between the others.

Jerome Monnet looked as colorless as always and the women, by complete contrast, had dressed up for the occasion—each, no doubt, wanting to outshine the other. Genevieve, looking worried, was in indigo and Adrienne in an unwittingly complimentary pale blue.

Lazareff and the doctor had settled themselves into

one corner as if forming an impartial, disinterested panel of experts ready to give their opinion if called upon to do so. Nadeau had a little file of notes under his arm, whilst Lazareff was, no doubt, wondering what the reading of the murdered man's will had to do with him.

When Lauriant entered, Marc Poulard started to stand. Seeing that no one else did, his mother pulled him down roughly, giving him one of her lethal glares which she reserved especially, it seemed, for undeserving males in general and for her own son in particular.

Lauriant felt sorry for him.

At least in due time, if Marc was as bright as the café owner thought, Françoise's rule might be a little less uncomfortable for him than his mother's reign. Who knows, maybe he would teach Françoise to read the things in the papers that interested him. Perhaps, like his father, in the end he would give up and run away to bigger and better things. Anything is possible.

Lauriant lit a Galloise from the fresh pack that the maid had just slipped to him before he left the bedroom. He took three or four paces into the room. He looked at each of them in turn and he saw anxiety in all of their eyes and a little fear in some. He let out a cloud of thick blue smoke.

Perec was about to begin proceedings, when Lauriant stopped him.

"We will not be following the usual process for reading

this particular will," he announced.

Perec was clearing his throat ready to start and could not reply in time to stop the detective from continuing.

"We are, today, going to do this my way."

He looked around.

"No objections, then," he said.

No one said anything. One or two looked away.

"I think," Lauriant said quietly, "that I began to come to the truth of this affair when I realized that Françoise," he paused and then explained for those who would not have stooped to know the girl by name, "the little hotel maid, was not unhappy."

Guichard looked at Lauriant as if he had sworn—not able to make any sense of it.

Lauriant was not surprised and, anyway, he did not care what his colleague felt. He would soon show Guichard.

The others appeared to share the chief inspector's conviction that Lauriant had gone slightly crazy. For the first time involuntary glances were exchanged between tables.

"That worried me a lot, you see," he continued. "However, its implications were not clear to me right off."

There was another, longer pause.

"I was making a mistake, you see."

No one appeared to be surprised by his admission. After all, the Paris policeman might be a little deranged.

"I was faced with the usual process of looking for both motive and opportunity. In other words, who would gain by the death of Emile Eckart and who had the opportunity to kill him last Tuesday morning."

Lauriant looked around the room.

"Also," he added, "I wondered why on last Tuesday and not on any other day."

With slow, almost heavy steps, he walked up to Perec. He had decided to start with the lawyer.

"When you told me, Monsieur Perec, about the contents of the German's will, two things came to me immediately."

Etienne Perec shrugged.

"And what two things came to you, may I ask?"

Lauriant's back was to Marc Poulard and, ignoring the lawyer's question, he turned suddenly to face the boy, who almost physically jumped, as the detective's face pushed close to his own.

"You will see Marc that I suspected you right away, because you inherit practically all of Eckart's not inconsiderable wealth!" he said brutally.

This time young Poulard did succeed in rising to his feet and his face, flushed and pimple ridden, registered surprise and incredulity in quick succession.

Next to him, Madame Poulard's great chest heaved quickly, massively, as she tried to recover her breath.

"Oh yes, Marc," Lauriant continued more smoothly,

"you are a rich man now."

A smile spread across Lauriant's face, as he straightened up.

"Now, my lad, you just sit down there and let that sink in for a bit, whilst I go on. Because apart from one other beneficiary and Etienne Perec, that about takes care of reading Eckart's will!"

Madame Poulard watched her son slip back into the chair. He looked as if someone had hit him.

She opened her mouth to speak, but for once in her life, on a threatening no-nonsense look from Lauriant, she opted for silence.

"Good, thank you, Madame."

Lauriant showed her his back as if to emphasize the unspoken instruction to shut up.

He continued to pace the room and talk without seeming to speak to any individual one of them in particular.

"As I said, motive and opportunity—it appeared that Marc Poulard had both. He was, after all, on the old track at the time of the murder. Close to the scene, if not actually at the very spot. But, you, Perec," Lauriant pointed his cigarette at the man of affairs, "let's get back to you. You told me, and you were being truthful, I know, that Marc Poulard knew nothing of the will's contents."

"That's right."

"And," Lauriant continued, "that removed his one

motive, although not his opportunity. So, nevertheless, I had to consider something else . . . another solution. Like, for example, that you did lie to me, Monsieur Perec, when we met. You said that only you and Eckart were aware of his legacy to the Poulard lad."

"That's right," the lawyer repeated.

"No, That's not right. That, of course, could not have been true. If it had been, none of what followed could have happened. I mean that there would have been no murder!"

"You can't call me a liar! You can't say that I was implicated in Emile's murder! It's not true! I protest!"

Perec, in his nervous state, the normally urbane manner completely gone, almost shouted out the words. Next to him Veyret and Harris looked uncomfortable.

"I would not protest too strongly if I were you," Lauriant replied very quietly. "Consider your position as I see it. Either you told someone else about the contents of that will or you yourself are surely implicated in the murder. Which is it? Which of these two alternatives am I to believe? Tell me, Monsieur Perec!"

"I have nothing to say." The man of affairs tried—and failed hopelessly—to look defiant.

Perec looked to Veyret for support, but found none forthcoming. The mayor merely stared down at his less than clean fingernails. Harris edged away from the two of them.

"Very well . . . for the moment."

Lauriant paused and added wickedly, "But also, I had

to keep in mind that Monsieur Perec admitted to me that he has no alibi for the time of the murder. He was quite proud of it. Interesting that, don't you think?"

Everyone turned to the lawyer, who began to look extremely forlorn.

Lauriant let him suffer for a moment or two.

"Still," he began again, "let me go on. I have plenty still to explain. I said that I made a mistake—and I will come back to that—and that mistake led me to consider next Monsieur Monnet."

Monnet's colorless face came up, his pallid eyes focused intently on Lauriant.

"After all, he hated the victim. That was common knowledge by all accounts; there had been an argument over Madame Monnet and I am sure," Lauriant returned the pale notary's stare, "that Monsieur Monnet is a particularly unforgiving man."

Monnet's eyes dropped and Lauriant continued.

"However, he claims to have been with his daughter at the time of the murder."

Jerome Monnet still did not speak.

"But Adrienne can't really confirm this."

The notary looked at his daughter but it was impossible to read anything into his expression.

"So," Lauriant sighed, "I could not rule you out, Monsieur Monnet."

Lauriant lit another cigarette.

"Also, of course, this applies equally in reverse: Monsieur Monnet cannot now provide an alibi for his daughter. I asked myself, and this was an important point, why had Adrienne not simply agreed that she had been with her father, thus providing both of them with an alibi? Why didn't you do that, Adrienne?"

The beautiful girl with long legs answered instantly.

"Why should I? I didn't kill Eckart!"

Lauriant was silent for a long moment, his eyes on Adrienne.

"I know," he said.

Lauriant had smoked quickly. He was tense. He put out the end of his cigarette in an ashtray as he walked past the Monnet's table, and immediately lit another.

"Now, let's turn to Mr. Harris, who said two things which gave me pause for thought when we talked. First, he claimed to be in his hotel room at the time of the murder. I accepted that at the time, but as things developed and I began to get a clearer picture, I knew that that could not be true."

Harris remained absolutely still. Unlike Perec—in complete contrast—he betrayed no emotion at being called a liar.

"That too meant that he also had no alibi, of course."

Harris still had not moved.

"The second thing: I asked him if the paintings which he was valuing and dealing with on Eckart's behalf were genuine and he told me that they were not forgeries."

Lauriant shook his head in mock confusion.

"It was a strange expression to use, when a simple 'yes' would have done from a man who confesses to be passionate about paintings even to the point of obsession."

Lauriant sneezed. Angry with his own weakness, he began once more to pace the room, as he raised his handkerchief to his nose.

"And that brings us to Monsieur Veyret, the mayor and the brother of Madame Monnet. He also has no real alibi. This is a case, you see, where too many people cannot account for their whereabouts and where almost everyone has lied."

"I have told you where I was," Veyret said rather lamely.

"Yes, but for the time of the murder, I can only be sure that you were close enough to have committed the crime. That you, like everybody else, knew of Eckart's habit of taking an early morning ride and . . . here I run out of ideas . . . what was your motive? Perhaps you hated him for some slight. According to Harris you are a peasant with a thin covering. You might nurture a peasant hatred and kill for that."

Veyret gave Harris a dirty look.

"Or was it was some shady business deal or some underhand political arrangement?"

Lauriant looked at the mayor, who after some initial confusion resumed his examination of his fingers.

"No? Well, there was no reason to think that you had been implicated in anything like these things, and frankly

I could not imagine Emile Eckart becoming involved with you in this way."

Veyret seemed relieved. It did not last.

"Remember," Lauriant added, "I've been in Eckart's shop. All the evidence there indicates that he was a careful man, ordered, and, if you see what I mean . . . very German. He would not, I think, have involved himself irrevocably with a man he would consider unintelligent, vain and rather unimaginative."

Veyret flared up in anger. Very red, he made his characteristic snorting noise, but there was no denying that his self-esteem had been dented and his pride hurt.

Perhaps, Lauriant thought, he was thinking about the damage being done to his chances in the next election when word of this got out, as it undoubtedly would.

Lauriant, on his part, hoped the mayor was thinking exactly that. He thought of it as a small debt repayment to Jean-Pierre and the other little people.

Across the room, Genevieve Monnet laughed.

"You see then that there were limited possibilities. First, Marc could have killed Eckart for the money. We have seen that this was not the case. Second, Monsieur Veyret could be the murderer, but there is no solid evidence to support this view and, anyway, for the reasons I explained," another look at the discomforted mayor, "it is most unlikely."

Lauriant moved back in front of the man of affairs.

"Thirdly, there is Monsieur Perec, the man without an alibi and fourthly," the detective moved to the next table, "comes Monsieur Jerome Monnet, a man with implacable hatreds—a man who hates the world in general, who makes his family's life something not short of a complete misery and a man who hated Eckart. He was a man with motive and a man with opportunity."

"But I didn't do it!" Monnet spoke at last. He looked panicky, but Lauriant ignored him.

"Then there is Mr. Harris."

Harris, with that movement which had become almost habitual to him, wiped his spectacles and replaced them on his nose.

Lauriant took a deep breath before speaking again. It was almost as if the whole business had wearied him now . . . as if it had become too much trouble.

15

A NICE LITTLE FRAUD

"During the war, for want of a better word," Lauriant explained, "Emile Eckart was a licensed thief. He traveled all over Italy about this work. He stole works of art for his government and, for reasons we need not discuss here, he would, Monsieur Lazareff has convinced to me, not dared to have stolen anything on his own behalf. But Monsieur Lazareff said something, quite accidentally, which put me on the right track."

Charles Lazareff's face clouded. He was evidently trying to think what he could have said that had assumed such importance.

Lauriant, meantime, felt the need to apologize in advance.

"Look, I'm not an expert in this, so bare with me whilst I do my best. Monsieur Lazareff," he turned to the art expert, "will correct me if I go wrong. Artists—and not just great artists . . . also those whose work over time has become less well regarded, but still valuable—had schools; groups of pupils and followers who came to them to learn their craft and, naturally, as a part of this, they imitated, consciously or otherwise, the style of their teacher."

Harris began to shift in his seat and a look of comprehension spread across Lazareff's face.

"Mr. Harris, of course, also knows this. Is that not so, Mr. Harris?"

Harris gave a jerk and nodded quickly without looking at Lauriant.

"Am I right about this so far, Monsieur Lazareff?"

"Yes. Yes, but," Lazareff added wistfully, "I had not thought of it."

"So you see, it was these pictures which Emile Eckart stole for himself."

Lauriant paused hoping that everyone was absorbing the point.

"You see?" he asked again. "Anyway, they were not paintings by major artists or by members of those artists' schools. They were paintings from the schools of less well-known figures. Eckart's stealing was never spotted, because in the scale of things in those days, these pictures were not valued by Eckart's masters in Berlin or by his own colleagues. But they were valuable to Eckart because being the clever man he was he could see the potential. He could also see before many others that the war would not end in Germany's victory. They were to be his insurance in case of the defeat which he saw, I am sure, as inevitable."

Turning back to Harris, Lauriant continued.

"Mr. Harris told me that art collectors collect to the limit of their funds and that sometimes they'd have to settle for what they can afford, rather than what they might ultimately desire. Many men, rich by most of our standards, fall into this category. They were Eckart's and Harris's customers. And their money, paid for paintings that cost him nothing to obtain, would, you would think, have been sufficient for Eckart. But he became greedy."

Only Harris and Lazareff seemed to be following Lauriant now, but as far as he was concerned, it did not matter any longer.

"Already considerable, the value of these paintings would be greatly increased if these days they were to be identified by a respected figure in the art world as not being by the pupils but," Lauriant paused for full effect, "by the teacher."

Harris had stood up.

"That is where Mr. Harris came in. Eckart and he got together and decided to perpetrate a nice little fraud! Eckart would provide the paintings—one at a time over a period so as not to attract undue attention—and Harris would then misidentify them and so value them up . . . no doubt they split the proceeds. Also, on occasions, to give a painting added authenticity, Harris would keep it in his own collection for a short period before selling it on to the unsuspecting collector or gallery."

Harris still stood motionless, but at last found his voice.

"No it was not like that! Well, not at first anyway."

He sounded choked and there was a note of appeal in his voice.

"I made a genuine mistake in identifying one of the paintings . . . early on. Eckart knew this and he let me sell it nevertheless, so that I became implicated."

No one looked at Harris. He stood in complete isolation in a room full of people. Lauriant thought that it was horrible. The man had begun to come to pieces.

"After that, you see, I had to authenticate the other paintings because Emile threatened to expose my error. Me! In my world, if that happened, I would be completely finished. Nobody would ever trust my judgment again. I would have lost everything including my own collection. As I said . . . it is almost my only passion in life."

Harris seemed to have grown smaller somehow. The arrogance and the self-assurance had totally drained from him.

Lazareff nodded, the only one really understanding the true depths of Harris's predicament. The others continued to look away.

"Sit down, Mr. Harris," Lauriant said gently. "I'm almost finished. You will not have to stand this much longer."

The detective crossed the room and quietly put his hand on the American's shoulder. "Please, sit down," he repeated, "I will have to talk about your other passion as well, I'm afraid."

There was a sadness in his voice as he gently pushed the American back into his chair.

"I believe, for what its worth," Lauriant said, as he turned away from the American, "that Mr. Harris has just told us the truth. He did get involved in this way. Then things got a great deal worse for him."

Lauriant signaled to Manod, who jumped out of whatever daydream was occupying his thoughts. "Get me a cognac," he ordered and, addressing no one in particular, added, "It's good for my cold."

Manod brought the bottle and a glass from the sideboard. After a sip at the brandy, Lauriant placed his hand back on Harris's shoulder and continued.

"At some stage the supply of paintings dried up; we have found none left. It was when the paintings were gone that Eckart moved into another game. This time Michael Harris, and Michael Harris alone, was the victim. Having recognized that one mistake, even a genuine error, was in Harris's view enough to destroy his reputation and his life's work, Eckart saw the effect that a whole series of misidentifications which were deliberate and not accidental would have on Harris. In short, with no more paintings to sell Eckart turned to blackmail . . . Harris paid up."

Lauriant removed his hand from the American's shoulder.

"That was it, wasn't it?"

The American nodded.

Whilst every other eye in the room was fixed on Michael Harris, Lauriant turned once more to Manod.

"Go upstairs and bring Mimi down from my bedroom."

None of the others in the room could possibly understand what the almost reclusive woman could have to do with any of this.

A few minutes later, Mimi, looking very smart with her hair piled high and dressed in her best, came in. She seemed, thought Lauriant, made for this moment. If

Adrienne Monnet had impact, Mimi certainly had presence. She stood in the middle of the room taking the measure of everyone in it.

"Mimi," he said, "when I sent Françoise to you yesterday, she asked you some questions for me. . . ."

Mimi, visibly enjoying being the center of attention, nodded.

"She did."

"Good."

Lauriant knew that he could trust to her understanding.

"And Mimi, what was the most important answer you gave to Françoise?"

"I told her that I had not seen Mr. Harris visit the notary's house over the last few days."

Her voice was flat and matter of fact. She was stating the simple truth and, Lauriant was sure, she knew exactly what the implications of her words were.

Jerome Monnet looked even more confused than ever and both his wife and his daughter looked at him, avoiding each other's eyes.

"Why was that important?" Lauriant asked Mimi.

"Because, he has visited the house many times on almost every other occasion he has come to our town."

Again the flat statement of fact.

"Thank you, Mimi. Just sit over there, will you."

Dignified, she selected a place near the window and sat, alert and awaiting developments.

"I have never seen or spoken to Mr. Harris in my home," Monnet volunteered.

"I would, frankly, be very surprised if you had."

Lauriant lowered his head and looked at the two Monnet women.

"I said at the start that I had made a mistake in this case. But mine was not the only mistake."

He paused. This part of his explanation would be amongst the hardest.

"Forgive me, Monsieur Monnet, but your wife has been the lover of Etienne Perec for some time, maybe even for years, and there were others before that. At some time during this relationship, Perec made the error of telling your wife about the contents of Emile Eckart's will. Probably, he did it with some good intentions . . ."

"Good intentions? I don't understand." Jerome Monnet still had not reacted overtly to Lauriant's revelation. He spoke like a man to whom his wife's infidelities were of no interest. But Lauriant hated to think what Genevieve Monnet would have to face on her return home.

"There is a bequest to your wife in that will, Monsieur Monnet, and Perec wished, no doubt, to prepare her for the difficulties she would have with you when this became generally known. I am willing to believe this was his intention."

Perec nodded. "Yes, I told her. It was much as you say."

"Why would Eckart leave money to my wife?" asked Monnet. "Was she having an affair with him too?"

"It was for spite. I don't think—I know—that it wasn't for any other reason," Lauriant replied.

Genevieve Monnet gave him a very weak smile of thanks.

"Did you also tell her about the legacy for Marc

Poulard?" Lauriant asked Perec.

The lawyer obviously could not see where this was leading. He shrugged.

"Yes, I did. Genevieve kept asking what else was in the will . . . just curiosity, I suppose. She's a woman after all. Anyway, I saw no harm in it."

"Nevertheless," Lauriant said, somewhat dramatically for him, "it was, as I said earlier, the trigger to murder."

"I don't see how . . ."

"Just one moment."

The detective lit another cigarette and took a long gulp from the brandy glass. He shuddered as the liquid hit his sore throat.

"Adrienne Monnet told me that she had a habit of collecting people."

The girl eyed him curiously.

"So. It's my turn now!"

Lauriant ignored her.

"She was a desperately unhappy young woman. She wanted to avoid the fate of her mother, a woman locked into an unhappy marriage, who was faced with no alternative but to stick it out. She wanted to get away."

"Wouldn't you?" Adrienne asked.

"And her mother, for reasons of her own, was happy to help her."

Genevieve Monnet did not look so grateful now.

"Perec's indiscretion about the will gave her the opportunity. For some time, Harris and Adrienne had been lovers. No doubt, Adrienne thought of him as a rich man who would be able to keep her comfortable until her father died and she obtained his money in her own right. But that was not important. What was most important of all, was that Harris would be able to get her away from here."

Lauriant searched in his pockets, but could not find another cigarette.

"You see, Adrienne couldn't wait. She could not go on standing that dreary house and that dreary existence, watching her mother quietly succumbing to whisky and avoiding reality by hiding out downstairs with the maid. And also, she could not go on living under the cruel conditions imposed on the family by Monsieur Monnet. It was frustrating. It was humiliating. Michael Harris was for her, you see, her means of escape . . . her ticket to freedom."

Adrienne crossed her long legs.

"So, you're right. So what? I wanted to get away and I loved Michael." She was impressively defiant.

"I am certain that he loved you!" Lauriant responded sharply. "But your plans went completely wrong, didn't they, when Harris was forced to tell you about being blackmailed and how Eckart had taken his money?"

Lauriant's shoulders sagged and he slowed down in his long explanation.

"It must have been quite a blow for you, eh Adrienne? Because no money meant no escape!"

Adrienne looked across at Harris and tried to smile. She got no response.

"And," Lauriant said, "that was where Marc Poulard came in."

16

THE END OF THE GAME

"Adrienne decided to collect Marc Poulard, as she would say, after Harris's revelation and, most of all, after her mother had told her Perec's details of Emile Eckart's will."

There was no reaction from mother or daughter.

"I thought at first that her new plan was this: If Marc was going to receive Eckart's money, he would be the alternative means of escape for her—that is, I thought of the simple solution. If Harris had no money, then as far as Adrienne was concerned there was no need for Michael Harris. She would switch her attentions to Marc Poulard, who, with Eckart's money, she would have reasoned would fit the bill just as well. But, it wasn't like that."

More cognac.

"I completely underestimated her and her evil. Adrienne did not want to be saddled with the local grocer's boy, no matter how rich he was! No! No! She wanted Harris with his world traveling lifestyle, and she wanted Marc's money as well. And, that is when she planned Eckart's death!"

"No! No! Please!" Adrienne protested.

Lauriant cut her short.

"I repeat! That is when you planned to murder the German. For you, after all, it must have appeared a simple process. Removing Eckart would eliminate the source of Michael Harris's problems and deliver the money to Marc Poulard. It was that elementary."

Lauriant took out his handkerchief and wiped his forehead. His cold and the brandy were making him sweat.

"So, Adrienne Monnet was the spring and the center of this vicious, this murderous conspiracy. You it was, Adrienne, who schemed, who twisted, who organized and who persuaded Michael Harris to actually kill Emile Eckart! For it was Harris who struck the fatal blow from behind!"

His eyes met those of the tall girl. She did not flinch.

"How did you do it? He was in love with you, of course. Did you convince him that what he was doing was fair, that it was some kind of just retribution? It doesn't matter. However it was done, it was easy for someone with Adrienne's talents for scheming and manipulation. Perhaps, as I said, Harris merely thought about it as a way of getting justice and some of his own money back. . . ."

Lauriant looked at the American, who nodded dumbly. There were tears in his eyes.

"But later, after the wedding to Marc, had you thought of this Mr. Harris . . . Adrienne would have found it impossible to stop there."

The American looked startled.

"Oh! You personally were in no danger—not immediately at least. But, more long term you would have been the only proof remaining against Adrienne and, I am sure, that she would have been tempted to tidy up that loose end, aren't you?"

The tears were now running down the American's cheeks.

"So, it would first be necessary to do away with Marc, so that Adrienne could, so to speak, reunite the money and the lifestyle. I doubt that Harris would have fancied that very much . . . just look at him. So Adrienne would, I am sure, have done this herself. And she would have killed Marc Poulard without a qualm."

Adrienne Monnet, still magnificently uncompromising, scoffed. Her mother looked at her as if seeing her for the first time. Young Poulard turned pale and sat with his mouth open.

"Genevieve Monnet told me about Jerome Monnet's heartless treatment of his own sister and Adrienne has inherited that heartlessness from her father. Killing Marc Poulard would have given her no concern at all."

"You can't prove any of this," Adrienne said positively. Her voice was quiet, almost disinterested. Very sure.

"Now to my mistake," Lauriant said, ignoring her. "You see, I thought all along that I was dealing with a murder that went according to plan and I was wrong. The murder did not go according to plan."

Lauriant tilted his head towards the stolid Manod. "Go and get Françoise, will you?"

Within a minute, Françoise appeared dressed in her usual worn black dress and wearing her white maid's apron.

"It's okay, Françoise," Lauriant began encouragingly, "Let me start you off. I know that you and Marc met in the back room of the café last Monday night and that Helène, the café owner's wife," he said by way of explanation to those who would not have frequented the place, "arranged it with some help from Beppo."

Veyret winced on hearing the name of his driver.

Lauriant smiled at Françoise. She was nervous, looking around the room at people she would normally never dare speak to, except to ask them what they wanted to eat or drink in the hotel.

"Yes," she said. "We did. We met there."

"And you argued about Adrienne Monnet?"

Françoise bit her lip and looked across first at Marc Poulard and then at Adrienne Monnet, who turned her head away from the maid.

"Come on, Françoise, Beppo told me all about it. So, let's not waste any more time. How did the argument end?"

"Marc agreed to break things off with her," the maid admitted brightly.

"That's right! That's what I did!" Marc added, backing her up.

"Oh, I know that! That is why, you see, Françoise was not unhappy. But later that night—tell me if I'm wrong, Marc—you visited the Monnet girl as usual."

Young Poulard nodded.

"This time, however, you had no intention of staying with Adrienne. You told her that things were over between you. Is that right?"

"That's right!"

"Imagine Adrienne's panic! In a few hours, Harris was going to sneak out of the hotel, down the servants' stairs, taking a weapon with him . . . by the way, what was it?"

"A poker," Harris said, his head lowered. "I've got a fireplace in my room, just as you have."

His head came up a little and he seemed to feel that he should add, "It was the only thing I could think of."

Lauriant approached his table of experts.

"Okay, Doctor Nadeau could a poker have done it?"

"Yes, it could."

"And would Harris have been able to exert sufficient force to strike the blow?"

"Yes—of course he could."

"Good. That, at least, settles that."

Lauriant signaled to Guichard, who moved a few steps closer to Harris.

"Eckart was, without doubt, surprised to see Harris on the track that morning. Harris somehow persuaded him to dismount—it doesn't matter much how—and engaged him in conversation. Perhaps they argued. Anyway, at some point Eckart turned his back on Harris, maybe in disgust or contempt, and that was his last action in life! For at that point Harris struck him. And it was all over!"

Lauriant's eyes turned once more to the Monnet girl.

"But back to poor Mademoiselle Monnet. Adrienne knows that her lover . . . her real lover, Harris, that is . . . will strike down Eckart during his morning ride! It's all been arranged."

Lauriant towered over the Monnet family table.

"But now, of course, she knows that it will all be for nothing because Marc, the wretched grocer's boy, has decided that he prefers a hotel maid to her! How, on top of everything else, her pride must have been hurt! In her terror Adrienne tries to reason with Marc, to change his mind. What else can she do? She is trapped."

Adrienne's eyes never flickered. She was quite capable of staring out the detective.

"She pleads and she argues," he went on. "No doubt, she tried every wheedling ploy at her command—used all her not inconsiderable charms. All night she tries without success. But in the end she fails. It is a disaster!"

Lauriant fumbled in his pockets and Françoise quickly handed him another pack of cigarettes.

"Worse, by then it is nearly morning. Marc, having for once in his life stood firm, makes his usual getaway over the back wall of the Monnets' house and Adrienne, to preserve appearances in case Mimi is watching—which of course she was." He smiled at her. "Adrienne waves him off as she did every other time. But now, left alone, what is Adrienne to do?"

Adrienne Monnet stood her ground.

"You can't involve me in any of this," she said. "If Michael killed that German pig, it was because he black-mailed him. It has nothing to do with me!"

"Just wait a moment, Adrienne, please. After Marc had left, it is my guess that you went downstairs from your room. You were in a frenzy. Somehow you needed to stop Harris. What was the point in taking the risk of killing Eckart now?"

"This is all rubbish," the girl said.

"Monsieur Monnet," Lauriant asked, "was your daughter dressed when you saw her on Tuesday morning?"

"Why, yes. I remember because it was so early for her to be dressed. She has my wife's habit of sleeping late."

"Okay. So Adrienne is dressed. Her first thought, therefore, must have been to go out, run down the track and either stop Harris at the hotel or somewhere along the path before he confronts Eckart. But two things happen which stop her: One, she meets her father in the house— and subsequently refuses to give him an alibi so that suspicion will fall on him and not on Michael Harris—and he delays her. And just to make sure that my suspicions stayed on her father . . . a master touch this: When I spoke to her, Adrienne made a great play of telling me that her father was too weak a man to contemplate killing Eckart. But of course, I already knew the kind of man Jerome

Monnet was from my discussions with Mimi"—all eyes turned to her—"and from my own talk with him."

Lauriant stopped, trying to collect his thoughts again.

"Also that morning, despite all the tensions and pressures she was under, she keeps her head. She thinks of Mimi, the woman who sees everything. Adrienne is sure that Mimi would see her leave at such an unusual hour and, worse, because of that, she would remember it!"

"I still say that you can prove none of this!"

"But, I can Adrienne. When you realized that you could not safely leave the house. You did something else. Françoise!"

He almost shouted the last word.

The maid looked startled.

"Françoise," he said more quietly, "what did Bertrand—the porter who was on duty at the hotel early on Tuesday morning—tell you?"

Françoise's face reflected the effort she was making to try to keep the information in order.

"That he had only one telephone call early in the morning and that was for Mr. Harris."

"Go on, Françoise."

"There was no reply from the room, so he assumed that Mr. Harris was showering and could not hear the telephone. After a while, the caller hung up."

"But, as we now know, Harris was not in the shower! He had already left the hotel. Clutching the poker behind his back, he was already on his way down the servants' stairs and along the track to dispose of Emile Eckart!"

He waited a moment and then asked the maid, "Right, Françoise, who did the porter say was the caller?"

"Adrienne Monnet!" she answered. Françoise was aghast at her own words.

Everyone in the room looked at the Monnet girl. She still did not flinch.

"So you see Adrienne, that is how you failed to stop Michael Harris committing an unnecessary murder—a murder which you inspired and planned—and in doing so you also implicated yourself!"

"Damn you!" said the girl with long legs.

"You see, Adrienne, without you and your ambitions, your schemes and your plans, but most of all, without your self-centered evil, Emile Eckart would still be alive and none of us would be here now."

Lauriant sighed heavily.

"Can I leave them both to you, Guichard?"

Fat Guichard and Lauriant stood together in the rain on the station platform at Sarcelles sur Mures waiting for the Paris train.

The rain was still dripping from the colored awnings.

"What do you think will happen to them?" Guichard asked.

Lauriant blew out his cheeks.

"Well, in my view, Harris has no hope, unless he can plead that he was being manipulated by Adrienne."

Guichard grimaced.

"So, if he wants to save himself, he will have to implicate her. It's as simple as that."

Lauriant contemplated the station bar, but decided to wait until he was on the train.

"What has she said so far?"

"Nothing. She is giving Servolin a hard time."

Lauriant shrugged—it could not have been otherwise. He was sorry for the examining magistrate.

"She insists that there is no evidence against her and her lawyer wants her released without further delay."

"Well, of course, she may have inspired and planned the crime and I am sure that she contemplated at least one other murder and probably two—certainly the death of Marc Poulard and, very likely, that of Michael Harris in due time, but she did not actually commit the murder of Emile Eckart."

Lauriant buried his hands in his overcoat pockets.

The train arrived and Lauriant heaved his case aboard.

He shook hands with Guichard, who was smiling warmly.

"Thanks, old man."

As the train pulled out of the station, Lauriant looked back from the window to see the chubby policeman waving.

Behind Guichard, the sun was coming out.

"One thing I don't understand," Mimi said.

The Restaurante La Langoustine was even emptier now. They were almost the last customers.

"It's worried me all these years. But I've never asked you about it."

"Now," asked Lauriant, "What could that be?"

"Why did Eckart leave all that money to young Marc Poulard of all people?" she asked.

"Yes . . . that puzzled me for a long time. Back then in Saint Sauveur, I had half a hope that you would be able to tell me."

Mimi slowly shook her head.

"It was, I think," he continued, "because, Marc was, as Eckart had been, a boy without a father—a boy having a hard time of it."

Mimi's face lit up. Her eyes sparkled in the dim light.

"Of course," she said quietly. "Of course."

"The irony of it is that Eckart actually loved and missed his father and Marc—well, Marc . . . he thought that his father's skipping out was the best thing the old man ever did!"

As Lauriant paid their dinner bill at the desk, she kissed him gently on the cheek.

It really had been a wonderful evening.

Detective Lauriant Investigates:

THE MURDER IN THE VENDEE

L'Ile Bois Aubrand

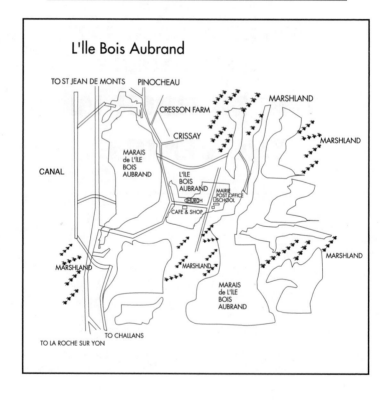

1

A VILLAGE OF FRANCE

"Destination?" Madame Letellier, smiling broadly, asked. Her pen was poised in anticipation over the appropriate box on her form.

"Vire."

Jacquot, the squint-eyed truck driver who lived in a ruin of a house on old Count Armand's land, for which Madame Letellier knew he owed at least two years rent, scowled. He was not a happy man.

"Okay," she said. "Route?"

If anything, Madame Letellier's smile grew more encouraging—even wider.

Happy, cheerful, young Madame Letellier and glum, doleful, old Jacquot faced each other on this hot Monday early afternoon, as so often before.

"Come on, Jacquot, have a red whilst we do this," she said, knowing her man, Josette Letellier had already half turned to the shelves. Without waiting for a reply she reached for a bottle from behind her and poured the old grouse an enormous glass of wine. A small coin passed across the counter, pushed reluctantly by a grubby finger.

Jacquot drank most of the wine in one swallow.

The weather was hot . . . very hot; the kind of Vendeé

summer day when the sun came down from the sky and sat solidly on your shoulders. Madame Letellier's little shop was mottled with sunlight and shadow and even the short journey Jacquot had made to the Letellier's in his battered Berliet truck had left him sweat-stained and even more irritable than even he was wont to be.

"Route?" Madame Letellier prompted with another encouraging smile, which, naturally, produced no response.

Jacquot thought hard. He had obviously made an effort to fix this important information in his mind.

"Cholet, Angers, Laval . . ." So far so good. There was a pause followed by a frown. ". . . Fougères, Mortain, Vire," he finished in triumph.

Jacquot, like many poorly educated people, had an exaggerated respect for—and fear of—official forms. He did not want trouble. Clearly, he wanted to get this right.

Without any change of expression, Josette recorded the information on her form. As she did so, with practiced dexterity, she refilled Jacquot's glass and another coin, a larger one this time, crossed the counter and went into the drawer. Pretty Madame Letellier, a picture of happiness and contentment, closed the drawer and forgot the change.

"Sender?"

"Max Cresson," said Jacquot, it seemed without noticing the oversight.

The man who sat at one of the tables, which gave the Letelliers' shop its other personality as the village café, knew Max Cresson to be one of the largest local farmers. The man, in the cooler darkness at the back of the room, smoked an American cigarette and had a beer in front of him which was getting quickly warmer and beginning to taste unpleasant.

It was the turn of the next box on the paper.

"Description of load?" he heard Madame Letellier ask.

"Apples," said Jacquot, adding quickly, "for the Cooperative at Vire, so they are paying the impost."

Lauriant, his feet and jacket resting on the chair opposite, pushed his beer away. What he was witnessing with little interest through his heat-induced drowsiness was a small skirmish in the continuing battle between the government of France to collect some of its taxes on one side, and the people of France trying to avoid paying all of them on the other.

Pretty Josette Letellier and ugly old Jacquot were foot soldiers in that particular war. She was the official intermediary for fiscal stamps and dues and he was the representative of the common man. Her form permitted Jacquot to transport his load of fruit to the cider mill without the danger of being stopped by the *gendarmes* and risking a substantial fine.

For this great courtesy, the government, of course, considered a levy was due.

The completion of the form, especially when Madame Letellier set the pace, could take some time. Although in Jacquot's case there were few pauses for pleasant conversation, this was not usually so. The tax to be paid was a ridiculously small amount, and Madame Letellier's commission for its collection, likewise, absurdly tiny. But filling in forms and collecting petty duties brought the people into the village—to her shop and café. And, with her cheerful personality, she was well able to make the most of this to the tune of a glass or two of wine, a beer or a calvados, or a small purchase or two from her stock.

The Letellier's establishment was the center of the daily life of the village—the place to buy, to drink, to relax and to exchange the latest local gossip.

And, Lauriant mused, at the center of the center was Josette Letellier, with her warmth and her ever-ready smile. She went a long way towards making the village what it was. She gave the place its character.

Lauriant had been in the western marshlands of the Vendeé for something over a year now.

As always, when some high profile felonies go unsolved or the crime statistics worsen, politicians and others in high places reorganize the police.

It creates a grand illusion of progress and convinces the newspapers, the television and the voter that "something is being done".

That is usually sufficient to diffuse protest until some scandal or society wedding diverts the attention of editors and public elsewhere.

This latest had been Lauriant's third—or was it fourth?—reorganization since joining the police. And this time, Lauriant had been, at least in the eyes of his colleagues remaining at headquarters in Paris, and in his own eyes at the time, a victim.

This time it was Lauriant, despite his record of success, who was banished to the provinces.

At first angry and resentful, Lauriant had been irrational. If they wanted to banish him, well he would make sure that he was banished!

He could have lived in La Roche sur Yon close to his office in the regional headquarters near his colleagues but no, that would not be enough—so, he had found this village, L'Ile Bois Aubrand, and he had gone to ground.

He'd found a landlady in Madame Simon. She was a widow—shapely, young, always well dressed . . . dressed with an edge to it, at least while Lauriant was around. Given any opportunity she fussed over him, tried to prepare meals for him, gave him drinks on his return in the evenings. In his mood, Lauriant wanted no part of it. He just wanted to slink off to his room and be left to molder.

His hostility and his chosen, self-imposed isolation had earned him no friends at police regional headquarters in La Roche. He had soon gained a reputation amongst his associates for being awkward, difficult, aggressive.

All that had been last year.

Now? Well, now he saw things differently. He had become used to the slow pace, to the quiet and to the country life.

The old Lauriant, he knew, would have kicked out in frustration and found some way to finesse himself back into the mainstream of police headquarters in Paris. But the new Lauriant was finding it harder and harder to see the point in it.

Despite everything, Lauriant was forced to admit to himself that he was happy, happier than he had been since his marriage fell apart.

The villagers, though a little suspicious at first, had been kind. Contrary to the general view of small communities, they had accepted him readily enough and without knowing it, had shown him that there was more to life than work, fame and photographs in newspapers.

Another pull at the cigarette and another sip at the warm beer and he put even the thought of going back to Paris aside once again.

Through the open window, which failed entirely to provide a breath of a cooling draft, Lauriant could see across the street Jacquot's old, once red, Berliet. A dusty canvas was drawn across the back of the lorry to secure the apples, and there were dried up streaks of dirt and water across the bonnet where Jacquot had recently made some sort of effort to clear the windscreen of caked-on earth and grime.

The truck was parked beneath a group of four or five equally dust-covered trees and next to it in sharp contrast was a white, shining new Renault 8—the butcher's latest acquisition. It slowly occurred to Lauriant, in his sluggish frame of mind, that butchers always seemed to have plenty of money. Perhaps Fouquet, the butcher, who had a van as well for delivering around the villages, would become, like Cresson and the men capitalizing on the growing tourist trade on the coast at Les Sables d'Orlonne and St. Jean de Monts, a success story in the new France of de Gaulle's Fifth Republic.

Outside a car stopped, partially pulling Lauriant's thoughts back from their sleepy reverie. He resented the interruption. The car was large and new and Lauriant, from under half closed eyelids, noticed that it had Paris number plates. A young couple got out of the car. They looked confused.

Helpfully, Madame Letellier excused herself from attending to Jacquot's form for a moment and went out to give them directions. She spoke to the man and a minute later the car was driving off down the street at high speed, leaving behind it a cloud of dust and poor Josette waving her arms and calling uselessly after it.

Official France in the village of L'Ile Bois Aubrand was represented by a group of stone buildings at the opposite end of the main street from the Letellier's shop. Clustered together and hazy in the vicious heat stood the school, the post office and the town hall, the Mairie. It was to the Mairie that Lauriant made his way that Wednesday two days after he had sluggishly watched from the back of her shop as Madame Letellier helplessly shouted after the car.

L'Ile Bois Aubrand, like so many of its kind, merited the smallest of entries in the PTT telephone directory for the Department. POPULATION: 906 the directory unhelp-fully stated and gave the names of the small number of people with telephones in and around the village. They included with the few others: the count, the Letelliers and, of course, the mayor.

The village was approached across the marais—that expanse of water, canals and marshland which is so typical of that part of the Vendeé—by a single road and was, effec-tively, a large island. Although in no sense was the district cut off or isolated, as almost every family had a boat which, along with bicycles, was used as everyday transport.

A tricolor flag, flanked by window boxes of colorful geraniums and brightly painted window shutters closed against the heat, hung loosely in the still air from the almost vertical pole above the door to the Mairie. The neighboring school was closed at this time of day and there were few cus-tomers at the post office. Not more than three bicycles and a dented Peugeot motor scooter leaned against its walls.

The Mairie itself contained just two rooms.

The walls of the large outer room, behind the decep-tively imposing main doors, had recently been repainted in gray, perhaps to make it more like commonplace pub-lic buildings the world over. Once a month, if the mayor decided it was worthwhile, the local council would meet in this room. On a shelf in one corner of the room was a bust of Marianne, "La République". The woman who represents democratic France now appeared overly white against her new unsullied gray backdrop.

Opposite the bust on the further wall was a notice

board on which were pinned a half dozen official publications—mostly tattered and curling at the edges. The mayor, these days, posted most of his new announcements in the Letelliers' shop where they were much more likely to be seen and even read.

A long table guarded the approach to the little door leading to the smaller inner sanctum room of the Mairie—this was itself the office of the mayor. The table, which had a trestle as a much-needed extra central support, was laden with documents and dossiers and with worn, seemingly much consulted ledgers. At one end was a circular rotating rack containing dozens of rubber stamps, the uses of which would have defied the most prolific imagination. Hidden behind a couple of large glue pots was an old telephone—the mayor's line to the outside world.

As a further shield for the mayor's privacy, one of the old school teachers—Lauriant did not know her name—sat behind the table scrutinizing, in her second role as village secretary, some newly received directive.

Along one wall were a small number of particularly uncomfortable wooden chairs, where those waiting to see the mayor on Tuesday and Thursday mornings would wait with varying degrees of patience for their audience with the man who was their "little prefect". Today only two people occupied the chairs: a young, but tired looking woman with a crying baby in a pushchair and old Jacquot, who had grudgingly nodded to Lauriant as the policeman was shown first into the mayor's office.

Georges Rocard, the mayor, was the power in the

place. He had been so for at least the last twenty years and some of the younger people who voted for him could remember no other mayor. He registered births, deaths and marriages, exercised the lesser functions of the state and organized enquiries into violations of the law. It was in this last capacity that Lauriant had come to see him.

"And that was the last time that you saw the young couple?" the mayor asked. "When you were in Josette's early last Monday afternoon?"

A big, heavy man, he had discarded his jacket and rolled up his shirtsleeves. There were large sweat patches around his armpits.

The windows of the office were wide open and the shutters closed, giving the room a comfortable, if gloomy atmosphere which was alleviated by little shafts of sunlight sneaking through the shutter gaps.

"The last time, yes . . . and the only time, so far," Lauriant replied. "Of course, the body had not been discovered then so they were of no interest to me officially at that point."

Rocard took a long puff at his tree trunk of a pipe. A majestic cloud of dense blue smoke lazed towards the ceiling.

"And you think that they collected the young count—I suppose we should call him the count now that his father is dead."

"I'm certain of it. When we find the young couple, we will also find Count Charles."

The mayor opened his cupboard and took out a bottle of Pineau de Charantes and two glasses. He filled them and gave one to Lauriant. He left the top off the bottle, keeping it ready for immediate re-use. The office was soon filled with a snug, pungent combination of pipe and cigarette smoke mixed with the grape must of the alcohol.

There was a silence for a moment or two as they drank and considered the death of old Count Armand, which had, after only a few days, already become the most celebrated case of murder in the history of the district.

"The car was a Vedette."

It was Lauriant who had begun again. The mayor looked doubtful.

"Big, two-tone paint. Flashy even," Lauriant felt he had to explain. "All right in Paris, but out here . . . well, it stuck out like a sore thumb. Every one who saw it remembered it. My inspector, Duverger, has interviewed eight people. We know its route in and out and the times—almost to the minute."

"Vedette?" asked Rocard. He had never heard of the make.

"Yes. Best of all, they only build a few. We should have no trouble tracing this one, especially as we can eliminate all those registered outside Paris."

Lauriant remembered the big car outside the shop window with Madame Letellier gesticulating and calling after it as it did its best to plaster her in dust.

"They asked Madame Letellier the way to the count's house at Crissay," Lauriant continued. "She told them and they jumped back into the car and drove off. It was only after a second or so that Josette realized that the old count was not there—that he was in Nice with his wife for the holidays. She tried to call after them, attract their attention but either they did not hear her or see her or, simply, they were not interested."

"You are, of course, certain that Count Charles was in the old count's house that day—at the time of the shooting?"

The mayor put his head on one side, blowing his own smoke away and studying Lauriant.

He was not sure that he liked incomers to his domain; he much preferred people he had known all his life. You knew where you were with them. There was, however, nothing he could do about this one, so he leaned forward and refilled the policeman's glass.

"Oh yes. The housekeeper . . ." Lauriant looked at his notes, "Madame Faure and the gardener, Pinay, saw him."

"Both good types—from the village," Rocard said.

"But, no one saw the old count. Also, no one saw Count Charles leave the house. That's against him. I have to assume that he was in the house at the time his father died."

They smoked in silence for a moment.

"And that he left the scene of the crime nevertheless!"

The mayor, Lauriant realized, had spotted an opening.

The detective merely nodded. At some stage he had expected Rocard to launch into his political speech against those—including the aristocracy—high up in society who thought themselves above good republican law, those who flouted their positions of power to the disadvantage of the ordinary folk. That stage had now been reached. This was it and it had to be endured.

The mayor had, Lauriant guessed, changed the speech hardly at all since he entered politics. And why should he? It had been getting him re-elected for over twenty years, and likely the same speech had got his predecessor into office for many years before that.

The mayor, it seemed, was still fighting battles on issues that Lauriant no longer understood—perhaps he never had. But at the very least this diatribe was preferable to Rocard's harangue against the clergy—a much more dangerous political stance to take in the very Catholic Vendeé. But even that seemed to do Rocard no harm.

"Count Armand must have been sixty, if he was a day," the mayor ended finally.

"Sixty-three," said Lauriant.

"And his wife?"

"She is thirty-five, well, almost. Her name, before she married the count, was Amelie Bergman. She's Swedish, and they met in Nice. That's why the count likes them to take their annual holiday there each year."

"I know. Still, that sort of thing—old, rich man and young, attractive wife . . . bound to cause trouble," mused Rocard.

"But we have no evidence that it caused a murder."

"Not yet, but it'll be in there somewhere, you can bet on it!"

2

JOSETTE & THE JUDGE

———————

Madame Letellier's night of the week was Friday. Her husband, André, was home. His week's work was complete.

On Friday night, she carefully laid the little table at the back of the café for their meal. In summer, it would be her country salad and lovingly cooked rillettes and a main course of chicken or duck followed by honey spiced bread. In winter, onion soup and a restorative daube would precede a tarte aux pommes.

Tonight, as she joined him at the table, after showing out the last of her customers, she thought that he looked particularly tired. His bottle of red wine was still half full and his plate was, well, less clear than she would have liked.

André's fair head was low. His eyelids were heavy.

She sat next to him and took his hand.

"You've had a bad week?"

He jumped slightly.

"Sorry. Not bad. Just busy."

Josette remembered when she and André had been at the village school together. She used to watch him in class. She knew that he was for her even then. She had loved him . . . even then. The other boys had been just boys, but André, he had been different. He would not answer back to old Mademoiselle Mournier, the teacher. Funny, she always thought of Mademoiselle Mournier as old, even older now when she delivered the mayor's official notices for display at the café. Then, Mademoiselle Mournier had seemed to Josette vindictive and cruel, especially to André. These days, when she brought the notices, Josette wondered if that was right. Was the woman just frightened like most of the world and, also like most of the world, assuaging her fears on those even less influential than herself? It may be that that was a part of a teacher's role, to prepare your pupils for a world that was barbed for those without cunning and privilege.

On Sundays André set off for the week in his car—a brand new Peugeot 204 supplied by his company. In the morning, Saturday, whilst he slept late, Madame Letellier would go outside and look at it. She would run her hands over the curves of its bonnet, admire the criss cross of its grill, wash its pale blue body.

From Monday to Friday, André completed his rounds of veterinary practices and farmers all over his area. He sold medicines for the animals. He worked for a company based in Paris! None of the other boys in their class could have done that! She was so lucky. What a man he was! What a man her man was!

Each week, there was a different route. It was so complicated. Where had he been this week? Somewhere in the south. Was it Poitiers? Perigueux? Limoges? Lyons? She could not remember.

But, on Friday, her André came home.

They sat together, and they ate together. She was happy and she was proud.

"Monsieur le juge."

Lauriant shook hands politely with the examining magistrate, whose office in the regional capital of La Roche sur Yon was far more luxurious than anything the detective was used to. Oil paintings and old prints in gilded frames hung on the walls. The carpet was, without doubt, Aubusson. The furniture was, without doubt, Second Empire. This room was, without doubt, no ordinary government office. De Bonvalet was, also without doubt, no ordinary government official.

The long windows were open against the heat of the morning and there was the faintest of distant rumbles as the traffic lazed past in the sunshine several floors below.

Judge de Bonvalet, a gray haired man in his fifties and a little overweight, withdrew his hand. He had heard of this policeman. Lauriant was disagreeable. Everybody said so. He was not looking forward to working with him. Had he been able to do so, he would have avoided the task. Circumstances were, however, as he fully recognized, against him. He no longer had the freedom of maneuver which he had once enjoyed in such matters. De Bonvalet was also sure that Lauriant would not have been chosen to investigate so difficult a case, if it had not been anticipated that they might both fail. Politics had been, as always and in every place, an unrewarding business for most—a godsend for just some.

Quietly in the background, music played. The judge found it a solace in an increasingly unpleasant world, a

world of which this policeman formed an all too obvious—
and intrusive—part.

"Rachmaninov," Lauriant stated simply. "Second
Piano Concerto."

This was for de Bonvalet a shock. It was a side of
Lauriant for which virulent rumor had not prepared the
examining magistrate.

Lauriant, aware of it and despite himself, enjoyed the
moment.

"You like his music?" the judge asked. There was no
disguising the astonishment in his voice.

"Yes, but I like others too. Particularly, at the
moment, right now, I am listening to Sibelius."

"You are able to appreciate different traditions I can
see," de Bonvalet said in the same bewildered voice.

Nevertheless, the examining magistrate visibly relaxed.
This detective exiled from Paris, with all that that implied,
might have a little of the gentleman in him after all. It was
something, at least, to which the examining magistrate felt
that he could cling. It raised his hopes.

More realistically, and perhaps less gentlemanly,
Lauriant recognized that he and de Bonvalet had found
common ground. That just might help both of them over
the next few difficult weeks. The detective was well aware
that this magistrate had the contacts and the power to bury
him forever in some dismal backwater and would do so
without compunction, if he chose.

"How are your investigations progressing into the
shooting, the murder of the count?"

"It's early days," Lauriant replied without exactly over committing himself.

"Have you anything more to tell me beyond what is in these papers?"

"The gun hasn't been recovered as yet, but the ballistics people say that it was a nine millimeter—probably ex-service—and, let's face it, after the last few years . . ." he paused very briefly, letting the examining magistrate absorb his meaning, "there's a lot of them about . . . unaccounted for, so to speak." His point, he was sure, had been taken. "Can't be certain there, though. But very messy."

De Bonvalet's expression indicated that discussion of such details in such tones was not normal in his office.

"I have, of course, sent for the countess from Nice, but I think," Lauriant added, "that I will make little more progress until I talk to the son."

"You think that the young man was involved?"

"Involved? Oh yes! A murderer of his own father? I don't know that—not yet, anyway."

The examining magistrate considered this without enthusiasm.

"Of course, the mother of Count Charles is still alive. She divorced the old count," Lauriant consulted his papers, "about eight years ago and is living near the sea at St. Jean-de-Monts. It may be that I will need to talk to her."

"Are you sure that is necessary?" De Bonvalet recovered himself and continued before Lauriant could reply. "The old count, you should know, was an important, very influential figure in the area," de Bonvalet prompted.

There was an exchange of glances between the two. It was clear to both that it was necessary to talk more frankly, but that the chosen expressions should be selected with care.

"He was, once, I understand," Lauriant began, picking his words cautiously, "a political figure of the right. Now, I believe, according to Rocard, our local mayor, that he is—sorry, *was*—a convinced Gaullist."

Lauriant had unconsciously slipped into the "our" without noticing it.

The examining magistrate paused for a moment before replying.

"Also you will understand from that, that the old count was an intelligent man. There have, of late, been others too who have made the same decision."

He thought that he had made his meaning fully clear to Lauriant. Lauriant thought so too. He took up the implication.

"Is it possible, *Monsieur le juge*," Lauriant began, "that some of his . . . old associates . . . shall we say, could have resented his defection—if that is how they would see it? Would they perhaps see his change of allegiance as a betrayal—that he was looking after his own and his family's interests at the expense of other . . . *greater* . . . things?"

"Of course, his old affiliations with the . . . terrorists . . ." Lauriant felt the word stick in the magistrate's throat, "were not unknown to many in our circle."

De Bonvalet, this time, despite every care, had made a slip and he knew it. His face was suddenly stiff and expressionless. But the words had been uttered and there was no going back. The magistrate consoled himself, and it was cold comfort, that his mistake at least offered an opportunity to measure whether this policeman really had the delicacy needed to deal with all the facets and implications which de Bonvalet knew were hidden in this case. If Lauriant was ever to get back to Paris, everything depended on de Bonvalet's conclusion.

Lauriant meantime did his best to look neutral. He tried very hard to give the impression of a man who had temporarily gone deaf. He even found himself rubbing his ear with the palm of his hand.

"I am sure that I can trust to your discretion," de Bonvalet said, looking as if he believed that he could do no such thing. "There have been many who have decided that their previous associations were no longer . . . tenable," the examining magistrate concluded.

"Count Armand's old affiliations are, shall we say, nevertheless, by no means averse to violence," Lauriant said.

It was not an encouraging rejoinder for de Bonvalet.

"True. They are not," he said simply.

"And they are by no means averse to revenge on their own kind."

"True, again."

"I am really asking you, judge, if I can rule this out as a possibility." Lauriant, forced to be blunt, looked de Bonvalet straight in the eyes.

"I am not able to say that you can," the examining magistrate, more uncomfortable than ever, replied.

He stood up and walked to the window. After a few seconds, he turned around.

"Look," he said, "the OAS is a spent force. We both know that. However, they can still be deadly in the vicious way of a cornered animal."

Lauriant nodded.

"Is the motive, from the point of view of these former associates of Count Armand, strong? Strong enough to kill?"

Lauriant pressed the point.

"They have killed," de Bonvalet replied, "and do kill all of the time and, of course, they blackmail, raid arms dumps and rob banks to give their operations the breath of life."

The examining magistrate had stated the obvious.

"So. I can take that as a 'no' to my first question. I can't rule this out as a possibility?"

"No—yes. I mean that you must keep this in mind."

"I want you to understand, *Monsieur le juge*, that I have no interest in politics. I have no interest in arresting terrorists, OAS . . . whatever you want to call them. That is a matter for other departments. But, I am interested in arresting a murderer. I ask you this question with that in mind. Who do I need to talk to—off the record if necessary—to find out if this was an OAS killing?"

"Officially, of course, I have no idea."

"Unofficially—as a man, not as a judge?"

"De Troquer."

Lauriant had never heard the name before.

"Colonel Pierre de Troquer. He knew Count Armand," de Bonvalet explained.

"Knew?"

"They were not friends—well, they were colleagues at

one time, if you understand me. De Troquer is, I believe, one of the true die-hards. Until recently, personally I was sure that there was no way in which he would accommodate himself to the realities that have been recognized by . . . some others." De Bonvalet shifted uncomfortably in his chair. "I include Count Armand in that," he added.

"Something has changed?"

"Yes. It is believed that he has become more realistic lately. Some accept it."

"And you?"

"I am still unconvinced."

"Where can I find him, this de Troquer?"

"He has a large house at Pinocheau. It's about five or six kilometers from Count Armand's home at Crissay— the scene of the crime. The man was in the army, of course. He lives at Pinocheau with his wife, Anna. They came back from the colonies some years ago. That, I am sure, is sufficient reason why they both feel so strongly about the question of Algeria and the . . . uncertain . . . future of France."

"The wife also shares these opinions?"

"Very much so."

"Thank you, *Monsieur le juge*."

Outside, Lauriant felt that he needed a drink and a place to think.

The little breeze from the morning had died away and the sun was growing even more oppressive as sultry morning blended into blazing afternoon.

Opposite the police headquarters there was a small bistro. It was old fashioned with checkered cloths and upturned glasses on tables which were lined along the pavement. Its name was painted in a semicircle across its deep windows. The menu, not changed for months, was in a glass case next to the entrance and there were metal grills covering the lower half of the upstairs windows.

Frankly, it was rough. A place de Bonvalet would have considered barely to be tolerated and the patronage of which completely out of the question. So Lauriant, while not feeling completely at home, had warmed to it during his visits to the town.

Every morning a few worn alcoholics waited for its door to open. That door mirrored the place. The blue paint was peeling and the brass locks were unpolished— had been so for years.

Like many of its kind, the little bistro served simple food, a few sandwiches and one hot dish each day. Mostly it survived on the sale of spirits. There was, however, for Lauriant, a charm about the place with its red awnings and its little round tables grouped between its faded barriers. Battered old speakers carried the noise of the RTL pop music station from the bar radio to the terrace.

He took off his jacket, glad to shed the formality required for a visit to the judge, and selected a chair on the terrace next to a table framed by two dusty bay trees in equally dusty pots. It was difficult to know how they survived surrounded by heat, traffic and dust. He lit another much needed Chesterfield.

Two young lads in shorts and T-shirts bearing the names of universities with which they could not possibly have any connection sullenly drank coffee at the other end of the terrace and tapped their feet to the music. At the next table a middle-aged woman with a lived-in face, and wearing a skirt too short for her years, wondered whether it was too early in the day to tout for custom.

"Beer?" the waiter asked, appearing as tired as the establishment.

"Fine. And a sandwich."

On the other side of the square, Lauriant watched his colleagues going in and out of the police building. One or two saw him and waved. More saw him and did not.

Realizing who he was, the woman at the next table lost interest and returned to her whisky glass and makeup repairs.

His beer and food arrived and the waiter paused to change the ashtray.

"Get me another beer as well, will you?"

The first beer was not bad. The second was better. It was pression—draught from the tap.

Lauriant placed his papers carefully on the table. He flicked through them without really registering their contents. Instead he quietly thought about Count Armand.

They had met just once at a dinner in the count's house at Crissay.

3

THE COUNT & THE CRIME

Lauriant recalled the count as cultured, urbane, well dressed. He was thin, and he did not look his age. Lauriant was sure that he was vain enough to dye his hair. Had his younger wife, directly or indirectly, been responsible for that? Did she make him feel youthful or did having her around emphasize the count's own feelings of advancing age—a condition to be righted by chemicals?

The dinner at the large house in Crissay had been formal. It too, like the bistro, had been old fashioned—but in a very different way. There had been waiters in black coats, hired for the evening. And during the week before, workmen had been called in to redecorate the salon in muted, somewhat out of place, pastel colors. Was that, again, the influence of the young countess?

There had been a printed invitation card. *The Count and Countess Armand . . . request the pleasure of the company of . . . Superintendent Lauriant . . . at Crissay . . . for dinner . . . Formal dress will be worn . . . RSVP.*

There had been expensive silver and glass and china on the enormous mahogany table. There were prim little cocktails and neat little canapés before the meal and expensive brandies and liqueurs to follow it. The evening was the sort of gathering for which diplomatic functions throughout the world had set the tone. Everyone, perhaps with the exception of Lauriant and Rocard—although even that was not sure—seemed very much at their ease.

But had Pierre de Troquer and his wife Anna been there? Lauriant, the newcomer, had been introduced to everyone. There had been too many to remember all their names. It was possible that de Troquer or his wife had been amongst them.

His thoughts, part way down his second beer and his third cigarette, returned to the count. It was hard to relate that cultured man to bombs and death. But even de Bonvalet, another man of culture, had admitted it. Count Armand had been the ally of brutal killers—terrorists. His motives were clear enough: a continuation of the old France, the preservation of a crumbling empire, a prolongation of faded French glory. Did he consider the price of it all, this man of culture?

Lives were being lost, men maimed and freedom—some people's defended at the expense of others'—being sacrificed. It was a deadly quadrille being danced to the music of the rock and roll generation.

Was it possible that the count saw none of this?

It was, perhaps, a part of the continuing dilemma of all Frenchmen of the count's age. They had faced it in 1940, then it was Vichy and Pétain on one side or de Gaulle and the so-called Free France on the other. Had the count, like so many others, made the same choice twice—once Pétain and collaboration and this time Salan and the OAS—against the Grand Zora's visions of a changed France?

Yes he had, at least for a while.

Then he had chosen again. At the third time of asking, he had chosen de Gaulle.

But did that alone constitute the cause of his death?

On the day following the murder, Lauriant had stood with Inspector Duverger next to Count Armand's body which was at the foot of the grand stairs in the house at Crissay. The old country house was very large and stone built. It blinked through its half-closed shutters at the wetlands and the marais proper beyond the gardens and the woodlands. The sunlight fell in great shafts from the windows and seared across the floor.

Both men had discarded their coats and ties long ago and stood semi-comfortable in shirt sleeves and light trousers. Duverger, short and thin, wore trousers that seemed too big for his little legs.

The corpse was spread on the floor, face down and legs crumpled beneath the torso. One arm was bent awkwardly around the back and the other seemed to be pointing accusingly at the double front doors, which were wide open.

Outside, the sun scorched the flagstones of the terrace and the count's dog barked at regular intervals. The reflections from the roofs of the police cars at the foot of the formal steps leading from the gravel drive to the terrace hurt the eyes.

Martin from the Forensics Department was saying, "The shot entered the man's back from above, hit the spine," a professional finger indicated the hole, "and diverted into the heart."

There was another expert swing of the finger.

"Death was as good as instantaneous. The doctor will have his report for you in the morning, but it won't tell you much more than that . . . he'll just use more words."

"Time of death?" Lauriant inquired.

"Last night—well this morning, actually. The doctor thinks around two or three o'clock."

"What was the count doing fully dressed at that time of the morning?" Duverger shook his head.

"And," added Lauriant, "Why was he not in Nice with his wife?"

The dog, knowing something was amiss, barked again.

"Anything of interest in his pockets?"

"No. There was nothing at all in his pockets."

"Range?" asked Duverger.

"Not close. Two or three meters. Suicides don't shoot themselves in the back as a general rule."

"Very funny. Were the front doors open like that?"

"Yes. We've been very careful, of course," Martin said.

Duverger added, "They were like that when Madame Faure, the housekeeper and Pinay—he's the gardener— found the body. They didn't arrive until the afternoon. Pinay rowed them both across the marais. With the family being away at this time of year it seems that they generally take it easy, you know, work less hours."

"From the angle and from the position of the body," Martin continued, "perhaps we were meant to think that he was shot down here."

"Has the body been moved then?" Lauriant asked.

"Oh yes and not very expertly. Look at this."

Martin bent down and pointed to small lines of blood on the carpet.

"I think he was coming down the stairs when he was shot from behind. He fell down a few steps, probably no more than that, so we can assume that someone, for some reason, wanted him down here in the entrance hall."

Martin, still bent at the waist, took two more paces and pointed again.

"That's why they tried to burn the carpet, to cover the blood streaks." About a quarter of the light colored Indian carpet had been scorched. "Also," said Martin, "That's probably why they dragged him down here. To put him on the carpet to burn it—and him."

"We keep saying 'they'," Duverger said. "Why?"

"No reason. No good reason, anyway."

"They," Martin continued to use the word, "obviously made off without making sure that the carpet was well alight." He kicked at a darkened corner of the Indian. It fell away as blackened pieces of wool. "Unfortunately for whoever did this, the fire died back. I guess they were hoping that the fire would destroy most of the evidence including the body. But bodies don't burn all that easily, you know."

"Made off, you say, how?" Lauriant asked.

"No idea," replied Martin honestly.

"Car tracks? Foot prints?"

"Loads—too many in one way. But the gravel, of course, doesn't take a clear impression . . . just lumps and bumps."

"And the terrace?"

"Nothing I can work with. And, we've had a good look elsewhere. No signs of a forced entry."

"Looks like they—or do I mean 'he' this time—had a key," said Duverger.

"Or Count Armand let his killer in," Lauriant said, as he threw the end of his cigarette out onto the terrace. "If Count Charles killed his father—forget the motive for a moment—would he have sat here with the corpse for ten hours waiting to be collected?" Lauriant asked.

"And then set fire to the carpet as he left," Duverger added.

"Not probable, is it?" Martin asked no one in particular. "Although, of course, he would have to have telephoned his contacts in the Vedette and it would have taken them time to get down from Paris."

"But not ten hours. And, anyway, he could have left here and met them somewhere else. It would have been much safer than sitting around with as blatant a piece of evidence against you as the corpse at your very feet. Also, how did he get here? There's only Count Armand's car in the garage. If the young count had his own car, why call his friends in the Vedette at all?"

The two policemen walked out on to the terrace and around to the back of the house. The garage containing the old count's Bugatti 101 Berline was a very elaborate stone building set apart from the house itself on a separate drive to the rear of the main building. The plastered parts of its walls had been washed a pale pink. Lauriant, when he had looked it over, suspected that this once more reflected the influence of the countess. There was room for four or five cars in the garage, but only the single space was occupied.

"The housekeeper, Madame Faure, and the gardener, Pinay, saw the young count here the afternoon before the murder," Duverger said as he and Lauriant walked back to the house, "but they went home around six o'clock. So we know nothing of his movements from then onwards. Neither of them spoke to him, by the way. They only saw him in the distance. Across the garden."

"Are they sure that it was him?"

"They've known him all his life. It was him."

"What was he doing?"

"Walking along the woodland paths towards the terrace. He had his hands in his pockets. He did that a lot it seems. His father didn't like it. Bit childish that, for a man of his age."

"How old is he?"

"Thirty-eight."

"Older than his step mother! This family set up could be a dangerous combination!"

Back in the hallway Martin waited for them. "Well," he said, "I've done my bit, the next part is down to you." The expert put on his hat. The skin on his bald head was already peeling from exposure to the sun. "And the best of luck."

"Thanks."

"By the way, can we get him out of here soon? Before long that," Martin pointed to the deceased count, "will be stinking pretty strongly in this heat."

4

THE YOUNG COUNT COMES HOME

They found the Vedette parked in a street off the Boulevard de Lannes. Half an hour later, they had picked up Count Charles and his two friends. The three of them had been strolling in the Bois de Boulogne.

"There was no resistance," the inspector calling from Paris told Lauriant over the telephone. "In fact, they seemed to be expecting it. The other two are married—Paul and Madeleine Sarrazin. They're on the way out to you—along with the car, just in case you need it. We've taken prints from the tires for you. Will you want them?"

"Send them anyway. We'll need to examine the car, but I don't think that it will help."

There was a short pause whilst the inspector made up his mind.

"How are you down there?"

"Still alive."

"When are you coming back? The way things are, we could do with some experienced hands right now."

Lauriant avoided answering that question.

For some reason which he could not pin down, Lauriant decided not to confront Count Charles straight away. Perhaps, he secretly enjoyed the idea of the aristocrat and his friends locked overnight in a police cell. If, however, it was a feeling of fulfilled vengeance, he could not quite think what was being avenged by his inaction.

He made a call to Mimi before leaving for the day. Getting the connection took an age.

He had first met Mimi several years before during an investigation in the little town of Saint Sauveur in the Southwest, where she lived. He had been immediately attracted to her and they had become friends. They had shared dinners together in Paris at intervals ever since. Alain, Mimi's husband, had been a regular soldier, a colonel, and now he was bedridden, paralyzed from a wound received in Indochina. Devotedly, Mimi spent her days caring for him.

"Does Alain, despite everything," Lauriant said, choosing the words carefully, "still have some old contacts in the army?"

"We both do. Both of us come from families with military traditions. We may not have much of an existence in Saint Sauveur, but we haven't completely lost contact with the wider world."

Absurdly, he felt hurt. The phrase reminded him that Mimi had another life of which he formed no part.

"Can you do something for me?"

Lauriant wanted some of his inquiries to stay out of official channels—for the moment at least.

"What do you want me to do?"

Ten minutes later, Lauriant put his head around the door to Duverger's office. The little inspector was almost hidden behind a paper-strewn desk.

"Apologize to your wife for me will you? You're going to be late home again."

This announcement produced a grimace and a resigned shrug.

"Can you find out if we have anything on the two Sarrazins? Anything, doesn't matter what. I've got a feeling about those two. Also, it's unlikely, but you'd better check out Count Charles as well."

"Okay."

"Want a drink before you start, Duverger?"

"Why not. Shall we walk across to the little bistro?"

"Why not."

Lauriant lingered over his drink before setting off for L'Isle Bois Aubrand. He was thinking of the inevitable encounter with his landlady.

As he had feared and expected, Madame Simon had managed to inveigle Lauriant into eating with her that evening. There had been no avoiding it.

"You can call me Nicole," she said over the coffee, leaning forward to better display the contents of her low cut dress and putting her hand on his. Lauriant jerked his hand away quickly. She ignored this, stood up and smiled in a way she no doubt thought inviting. While clearing the plates she managed to brush her breast against his shoulder and briefly against his cheek.

Had she taken the plates to the kitchen, Lauriant would have made for the door and safety, but he was not given the chance. Nicole poured them each a cognac, performing her little intimate ritual once more as she placed his glass in front of him. Provocatively she swung her hips close to his face covering the action by refilling his coffee cup. Lauriant could smell the strong perfume and sense the movement of her legs inches from his elbow.

He smiled weakly and drank the brandy in one swallow.

Escape had not been easy. It was over an hour later when he made it to the security of his room. As he turned the lock, he heard Nicole's door across the landing angrily slammed closed.

Next morning, to avoid any further complications, Lauriant, in cowardly mode, had skipped his breakfast and had left L'Ile Bois Aubrand early.

Count Charles, when he was escorted into Lauriant's office in La Roche sur Yon, proved to be a tall man, slender with dark hair. Like his father, he had, on the surface at least, a quiet confident manner.

He appeared very self-assured despite his situation and sat in the chair opposite the detective without being told. Lauriant nodded out the *gendarme* who had brought the count from the cells.

Lauriant offered him a cigarette which he took gratefully.

"They took mine away yesterday," Count Charles said simply, "along with my jacket, my tie, my belt and my shoelaces. They even took my wallet. God knows what they felt they would find in it."

"That's normal procedure, I'm afraid. It applies to counts and to . . . pimps."

Count Charles grimaced and Lauriant knew that he had been unnecessarily brutal. He found a sudden, though brief fascination with the marks on his desktop. When he felt ready, he looked up again.

"I have to ask you some questions about the murder of your father," Lauriant continued. "I met him once. I am sorry."

The young count brushed this aside, as if his father's death was of no real consequence to him, and also that the feelings of a policeman about his demise—whatever they were—were of no relevance at all.

"Go ahead," he said. Melodramatically, he blew smoke towards the ceiling. It was, Lauriant thought, a silly gesture.

"You were at Crissay on the afternoon before the killing?" Lauriant eyed the man.

"Yes I was—you must know that. I'm sure that Pinay or Madame Faure would have told you. They both saw me."

Again, there was the simple, straightforward, apparently confident statement of fact.

"Why were you there?"

"I live there. It's my home," said the count.

Angered for a moment, Lauriant decided, nevertheless, to let that pass.

"Okay. Tell me, how did you get to the house? I ask as there was no sign of your car."

"No, I didn't use my car. I walked over through the woodlands."

"Walked over? Walked over from where?"

"Max Cresson's house."

"Cresson?" Lauriant made a note on his pad. "And what were you doing at Cresson's farm?"

"I had some unsettled business with the man . . . well, with his family actually."

"What business?"

The time had come for some straight talking and they both knew it. Lauriant stared hard at the prisoner. His face quivered slightly. For the first time, there was a glimmer of a crack in his composure—a glimpse at the real man underneath the thin assurance conferred by breeding and training. The superintendent was suddenly convinced that he was facing a man whose nerves were near breaking—approaching the end of the road.

"Can I have another cigarette?" Count Charles asked.

Lauriant pushed the pack and his lighter across the desk. The count lit a second Chesterfield.

"For some time, I have been . . . involved . . . with Monique—she's Cresson's daughter. Very pretty. Blonde. Shapely, nice figure. Well, things got out of hand, so to speak, and she's pregnant. Her father and brother, as you can imagine, are furious with me."

"Are you the child's father?"

"Could be."

Lauriant thought about this for a moment. He reached a decision and then changed track.

"Where's your car now?"

"It's in Paris, garaged. Paul—Paul Sarrazin—he's the friend you've got locked up downstairs . . . arranged it. He's always got contacts of some sort. He's that sort of man. I'd left the car near the Cresson's house, well back from the road on a track. I doubt that anyone saw it. Paul picked it up and took it back to Paris."

"And you and Madame Sarrazin went back in the Vedette."

"That's about it. Yes."

"Why did you hide your car?" Lauriant asked.

"I wanted to see Monique and I didn't want to see her brother Michel or Cresson himself. I wanted to try to sort things out with her."

"All right. But why spirit the car away to Paris?"

"Well under the circumstances, I wasn't thinking too clearly. My father was dead and there was the Cresson business. . . . Paul just said something about not leaving loose ends untied and I went along with it."

"When you went to the farm, did you see the girl—Monique Cresson?"

"Not alone, no."

"Who did you see with her?"

Count Charles shuddered, remembering things

that he would far prefer to forget.

"Both of the brutes—Max and Michel. Michel must have spotted me making my way towards the house. He came out with a shotgun and ordered me in. Monique and her father were there in the living room."

"What happened?"

"They wanted me to marry her."

"And?"

"The shotgun and those two big men were pretty persuasive." The count gave another shudder. "It was no time to argue. Anyway, the Cressons, everyone thinks, are a bit crazy. So I said I would."

"Did you mean it?"

"No, of course not. Monique is, as I said, very attractive physically. But she is just a country girl. How could I contemplate spending the rest of my life with a woman like that?" He paused before ending, "Damn it! Her father is a farmer!"

"But, so was yours . . . in a way," Lauriant pointed out reasonably enough.

"Cresson actually works on his land! You would hardly call my father a 'dirt under the fingernails' farmer!"

Count Charles looked insulted.

"Go on," Lauriant urged, trying to keep his voice expressionless.

"I said I would marry her—only to get out of there. They made me sign a paper saying, as far as I can remember, that I'd agreed to marry Monique. They had the paper ready. They must have known that I'd show up sometime. Then they let me go and I walked home—I was a bit shaken up. I didn't think about the car then."

"All right. So you didn't sort things out as you wished?"

"No. I was going to try to come to some arrangement." He hesitated and then added quickly, "A financial arrangement—for Monique and the child, you see."

"Even though, from what you said, you feel that you might not be the child's father?"

"Yes. How can you know for sure about these things? That's what Paul said. I only wanted to remove this . . . complication from my life."

"And you thought that money was the way to do it?"

"Yes—it usually works," the count replied and, then, added quickly, "So I'm told."

"Told by Paul Sarrazin?" Lauriant asked.

"Yes."

"Are you telling me the truth about this?"

There was something nagging at Lauriant. It was nothing definitive, but he had a bad feeling about Count Charles and his friends.

"Yes!"

The policeman had more than half expected a long outburst on his insulting the young count's honor and pride, but, strangely, he felt, it had not come.

"Your father, now. Let's look at that part of your activities," Lauriant continued. "Did you see him at Crissay on the day of his death?"

"Not before . . ." Charles lowered his eyes. "I mean that I only saw his body."

"And, despite your car being close by, you sat with the corpse of your own murdered father for hours, waiting for the Sarrazins to arrive?"

"Yes."

Again, there was that troubled feeling within Lauriant.

"Do you want to think about that answer again?" he asked quietly.

"No. I have no reason to say anything else. The truth, I believe, is usually best on these occasions."

The slight hint of defiance had returned.

"Why do you think that your friends the Sarrazins took so long to arrive from Paris?"

"I don't know."

"Weren't you desperate for them to arrive?"

"I was waiting for them. Desperate is not a word that I would use to describe the circumstances."

5

THE FAMILY OF FARMERS

Next morning, Lauriant walked slowly down the main street of L'Ile Bois Aubrand. It was near midday. There was no breeze off the marais and it was much too hot to hurry. At the top of the street a few brightly painted boats, vivid in the sunshine, sat languid at the water's edge with their oars dragged up the bank and racked safely away. A young man on a Peugeot motor scooter swung noisily into the side road for Crissay. Lauriant recognized Michel Cresson.

Everyone else in the village, it seemed, had gone to ground for a few hours. Only the Letelliers' shop contained any noticeable signs of life as Josette moved a few boxes off the pavement and into the little shade offered by the bleached awning over the shop door.

Lauriant went in and settled his elbows on the counter and watched several elderly village women meet for their noontime drink and gossip.

It looked as if the going up to that point had been ponderous, but it was awesome to see the effects of even one glass of strong red wine.

At first they had all looked at the glasses in front of them as if they had no idea what they contained—almost daring each other to take the first sip. One of them, her handbag clutched on her knees with one hand, actually appeared to be waving away such temptation with the other until she felt that she had protested as much as decorum demanded. Then, with a little laugh and a joke, no doubt often repeated to her neighbor, she drank a good measure from her glass and was immediately followed by her companions.

This clearly was a regular little ceremony amongst them. It was not long before the glasses were empty and being refilled from the liter bottle, which Madame Letellier had thoughtfully left on their table along with a plate of paté and some bread.

"Cold beer, please," Lauriant ordered as the pretty proprietor joined him inside the shop. Madame Letellier poured the beer and was about to retreat to the old women's table to gentle them into a second bottle when the detective asked, "You've lived here all of your life, Josette, tell me about the Cresson family."

Seeing Michel had prompted him to ask the question.

She thought for a moment, brushed her dark hair back from her face with one hand and then pulled him to the end of the counter furthest away from the women.

"Mixed bag, I suppose I'd say," she began with her delightful smile. "But mainly bad. Max, the father, is a crude, physical sort of man. Also, I am sure that he would be a hard man to cross. He has been investing heavily in the farm for a couple of years now. He even bought some land off Count Armand—God rest his soul," she added quickly. "I don't think that the count particularly wanted to sell it, but Cresson kept at him for months. He can be very persistent, that one. He usually gets his own way in the end. Anyway, he found some way to lever the deal out of the old count." She poured the rest of Lauriant's beer from the bottle into his glass. "One way and another," Josette ended, "Cresson has become the largest farmer in the area."

There was a look of disbelief in her eyes and she shook her head.

"You're surprised?" the policeman asked, lighting a cigarette and offering one to Josette at the same time.

"Yes I am. It takes money to buy land and tractors and machinery and to build new barns and to plant new orchards and new crops. And he's bought new stock to improve his herd. He must have spent a lot. It could be Common Agricultural Policy money, I guess."

Lauriant lit her cigarette.

"What about Michel Cresson, the son?"

"He's another bad sort—and that's not just my view. He always was a bit wild. You know, the type who likes to settle arguments with his fists. Most of the lads around here of his age have been on the receiving end at some time or another. Not what you'd call popular, young Cresson. We all think that he's a menace and I'm not sure some don't think worse than that. Anyway, there's a vague feeling of unease when he's around. Do you know what I mean? Like living with a ticking bomb."

The superintendent nodded.

"When he comes in here, which isn't often, especially since André has had his new job," Josette continued, "some of my customers finish their drinks as quickly as possible, pay up and leave."

This obviously made her very sad.

"Although," she went on quickly, trying to be as fair as she could, "I have to say that he's never caused any trouble in here, but he's certainly not good for business. And, if anything, he's gotten worse since his mother was killed."

"Killed? How was she killed?"

"Oh! Of course, you wouldn't know!" Josette exclaimed. "He—Michel that is—shot her. Oh, it was an accident, they all said that. The father and the sister, Monique, backed him up. He was cleaning a shotgun and it went off—that was their story."

Madame Letellier paused, wondering whether she needed to explain further. She decided that she did.

"You're not a countryman yourself, so you won't understand what that means. No one around here believes for a moment that anyone would rack or take to cleaning a gun without checking if it is loaded first! So nobody believed the story at the time."

Lauriant, smoking thoughtfully, waited until she went on.

"But it was difficult to prove anything else, there being no other witnesses. And it's very hard to believe that a son—even Michel—would deliberately shoot down his own mother." Josette shuddered. "Michel took off for a few years after that. He was probably wise, the way feelings were running. People liked his mother, you see. They felt sorry for her too, being married to Max."

She slipped away to put another bottle on the old women's table.

"But Michel's been back here for about two years now," Josette explained when she rejoined Lauriant. "Everybody, under the circumstances as you can imagine, avoids him as much as possible."

"Do you know where he went when he was away?" Lauriant asked.

"No. I don't know what he did then."

"And Monique?"

"Pretty girl. Quiet. She looks like her mother used to. Overawed by her father and her brother, I'd say. Not much more to her than that. Her life would have been better when her mother was alive. For a while she got away with short dresses and a little makeup, but the men in the family soon put a stop to that. I see her once or twice a week. She comes in here to do some shopping. Only small things, when they run out. They get most of their food from the supermarket in Challans and they buy their meat from Fouquet."

She nodded through the window at the butcher's shop opposite which was shuttered up over the lunch hour, although Fouquet, a muscular man in his late twenties, was now outside loading meat into his van for delivery that afternoon. In one hand, he was holding a blood-soiled list.

"He's doing well for a man whose only been here

for a couple of years. New car too!"

Lauriant thought that he caught a little professional shopkeeper's envy in her voice.

"But back to Monique. She can't be much good as a housekeeper, running out of things all the time like she does," said pretty Josette.

"Perhaps she just needs to get out—or arranges to meet someone and uses the shopping as an excuse."

"Could be. I would if I was her. She comes down the marais in the boat. Somewhere on the way down, out of sight of the farm, she hitches up her skirt—nothing vulgar, mind, just to look a little bit less the farm girl and a little bit more fashionable—and tidies up her face and hair. On the row back, she no doubt does it all in reverse. She can't drive; that's why she uses the boat."

"Have you seen her lately?"

"Not for days. Actually, now you mention it, she's, so to speak, overdue."

"Have you seen her since the murder?"

"No, not at all—no I haven't."

Lauriant looked very serious.

"Try to think. Has she ever been this long between visits before?"

"No. No, I don't think that she has."

The two small black and white painted Renault police cars swung to a halt in a cloud of dust and shale outside the Cresson farmhouse.

Duverger was out of the first of them instantly and was knocking with both fists at the front door within seconds. Two uniformed *gendarmes* chased him to the house.

Lauriant, following in his Citroen, was slower off the mark. He arrived at the door just as it was opened by Michel Cresson, a big, broad shouldered man with short cut blond hair. He looked surprised.

Duverger seized the man's arm. It was ridiculous. The little detective was brushed aside by Michel as if he were an annoying insect. Duverger went down with a fearful noise. Lauriant was sure that he had broken a bone.

"What the hell is going on?" Michel Cresson shouted as the two *gendarmes* jumped on him. Even with two of them, they could not bring the big man to the ground.

During the scuffle another equally massive man, dark, with a fat nose and a brick red complexion, appeared in the doorway. Taking in the situation quickly, he took a swing at Duverger just as the inspector rose from the first blow. The big fist struck home and this time Duverger did not get up. He stayed on the ground.

More *gendarmes* hit the second man hard, forcing his arms behind his back and into the cuffs. But the younger man continued the struggle, hitting out at one of the *gendarmes* and administering a savage kick at the prostrate Duverger as he did so.

Lauriant stepped up behind him and reluctantly pulled out his pistol. There was no time for pleasantries. He hit Michel hard across the back of his head. The man dropped, still not senseless, but very groggy.

"Cuff him too, for God's sake," Lauriant ordered and he ran inside the house.

"Monique! Monique!" he called.

There was no reply. He stood in the hall. He shouted up the stairs and into the kitchen. Nothing.

Back outside, he grabbed Max Cresson.

"Where's the girl?" he demanded.

"Not here."

Max Cresson had a fat lip and a loose tooth.

"I'll ask you once more. Where's the girl?"

"I don't know—I haven't seen her for days." Lauriant looked angry enough to hit him. "She ran away," Max added quickly.

With his arms secured behind him, Max Cresson adopted the only aggressive response he had left to him and tried to kick the detective. He missed, narrowly.

"You're under arrest," Lauriant said unnecessarily.

"On what charge?"

"Assaulting a police officer will do for a start. Get them out of here."

The two prisoners were pushed, none too gently, into the back of one of the Renaults.

Lauriant bent next to Duverger, who had sat up and was holding his head with one hand. He was bleeding badly from a gash where he had taken the blow from the boot in his temple. His left arm was hanging at an awkward angle.

"Hospital for you my lad," Lauriant said.

The little inspector screwed up his eyes and nodded

dumbly. He was covered in dust and his shirt was ripped across the chest. He was quite breathless.

"I could have got him, you know. Just bad luck."

It was part whisper and part hiss.

"I know."

Two of the *gendarmes* helped Duverger into the other Renault and sped away towards Challans.

"Do you want me to stay?" asked Bosquet, one of the uniformed men.

"No, help the others with those two." He pointed to the two Cresson men in the Renault. One of them was kicking at the seat in front of him. Lauriant heard the cloth tear. "Off you go, Bosquet, before they wreck the car completely. I'll just have a look around."

The *gendarme* made for the car as Lauriant called after him, "Keep them in separate cells when you get them there! They're as likely to kill each other as anyone else!"

A quick but thorough search of the farmhouse showed no sign of Monique.

None of the rooms were locked and the attic, although full of years of collected dust, junk and old clothing, contained nothing else. Lauriant looked around the old outhouses and the cowsheds before searching the new barn. Still nothing. Apart from her dresses and other clothes in the wardrobe, there was no sign of the girl. Her bed was unmade, but so were the others.

Three shotguns were in a rack on the scullery wall.

He checked them all. None were loaded.

Lauriant sat at the table in the huge kitchen with its flagstone floor.

There were unwashed dishes stacked in the sink that had been there for days. The pantry stock was low. Monique, obviously, had not been around for some time.

Lauriant found his cigarettes. They had been crushed in the struggle, but he lit one nonetheless.

In the cupboard he had found a bottle of farm cider without a label. He opened it and washed himself a glass.

Now, smoking and sipping at the raw cider, he contemplated his position.

He was in trouble. There was no doubt about that. He had filled up the cells in La Roche—Count Charles, the Sarrazins and now the Cressons.

And he had lost Monique.

On top of that he had his inspector in hospital, by now being stitched up. The examining magistrate would soon be wanting answers, or he would be forced to release the prisoners—apart from the Cressons. Where did he go from here?

6

THE YOUNG COUNT'S FRIENDS

It was time to get down to basics. In the end it would all come down to evidence—evidence that would stand up to cross-examination in court. Ruefully, the detective pulled a face. Up until now, in the case of the count's murder, he had none to offer. He could imagine de Bonvalet's reaction, if he told him that.

The examining magistrate was watching every move Lauriant made. He was sure of that. De Bonvalet might even be waiting for the mistake that would finish the detective's career for good. It was unnerving.

Lauriant needed to collect well-substantiated and provable facts, with details that would survive scrutiny. He needed badly to build a case. And he had a sinister feeling that he was running out of luck.

Where to start—or, more correctly, restart?

Well, basics it had to be!

And basics this time meant the Sarrazins. Lauriant decided this on his drive back to the La Roche headquarters. And, through the Sarrazins, Count Charles and his stepmother. Pierre de Troquer and the old count's first wife would have to wait. And, for the moment, the Cressons could wait too. A spell in the cells would do them both good.

There were just not enough men to search all of the Cresson fields and orchards and the surrounding woodlands and to drag the marais for the girl. Every waterway and canal would need a dozen men—and some of them trained divers—to do the job properly. Even then Monique's body could be anywhere in the reed and weed clogged expanse that formed a large part of the marais. It might never be found.

Secretly, he was hoping that they would not have to search at all. He was hoping that Monique would turn up. Long shots did sometimes pay off.

More realistically, he knew that at some stage he would have to break down one of the Cressons.

The reports on the Sarrazins and Count Charles were on his desk when he arrived back at his office.

"Has someone been along to see Duverger's wife and children?" he asked Bosquet.

"Taken care of."

"Good. Let me know how he is as soon as you hear anything."

"Okay."

Lauriant fell into the chair behind his desk and telephoned Mayor Rocard.

"I've arrested the Cressons—apart from Monique that is, who is missing—"

"Only missing?"

"So far, yes. Can you get someone over there to look after the place? For a start, the cows will need milking tonight."

"Leave it to me. I'll send Jacquot over there. Looks like we might make a countryman of you yet."

"Not very likely."

There was a pause.

"Well? Did one of the Cressons kill the old count then?" Rocard asked.

"I don't know yet," said Lauriant honestly.

"De Bonvalet's been sniffing around. Of course, I've told him nothing. As far as I know there is nothing to tell yet."

Lauriant put down the telephone and gloomily looked at the papers on his desk.

The Sarrazins' files did not surprise Lauriant. That there was one on Count Charles did. The count had been arrested only a few weeks before for not paying his bills. It had not gone far before his father had settled his debts and the action had been dropped.

Madeleine Sarrazin had been caught in a Vice Squad round up in Paris over five years ago, before she was married. She had been released immediately. The police had decided that, at minimum, there had been no case to answer or, at best, that she was an ordinary young woman going about her lawful business who was in the wrong place at the wrong time.

There was no record that she had made any fuss or complaint about it. That, for someone who was innocent, was odd.

Her husband, Paul, had been accused of fraud when he was employed by a Paris bank. From the notes, the police were sure that he had taken some very considerable amounts of his employer's and their customers' money, but they had not been able to prove it. He also had eventually been released without charge. His arrest had taken place about two years after his wife's.

Paul Sarrazin sat well back in the chair, leaning away from the desk to make room for his long legs. His wife—dark, attractive and well dressed showed little sign of two nights in custody. Both wore expensive clothes and both were wary. They did not trust Lauriant an inch.

"Was it you who got Count Charles into trouble with his finances?" Lauriant began.

"So you know about that. It was simple enough—we backed the wrong horses in both senses." Sarrazin grinned. "We lost on our investments in some stocks which should have been good, but weren't. And we lost at the races too."

"How did you survive?"

"I always survive, Superintendent. I never risk what I can't afford to lose."

"Even when it's someone else's money?" Lauriant asked.

"So you know about that little business too, do you? I

thought you might. Then you know that the case against me was thrown out—never went to court."

"What is your line of business these days?"

"I arrange deals. I give advice. Not always good advice as Count Charles will tell you; and I fix things for people. You can say that I am a negotiator—a tidier up of other people's messes. And," he added with heavy emphasis, "I keep my own nose very clean."

Lauriant thought for a second, before asking, "And you and Count Charles stayed friends even though you lost him his money?"

"It was nothing personal. Anyway, it wasn't all his money by any means. It just left him . . . shall we say . . . embarrassed, for a time. He knew the risks just as I did. He didn't care that much anyway. His father has more money than he knows—knew—what to do with. And at the old man's age—particularly with that wife of his—he couldn't last much longer."

"If he died, wouldn't the money have gone to Count Armand's wife?"

"As I understand it, and you can take my word for it in these sorts of things, Superintendent, only the legal minimum was set aside for the wife. The old count's first wife, strangely enough, stood to get more from his death. But still most of it—all the rest of it, apart from bits for the servants, was going to Charles."

"So knowing this, in your role as friend, you came down to the Vendeé to help out Count Charles with the little local difficulty of his father's murder."

"I always like to help out where I can."

Paul Sarrazin looked more relaxed and self satisfied than at any point during the interview so far.

"What happened when you got here?"

"We drove down and eventually found the place—which is impressive, I must say—picked up Charles and his car and went back to Paris."

Sarrazin, shrewdly, was keeping it simple.

"Did you go inside the house?" Lauriant prompted.

"I did. Madeleine stayed in the Vedette."

"Go on."

"Count Charles was in that big hallway with the body. He looked awful. Must have been a mixture of the shock and the cognac . . . and the whisky."

"Had he been drinking?"

"He really had been. I've seen him drunk a time or two, but never like that!"

"Where was the body?"

"On the stairs."

"Go on," Lauriant prompted again.

"Well we—me and Charles, mostly me, the way he was—dragged it down the stairs into the hall. It was getting stiff."

"Why did you move the body?"

"I—at least I think it was me—suggested we go through his pockets."

"Why?"

"I don't know . . . well, you never know what useful little something you might find. But it didn't matter. Someone had been there before us. His pockets were already empty. When we'd finished we left the corpse there in the hall."

"Was the carpet already burned?"

"Burned? The hallway carpet?"

The detective nodded.

"First I've heard of that. The carpet wasn't burned. That's not the sort of thing you'd fail to notice—even in those circumstances, body lying around and Charles too drunk to take much in."

"He wasn't so drunk that he missed a chance to search his father's pockets," Lauriant pointed out.

Sarrazin shrugged.

"I've told you how it was," he said.

Lauriant turned to the wife.

"Well, Madeleine, whilst all this was going on, you sat quietly in the car getting hotter and hotter in the midday sun."

"That's right," she said. Her dark hair framed her face, which although attractive had a hardness about the eyes.

"You never got out—not even to cool down a bit or maybe find a little shade?"

"No. I stayed in the car."

She looked at her husband.

"I didn't like the thought of seeing a corpse," she explained. "Anyway. Paul was back out in a minute or two, and Count Charles wasn't far behind him. He almost fell down walking across the terrace. Paul went back to hold him up. I only wanted to get away from there and we did, pretty fast."

"You drove the Vedette back to the Boulevard de Lannes?"

"Yes. Paul brought the count's car back. There was no way he could have driven it."

"Do you have a job, Madeleine?" Lauriant asked, changing direction.

"No. Not now. I used to be a nurse." She smiled. "And I was good at it too."

"But," said Lauriant with some venom, "it seems that you were a nurse who could not look at an old man's corpse."

Back in L'Ile Bois Aubrand that night, Lauriant received two telephone calls. The first was from Rocard, who found him at the Letelliers' shop smoking moodily and contemplating a further beer before dodging another meal with Madame Simon.

"The old count's wife is back from Nice," the mayor announced.

"Is she alone?"

"Yes, as far as I know. She's at the house in Crissay."

"Well, she's got courage to stay there, you have to give her that," Lauriant said.

"Or no imagination," Rocard replied. "Maybe, she just doesn't care."

The second, much more welcome call came later from Mimi. It had been only six weeks since their last dinner together at the Restaurante La Langoustine. It seemed much longer.

7

THE COUNTESS & BRUTAL POLITICS

It was an ugly statement, but it had to be made.

"Your husband's body is at the mortuary in La Roche sur Yon. You can make arrangements for its collection and for his funeral as soon as you wish."

Lauriant and the young countess stood together in the ornate chateau-like sitting room of the house at Crissay. Above them, a large chandelier hung from the baroque ceiling and the wood paneled walls exuded age, patina and polish. Nonetheless, this was a room which showed every sign of daily use.

On one small oak wine table, there was a pile of fashion magazines with thumbed edges and on another several romantic novels had been discarded. In one corner, there was a tray with the remains of the countess's breakfast and the old count's dog slept peacefully on a settee. The curtains had been roughly pulled back—rather than carefully drawn—so that they hung untidily in a manner unsuited to this refined room. As a final touch of domesticity, Madame Faure had left a box of dusters and brushes near to the heavy door, ready to resume work on the departure of another pestilential policeman.

Neither Lauriant nor the countess seemed to want to sit down.

The countess—the woman who had once been Amelie Bergman—was very much as Lauriant remembered her from his one visit to the house at Crissay during Count Armand's lifetime.

Tall, strikingly blonde and with an exceptional figure, she was beautifully, if a little conservatively, dressed for her age. Her dress, which rather unexpectedly was not short, accentuated the curves of her body. It was a pale pastel yellow and it was without sleeves and cut low at the front. Pinned on the dress was a diamond brooch, which perfectly matched her earrings. The hands were delicate and the nails flawless. The suntan from the weeks in the south was very evident. But, jarringly, the blue eyes were misty and lacked any sparkle and there was a remoteness—but not coldness nor anything like it—about Amelie Bergman.

"Forgive me, but would Charles not take care of such things?" she asked vaguely. Her voice indicated only bland inquiry.

"I'm afraid that for the time being at least he will be in no position to do so."

Lauriant was not sure whether she was startled by his statement or merely daunted by having to undertake anything more complicated than arranging her wardrobe or commanding others to prepare a meal.

"You see," Lauriant explained, "at the moment I need your stepson's help and, for a while, I will not be able to . . . spare him."

"I will do it," she said simply and with a hint of child-like resolve in her skillfully made up face.

"Thank you," Lauriant said, and to his surprise, he did feel grateful.

"Now," he continued, more determined to get about his business, "can you tell me why your husband came home from Nice without you?"

The countess adopted a puzzled frown and fingered one of the romantic novels as she walked past the little table. She flicked through the pages and said in a bewildered voice, "I didn't know that he had until the police came to our hotel and told me about his death. Why are you asking me these things?"

At last she sat down and, relieved, Lauriant sat opposite her on the over stuffed couch.

"You didn't know that your husband had left Nice?" Lauriant sounded, and must have looked, incredulous.

"No, I knew that he had left Nice. I meant that I didn't know that he had come home," she explained rather dreamily. She looked at him as if he was being particularly stupid.

"What reason did he give you for leaving Nice?" Lauriant asked.

"He only said that he had some matters of business to attend to and that he would be away for some days."

"That's not very specific."

"My husband's business interests were not a matter about which we talked. I've no idea about his finances at all—except, naturally, that there was always every indication that they were adequate."

She looked into the distance and the slightest of smiles caught the corners of her mouth.

"We always talked of other things . . . holidays, my clothes, presents, romantic weekends and love," she continued. "He thought—it was his strong conviction—that business was a matter for him and that I should neither have nor want to have any part of it. I didn't anyway. It was, he said, a continuation of the family history to which he was only a present contributor and, as such, a mere temporary custodian. That's how he said it. I tried to understand his views on this and so, as I said, I had no part in any of it. It wasn't important anyway. I wasn't interested. I think he would've talked to Charles about it, though, don't you? You should ask him."

"Did you know that Count Charles had lost some considerable sums of money on bad . . . investments . . . lately?" Lauriant asked her.

"Maybe. It's possible. I think I was told—or maybe I only overheard it. In any case, I would not have been involved in any discussion on the issue."

Lauriant wondered what kind of dreamy, fluffy world Amelie inhabited.

"You have not dressed in black for your husband?" he asked.

"It is not necessary. There will be others ready enough to do that for him. My dressing in black would be superfluous . . . perhaps even in bad taste in some people's eyes."

"Those of his first wife, for example?" Lauriant suggested.

"Yes. She particularly."

"You don't like her?" he asked.

"I have never met her."

Again there was a little frown, as if these difficult things had nothing to do with her.

"And her relationship with your stepson. Was it a close relationship do you know?" the detective asked.

"Not in the way that I, and probably you are used to." Amelie paused before adding, "They were close in their own way, I think, but it was all very formal; very ordered, structured. I am a person who is devoted to feelings, you see. I must show my feelings!"

"Their apparent coldness was strange to you?" Lauriant inquired.

"They did not show much feeling of any kind towards each other—at least, that is the impression I have, but it comes only from Charles. It may be that his mother saw things differently. But I doubt it. I can't come to terms with a relationship without love."

"Is that how you saw it?"

The countess shrugged.

"My father is a businessman. He owns factories. It's very boring. My mother thought so too. She ran away from him and lives with an actor now. He let her go. I don't think he could have loved her. If he did, he would not have done that. I would fight for the man I loved and if necessary make the ultimate sacrifice!"

It was like a little scene from one of her romantic novels.

"And your husband?" Lauriant asked, "How was his relationship with Count Charles? Was that on the same lines as his mother's?"

"Not much different." She took a short pause before adding, "Charles was always under scrutiny—under training, almost. It irritated him very much, I think. He would, it seemed to me, deliberately antagonize his father sometimes as a kind of revenge. Once in a while, he would break free—go off. Mainly, he went to Paris."

The vagueness in her manner was becoming even more pronounced and she seemed to be losing interest. She picked up another of her books.

"Did this, too, cause problems?" Lauriant prompted.

"Armand would never have talked to me of such things, but I think that he was very unhappy with Charles and with the sort of friends he had made."

"And your husband was anxious about this?"

"My husband realized that, at his age, it would not be long before . . . before Charles would take up the custodianship of the family history. That's how he would have seen it. He was not sure that Charles was ready for the responsibility, but he was sure that he personally was running out of time."

There was a silence, whilst she gathered her thoughts and sought the right words to explain her idea further.

"Armand, I think, thought that he had failed in what was for him the most important task of his life—getting Charles ready."

It was a sad statement, thought Lauriant.

"Do you like your stepson?"

"I like him very much. We have helped each other to get through some difficult times."

Lauriant wondered what in her world could possibly have constituted a difficult time.

"And your husband? Did you love him?"

"I loved Armand. As I said, I am devoted to feelings. If I had not loved my husband, I would not have married him."

As he left the house, Lauriant knew that he would struggle to understand Countess Amelie. Did she really live in a world of her own creation or did her manner hide a harder, deeper person, a person who would, as she put it, make the ultimate sacrifice in the cause of love?

As he got back into the car, the superintendent found himself shaking his head.

On his way back from Crissay, Lauriant pulled the Citroen over to the right and parked. He wanted time to think over his telephone conversation with Mimi of the previous evening.

On one side, the marais stretched away in what was, for him, becoming its usual torpid mood. Beyond the lush lime-colored reeds, the water was completely still—totally unruffled, and the sun reflected back brightly, listlessly from its surface. He could see a couple of boats through the heat haze, with their owners huddled under canvas covers to avoid the sunshine. The men's fishing lines hung limp. It seemed that even the fish were finding it too exhausting to play the game—food for the fish or food for the man—of life and death today.

With the windows of the car down, Lauriant looked at the swathe of wild flowers— white, yellow, pale blue and, here and there, the crimson red splash of a native poppy, which covered the gentle slope in front of him and swept up towards the dusty trees. Then, he closed his eyes. He conjured up an image of Mimi's face. He could clearly see the violet blue eyes.

"There are men who are only interesting," Mimi had began their telephone conversation, "but, then, there are men who are really interesting."

"Oh?" Lauriant had replied rather dumbly.

"Now, your de Troquer is one of those . . . the really interesting sort," Mimi continued.

Lauriant morosely speculated where, for her, he would fit in to this analysis of interesting men.

"Do you remember that big explosion at Maison Blanche, the airport at Algiers, a couple of years ago?" she asked.

"Of course. It was in all the papers. One of the biggest OAS attacks of them all."

"Well, I've spoken to some of Alain's old colleagues in the Armed Forces Ministry. Did you know that he was posted there for a time?"

"No. I just hoped that you would be able to talk to one or two of his friends."

"Rumor—strong rumor, shall I say?—reckons it was de Troquer, who was behind the Maison Blanche bomb."

"So he was a big time kind of operator, was he?" Lauriant asked.

"Yes. And that, as far as I can learn, was the last straw. De Troquer had already been in trouble with the government. A couple of people at the Ministry say he was involved on the fringes of the Generals' Revolt in Algiers— the one back in sixty-one with General Challe, Zeller and Godard and the others. When he was ordered to, he refused to move his soldiers against the rebels. He supported them all right, but he pulled well back, before it all went wrong. They put Challe and Zeller on trial, if you remember and the two were given prison sentences. But in the end, the government decided to give de Troquer the benefit of the doubt. After all, they must have thought, he's only a colonel and we've enough rebellious generals to cope with. So, at that time, it seems, they let it pass."

Mimi must have been looking at a note, because she took a second or so to continue.

"A man named Lucien Bitterlin, who headed the *Mouvement pour la Coopération* in Algeria—have you heard of him?" she asked next.

"No." The name meant nothing to Lauriant.

"He was anti-OAS and was on the receiving end of de Troquer's attentions at one time. He escaped the thugs, but only just. It seems that there were bullet holes—nine millimeter—all over the car he was in. He was a very lucky man. But that got everyone riled up, and de Troquer was, from then on, on borrowed time as far as the government was concerned."

"But, he was kept in the army and he didn't slip off to Spain or somewhere with the likes of Salan or Sousini?" Lauriant inquired.

"No. But, anyway, he was behind the Maison Blanche bomb, without a doubt, and they, the Armed Forces Ministry men—this depends on your point of view—victimized him or punished him by throwing him out of the army before he could do any more damage."

Far away, in Saint Sauveur, Mimi, thinking this through, paused again.

"That was, I think, on balance, a mistake," she continued. "In the army they could have kept a closer eye on him, especially as everyone knows that he has strong OAS links."

"I see what you mean," Lauriant added. "But surely they tracked him? Placed someone to watch him."

"May have done. Nobody said anything about that," Mimi continued. "When Maurice Gingembre, the treasurer of the OAS, was arrested, a lot of people think that de Troquer took over a large part of the organization's funds. If he did—and it's only rumor around the army—he will have become a very important figure in the OAS in France."

"I can see that. Money equals power, even for revolutionaries."

"Counter-revolutionaries," Mimi corrected him, "At least I'm told that's how they see themselves. With that background you can see why some of the people in the army and at the Ministry would like de Troquer out of the way permanently, but they can't act without authority, which, so far, has not been forthcoming."

"But he must still have influence or some protection somewhere high up," Lauriant said. "There are enough government toughs available to take care of an issue like that quietly enough."

"I suppose that they think that the OAS is only of nuisance value these days and that another show trial—which the government may not win—would only bring the OAS more life-saving publicity. That's just a guess. Also he's a veteran who fought in the Mediterranean with the Free French in the war. That's bound to help him some. Alain says that there are a lot, sometimes too many old ties of perhaps misplaced loyalty in the forces."

This casual reference to her husband irritated Lauriant.

"And," Mimi went on, "de Troquer is said to be tough, ambitious and a man who knows how to hold his tongue. Also he's well read—Clauswitz, Trotsky, Jomini, Arendt and Mao Tse Tung—it's a heady combination. He knows a lot about revolutions and counter-revolutions, and, as a result, he is very skeptical about the political and revolutionary potential of the OAS nowadays here in France."

"He's right to be—they've missed their chance. But,

that, as I've been reminded recently, doesn't make them any less murderous in individual cases when they choose to be."

Lauriant was thinking about his discussion with de Bonvalet.

"Still," Mimi said, "his attitude, of course, means that he is less than totally popular with the other hard line men on the OAS side as well. And they probably don't like him having his hands on a lot of their money."

"He might be bright, but it seems to me that he must realize that any political and military ambitions he had are finished. And," Lauriant added, "he has left himself terribly exposed."

"Now," Mimi continued, "that reminds me, he will have a bodyguard or two around. That's been his pattern even in the army according to my sources." Her voice softened perceptibly. "So please, look after yourself. Promise me—no unnecessary heroics!"

"What about Count Armand?" asked Lauriant, happy that she worried about him, though he anticipated ignoring her request.

"Not in the same league, I'm afraid," she replied.

There was disappointment in her voice. The count was clearly, in her opinion, not one of the really interesting kind of men.

"He was a Vichy official whilst de Troquer was fighting with the Free French. Some of the people I have talked to think he was associated with the deportation of French Jews back then. I wouldn't put it past him. OAS links, well, maybe. . . ."

"He had them. I've learned that." Lauriant was glad to be able to impart at least some information.

"Politics and violence breed strange bedfellows," Mimi mused. "So the pair of them must have rubbed each other up the wrong way recently since the count switched sides to the government."

"Count Armand seems to have been consistent in only one thing: looking after his own interests," Lauriant told her.

"I agree." She wavered a moment. "Will you be seeing de Troquer?"

"Yes—I've no real choice."

"Do you think that he was involved in the count's murder?" Mimi asked

"I am completely without bearings in this case."

Lauriant was being honest with her.

"I can't seem to get a feel for things. I'm having difficulty seeing how to go forward. I'm really working in the dark."

"Take care of yourself," she said gently.

"You too."

He heard her little laugh down the line, lightening the mood.

"You'll work it out," she said confidently.

As he had replaced the receiver, Lauriant was acutely aware that he did not share her confidence.

8

THE OLD MISERY & THE COLONEL

Jacquot's antiquated red truck was clearly visible as Lauriant drove up to the Cressons' farm. It was parked outside the farmhouse not far from the place where poor Duverger had taken his beating.

Lauriant left the Citroen in the shade of the cowsheds and stood for a couple of minutes in the sunshine calling for the old man.

When Jacquot turned up, he looked considerably less miserable than usual. A result, Lauriant thought, as a previous devotee of a few hours acquaintance with the strong farm cider. He smelled terrible.

"Let's take a walk," Lauriant suggested tactfully. "You picked up a load of apples for Vire from here on the morning following the old count's murder," he began, positioning himself carefully upwind as they walked towards the new barn.

"Yes."

Squint-eyed Jacquot actually smiled for a fleeting second, and Lauriant realized that he was witnessing something very rare.

"I owe him . . . the old count . . . some rent, but I suppose he'll not be wanting it now."

"No," Lauriant agreed, "it's not very likely. But Count Charles will want to collect."

"Not him," said Jacquot confidently. "He's a soft touch compared to his old man. I had to avoid the old count once in a while. I used to dodge away every time I saw him. It was easy enough. Count Armand was never really willing to face me out. But the son—he won't tackle me at all. He just hasn't got it in him!"

A sudden cloud passed across Jacquot's face as another thought took root in his befuddled brain.

"Of course, he could appoint a factor. Then I will be in trouble."

"You'd better hope that he doesn't," Lauriant said. "Factors need to justify their wages."

Predictably, the customary miserable look settled again upon old Jacquot's features. The cider-induced contentment had vanished even more quickly than it had appeared.

"Did you see anyone or anything unusual that morning when you were collecting the apples? Better still, did you see Monique for instance?" Lauriant asked.

"Didn't actually see her," Jacquot said, "but Max called to her from out here. She was in the house. Of course, I saw Max and I saw Michel—he helped load the apples. One thing though, they both looked a bit jumpy."

"Jumpy?"

"Kept eyeing each other. That's not unusual, of course, but I thought that they had been arguing before I arrived and couldn't wait for me to go so that they could finish off the row."

"Anything else?"

Jacquot shrugged and wiped his sweaty forehead with the back of his hand.

"Fouquet the butcher turned up in his van," he said. "He normally delivers in the afternoons, so that was a bit strange, seeing him around outside of the village before noon. But I didn't give it much thought at the time. I was hot and I wanted a drink—which meant the Letelliers. The Cressons wouldn't offer you anything like most of the others do."

Jacquot fell silent for a moment, contemplating the utter meanness of humankind as represented by the family Cresson.

"Also," he had thought of something else, "Fouquet didn't go in to see Monique. You'd think that she was the one who would be interested in his meat, wouldn't you? He was still speaking to Max out here—must have been talking for about twenty minutes when I drove off with the apples lashed down to report to the Letelliers. You remember that, you were there."

Lauriant nodded. "Yes, I remember. It was hot as hell and you and Josette filled in the forms."

They had reached the barn and turned to retrace their route. Lauriant carefully changed sides, keeping upwind. After a few paces, Jacquot stopped suddenly.

"You said about noticing things that were unusual. . . ."

"Yes."

"Well, after I left the café for Vire, I took the route back through here and passed Crissay and that house at

Pinocheau, the one where that high and mighty colonel lives. André Letellier's car was outside the big house. Funny that. He should have been miles away doing his round."

"Are you sure that it was Letellier's car and not just one like it?"

"Well, it looked the same. It was a Peugeot, the right model, I think, and the right color. I couldn't swear to it, but it's new and there's not another one around here like it."

"I wonder why the old man came back from Nice—why he was here in Crissay at all."

Duverger, his arm wrapped comfortably in a truly majestic sling and his head embellished with an oversized plaster of the kind only overzealous young doctors apply, looked at Lauriant who was leaning forward over his desk.

If he hoped for some better answer from Lauriant than he got, he was disappointed.

"No idea!"

Lauriant was looking morose. His expression would not have disgraced old Jacquot in one of his darkest moods, but then Lauriant had not had a few days unfettered run at the Cressons' cider.

"His wife doesn't know," Lauriant continued, "his son doesn't know. He, most certainly, can't tell us."

"Still," Duverger suggested, "there must have been a reason—and a good one—to drive all this way back here and leave that lovely young wife of his behind, to her own devices . . ." he paused to add emphasis to his next words ". . . on the Riviera."

Lauriant was sure that Duverger, who, rather theatrically, used his other hand to reposition the injured arm, had misread that particular part of the situation, but he said nothing.

Lauriant pushed the pad on which he had been scribbling absentmindedly away from him and placed his elbows on his desk.

"I'm going to have to ask Colonel de Troquer about that," he said.

"Are you going to lay a charge against Count Charles?" de Bonvalet asked. There was a strong note of irritation in his voice and it was clear over the telephone line.

Obviously, outside obligations had already begun to sour the relationship that had begun to be built up between the detective and the judge. It had not taken long.

Lauriant knew what was coming next.

"His lawyer—"

"A man who is definitely well known to you," Lauriant interrupted.

The examining magistrate was dumbfounded and merely contrived to reply, "Yes . . ."

"Wants," Lauriant went on, "him released and has been putting pressure on you to do so. I suppose that's it—more or less."

"Yes it is. Have you any grounds on which to charge him with the murder of his father?"

"None that I can, at the moment, put before you. I can, however, hold him for leaving the scene of a crime, in this case a none too insignificant crime."

"Is that what you intend to do or will you agree with me that he should be released?" de Bonvalet asked.

"Yes. On condition that he stays at Crissay and does not go running off again. Will that satisfy this lawyer—to whom you should explain that his client's previous behavior is very much against him?"

"I will."

Lauriant was about to replace the telephone receiver when de Bonvalet added quickly, "And the Sarrazins?"

"Same lawyer?"

"No!"

"Them too. You can release them if you must, but on the same condition—that they stay in the area. But, not at Crissay. They can stay in a hotel at La Roche and they can have the car back. We've finished with it."

Lauriant felt very angry, and he worked hard to stop himself from banging the receiver back into its cradle.

Lauriant's audience with Colonel Pierre Alexandre de Troquer was arranged after a telephone call to his wife.

"You may go now, Roland," the colonel told the man with the physique of a body builder who had shown Lauriant into the room.

"Please sit down," de Troquer said, indicating one of the only two chairs in the room.

If the colonel had hoped to recreate the atmosphere of the *caserne* and of his lost career in this room, he had failed.

The walls, painted a plain white, and the basic pine furniture gave more of an impression of a monk's cell than an army barracks. The feeling was only relieved by a row of bottles and a few shot glasses on a side table which had been positioned with military precision against one wall. The bottles and glasses themselves looked as if they were on parade and awaiting inspection.

On hooks near the door hung a long brown coat and the distinctive white kepi of the Foreign Legion. Lauriant wondered if, when and how the colonel had won the right to wear it. As far as the detective knew, regular army officers like the colonel only received the sacred white kepi at the end of a period in command of an elite Foreign Legion formation. Even then the officer needed to earn it, as its award was solely decided by the regiment.

The colonel himself was a spare, short man, still with a close shaved army haircut. With a wide barrel chest, he looked remarkably fit. His arms were muscular and his shoulders were square set. The khaki shirt was perfectly pressed and appeared to only require the shoulder patches and epaulettes to complete its military appearance. The trousers, pulled smartly in at the trim waist by a brown belt, were absolute copies of army issue.

He was a man, it appeared, unable to live without the

outward trappings of order and discipline instilled by an adult lifetime of military service.

He was also a man whose presence was greater than his physical size, he had that rare aptitude for quiet intimidation. Lauriant was certain that many soldiers whether ordinary conscripts or important generals had splintered before it.

His aura implied a distinct, if half hidden, lurking menace. It made Lauriant uneasy.

The colonel wore a white T-shirt beneath the khaki and dark chest hair showed above it almost reaching his neck. He exuded the kind of animal maleness, which Lauriant knew that he could never possess himself, no matter how much he wanted it.

Narrow faced with a pointed, almost Roman nose that was bent off center, de Troquer had piercing blue eyes, which somehow dominated his other features. These eyes examined the detective, slowly registering every essential. Then unexpectedly the colonel smiled.

Lauriant was not used to army officers, even ex-army officers, smiling.

It made him even more uneasy.

"You are here about the death of the unfortunate Count Armand," de Troquer began without introductions.

"Unfortunate?" Lauriant asked.

"Only in his death" the colonel explained. "At certain

times in his life, he has been a fortunate man indeed."

"In what way?"

"He has had the honor to serve France. To do his duty to our country as he saw it."

Lauriant looked the colonel in the eyes. It was a sincere answer.

"Do I understand from that statement that you did not always agree with him on where this duty lay?"

"You can understand that if you wish."

Lauriant decided that it was time to clear the air.

"Colonel, I know that you think that you are in some way in a privileged position and I am willing to believe over some issues that you are."

Lauriant watched the ex-soldier, but the expression on his face was unchanged, so the detective continued.

"I am only interested in solving this murder and, incidentally, the disappearance of a young woman. . . ."

"Monique Cresson," the colonel said. His voice was bland.

"I see that you keep well informed," the superintendent observed dryly.

"For me—for many reasons—keeping well informed, as you call it, is essential. And I know, for example, that Monsieur de Bonvalet has been appointed as examining magistrate for the case. Am I right?"

The detective nodded and the colonel looked thoughtful for a moment as if thinking this over before shrugging his shoulders slightly.

"Under the circumstances I would have done the

same," he admitted. "Tell me, have you heard the expression poacher turned gamekeeper?"

"Yes."

"Then, I think we understand each other."

Lauriant absorbed this before continuing.

"What was your relationship with the old count?"

"We were, for a brief time, colleagues."

"Colleagues in the OAS?"

"You cannot really expect me to answer that question."

"Would it help, colonel, if I said that any political issues we discuss here are of no interest to me—will go no further than this room unless, naturally, they impinge upon the investigation of Count Armand's murder?"

"I have your word for that?" the colonel asked.

"You have it."

"But, you'll forgive me if I wonder if that is also de Bonvalet's view."

De Troquer stopped and put his hand to his lips in a gesture that enjoined silence and secrecy the world over.

"Very well," he said before continuing, "Count Armand was, in my opinion, a Fascist pig. That is not despite all the culture and the excessively good manners. In many ways they were a part of it. When we were with de Gaulle fighting for France, he was working with the Germans. But, as your friend Mimi will have found out. . . ."

Lauriant's shock showed clearly in his face, but the colonel only looked at him in a sympathetic way, making a dismissive movement with his hand. He smiled again. It was an almost instinctive gesture.

"We agreed a moment ago, didn't we, that keeping well informed is fundamental?"

"Yes, but . . ."

"There are still people in the Ministry whose hearts are, as far as I am concerned, in the right place. Some of them are not only former associates of her poor husband and because of this spoke to your friend Mimi, but some spoke to me by and by as well."

De Troquer let this register with the superintendent.

"Also," he continued, "from what they tell me, I can take your word—once given. Without that, as you can imagine, we would not be having this conversation."

Lauriant's thinking moved—not without creaking as it did so—from astonishment to a degree of self-satisfaction.

"So," the colonel continued, "we, the count and I, came to the resistance movement against de Gaulle by very different routes."

De Troquer stood up and paced the small room. He clasped his hands behind his back pausing once or twice to look out of the window at the garden. Lauriant saw the muscles in his bare arms flex. Suddenly, his mind made up, he turned around to face the policeman.

"I have never liked the count's kind and I have never taken any trouble to hide that dislike. Essentially, he was always out for what he could get. If that meant Vichy and the Germans, so be it. If it meant an accommodation with the Allies, well that was fine too. When he thought that the OAS would win, he was for us. When it became clear that we would lose, he turned to the Gaullists. If I had had the opportunity I would have crushed him long before that. But even I was subject to outside constraints then. But, I should have done it nevertheless!"

The colonel paused. He faced Lauriant squarely, looking down at him. The ex-soldier's face was set, a grim, impenetrable mask.

"As I said," de Troquer concluded, "at certain times in his life, Count Armand has been very fortunate indeed."

"Did you . . . I'm sorry, the OAS . . . ever contemplate his . . . removal? I mean later at the time of what could be considered his defection?"

The colonel sat down heavily, sitting stiff-backed in his chair.

"There were many defectors at that time. Some were quite rightly killed, but I have no knowledge of anyone in the organization considering the count as being important enough to merit execution. It's an unusual kind of distinction. As I said, he was a very lucky man. It might so easily have been otherwise."

"Can you say, then, that he was not killed for political reasons?"

"No. Not absolutely. The organization is fragmented now—there are all kinds of little groups and even individuals carrying out . . . deeds . . . in the name of the OAS. But I can say that he was not killed by me or by any of my own . . . associates . . . as far as I know. So, the possibility is just that, a possibility. But I think it is a most unlikely one."

"Have you made inquiries of your own about this?"

"Yes."

"I am grateful for your honesty," Lauriant said.

The colonel acknowledged this with a slight nod of his head.

"Now, do you know why the old count returned from Nice?" the detective asked.

"No. I don't. But I can say that it was most certainly not at my request."

The colonel looked at his watch.

"I'm sorry, but we have family friends joining us for lunch. Have you anything else to ask me?"

The normality of this little domestic statement seemed to be wholly out of place in the middle of a discussion of terrorism and murder.

"You knew the Cresson girl by name just now."

"Yes," the colonel answered.

"Did you know that she was pregnant and that there is every possibility that Count Charles is the baby's father?"

De Troquer shrugged.

"It is the sort of stupid mess Charles would get himself into," he said. "Did he spirit the girl away do you think?"

"I'm not sure that she was spirited away," Lauriant replied.

"Ah!" The colonel looked thoughtful. "You suspect, therefore, that she too has been murdered and that the two deaths are connected."

"It's a possibility which I cannot ignore."

De Troquer was silent for a moment.

"I'll go one step further with you," he said finally. "Particularly as you will no doubt inform our friend de

Bonvalet that I have been useful."

Lauriant nodded, grateful for any help.

"The girl's brother, Michel, has not been entirely without his uses to us," the colonel resumed.

"I have seen how tough he can be."

Lauriant remembered Duverger's sling and plaster.

"Not just tough! He has a surprisingly good brain, even if his . . . er . . . personality . . . might be more suspect. He is an excellent organizer, for example, but he disguises his abilities very well. That, I can assure you, is quite deliberate. The toughness about which you spoke is not entirely a façade. He can be violent. But there is a better side to him. I understand that Max, his father, was something of a brute to the children when they were growing up, which may account for the less . . . attractive . . . attributes he has. And, before you ask, I am perfectly well aware of his reputation locally and about the terrible business of his mother's death."

"Has he done some . . . organizing for you?" the detective asked.

"I can give you no details, but we have always been happy with his efforts."

De Troquer paused again.

"There is one other thing."

"Yes?"

"He hates his father."

"Apart from being beaten as a child, do you know if there is some other reason?"

"No. Not apart from his flawed upbringing. I have

never inquired further. It was of no interest to me or to us as an organization and it didn't hamper Michel in any of his activities on our behalf."

"I see," Lauriant commented, somewhat inadequately.

"But, the tables have turned," de Troquer added, "and Max is now the one who is afraid of his son. It's funny that Max's sort of man never seems to contemplate that their kind of physical tyranny can only be temporary—that, as they each get older, time is against the bully."

Lauriant contemplated this wisdom from the military man for a moment.

"Can you tell me why André Letellier's car was here on the morning after the murder of Count Armand?" the superintendent then asked with an abrupt change of subject.

The colonel looked puzzled.

"Letellier? Letellier—ah! Yes, the man from the shop in L'Ile Bois Aubrand. I've never spoken to the man more than three or four times in my life, and I certainly didn't see him on that morning. I can only suggest that you have been misled."

"Thank you, colonel, for being so . . . frank," Lauriant said, contemplating this answer, "I have only one other thing to ask you. Are there any guns in the house? I'm particularly interested in nine millimeter hand guns."

The colonel gave Lauriant another of his intimidating twisted nose smiles.

"Of course. Roland, for instance—the man who showed you in—carries one as a matter of course. So do I."

De Troquer opened a draw in the table and pulled out

a gun. He handed it to Lauriant.

"Not fired recently," he informed the superintendent, "and, if you wish to check, Roland's will be the same."

The menacing smile crept back.

"Of course, if either of us had shot Count Armand, I think that you would accept that we would be professional enough not to hang on to the murder weapon. We have had some experience in these matters!"

Lauriant stood up and the colonel offered him his hand. Lauriant took it.

"There," said de Troquer, "in the final analysis, even though we are very different—on different sides of the fence, so to speak—we can cooperate."

He showed Lauriant to the door.

"By the way," he said as the detective walked to his car, "when you find anything out about Monique Cresson, tell Michel as early as you can. I think that he'll be very worried."

9

ANOTHER KIND OF COUNTESS

Lauriant had taken the back roads from L'Ile Bois Aubrand across the Marais de Challans and then on to the Marais de Monts. He had swung the big, smooth, frog nosed Citroen DS though the little towns of St. Urbain and Sallertaine and had crossed the Canal du Perrier near La Cailleterie.

The superintendent enjoyed the drive, reveling in the comfort of the car and the bliss of the day. It was a relief to get away.

He had stopped for a good lunch at a roadside restaurant outside St. Jean de Monts, which catered mainly for the tourists. The Citroen, parked on the gravel between a Peugeot loaded with a family's holiday luggage, and a little Renault Dauphine, flopped gently to a stop, lowering itself on its pneumatic suspension system like an exhausted whale.

It had been Count Armand's first wife who had suggested that they take an afternoon walk through the spacious town square at St. Jean de Monts and down to the ocean. It was another perfect sunny day.

The countess was a small woman, approaching sixty, with short, neatly cut gray hair, which she made no attempt to dye. She had a little, bird-like habit of cocking her head to one side after speaking and then looking at you, carefully waiting for a reply.

To the detective's surprise, she wore blue jeans and a loose, oversized top. Again, there was no sign of mourning clothes for the old count.

"Oh, the Bergman girl was not important really," she said, after Lauriant asked how she felt about her husband's remarrying. "She was just the usual attempt by an aging man to relive his youth through the attentions of a pretty enough young woman. Armand," she added, looking wistful, "was only foolish, not wicked. But a lot of men behave that way or at least would like to. Armand went further than most, I suppose. You could say that his sin was one of excess."

Lauriant, hot and sticky, took off his jacket and held it across one shoulder.

"Are you telling me that he was infatuated with the girl or not?" he asked.

"That depends how you look at it. I'm telling you both, I think," she replied, dodging two children chasing after a gaudy beach ball. "He was infatuated, particularly at the start. And as she was the empty-headed type who would adore him without putting too many demands on him, he couldn't help himself. She would not ask too many questions, you see, and she would not pressure him about his thoughts and actions or be inquisitive about his business affairs or politics. I doubt that she would understand much of it either! She would dote on him and ask nothing much in return. He would like that."

They took a few more paces before she continued.

"Armand was never good under stress. He always had an instinct for taking the easy way, even if the hard road was entirely the right one. I guess I let him see that I knew him too well after all those years. It was my mistake. You see, it made him uncomfortable."

She looked very thoughtful.

"It's possible, probable even that I drove him to the Bergman woman. He needed a rest from me and my ways."

"And Amelie Bergman seemed to him to be the solution?"

"Solution enough to marry her," she replied.

There was some bitterness and not a little disgust in her voice.

They walked by a little bookshop selling *Marie Claire*, *Elle*, and *L'Express*. Outside one of the cafés, there were cheerful blue and red umbrellas with CINZANO printed on them and beneath them laughing families and couples, with eyes only for each other and barely touched drinks.

"Look, superintendent, I don't want you to misunderstand what I say. I loved my life at Crissay and I liked the people of L'Ile Bois Aubrand. They were always good and kind to me—in the way of things in a village, we were all, in a manner, friends. On the whole, we helped each other when it was necessary. You, as I'm told you now live there with Nicole . . ." did Lauriant detect a slight pause and a quick look before she continued? ". . . will, I'm sure, know what I mean. Between them, my husband and Amelie Bergman destroyed all of that for me. Being forced from your home and your possessions is like a bereavement for some people. It was like that for me; like losing your memory and having a part of you, your own past, removed."

The countess sadly shrugged her shoulders, remembering these painful things.

"But," she continued firmly, "Armand would keep Amelie Bergman at arms length as far as the business of the family is concerned." Another troubled, split second expression crossed her face before she went on. "He kept her, I believe, towards the end especially, for decoration, so to speak. But he always discussed family issues with me."

Some families dressed for the beach came towards them, the men in shorts and bright shirts and the women in sundresses and swimsuits with children running around their legs. Lauriant waited until they had passed.

"When was it that you last saw Count Armand?"

"We last met about . . . let me think . . . about three weeks before his death. He was taking the Bergman girl down to Nice just afterwards. She liked it there and he liked to do what she liked for her. I'm sure that it made him feel good, feel big."

"What did you talk about that last time?"

"Just family matters to be frank. We talked about our son. Armand might have been witless about his new wife,

but Charles has inherited that part of his father's character in large measure, I'm afraid. My son, superintendent,
can be extremely stupid over many things when the chance
presents itself."

"You've heard, then, about the business of losing
money on stocks?" the detective asked.

"Oh yes. Armand was angry with him—very angry. It
wasn't just the money. For him it was the final indignity.
Armand and my son had never been close, but he and
Charles had really been at loggerheads lately. When he was
under pressure, Armand was always quick to lose his temper—he was that sort of man. He and Charles had argued
pretty fiercely over the last few months. Charles, too, you
see, can be very . . . tempestuous."

"The father, then, did not just think that his son had
been unlucky in his investments and that was that?"

"No! Armand and I both suspected that these stocks of
our son's figured more strongly at Longchamps and St.
Cloud rather than on the Bourse. No, superintendent,
these stocks had four legs and, unfortunately, all too often
those legs were not as quick as the legs of the competition.
That was the source of Charles' problems!"

The countess paused for a moment. She frowned,
shook her head slowly and for the first time spoke
dejectedly.

"Also," she said, "the relationship between Armand
and our son was . . . soured, because Armand was very well
aware of the attraction that the Bergman woman held for
Charles."

"So, your son loved his stepmother?"

"In a doting sort of way. If Charles had not been over thirty, you'd have called it puppy love. It was, I think, just that fatuous. There was, in my estimation, nothing physical between them."

The countess raised her hands in a despairing gesture and slowly dropped them to her sides before continuing.

"But it was all a constant source of annoyance to Armand—you know, seeing Charles around the place looking like a love-sick camel all day."

"Did your son turn to you for help with his money problems?" Lauriant asked.

"We talked about it, but he knew that I was in no position to be of any financial use. Armand gave me ample for my needs following the divorce—it was a part of his conditions. I, in return, agreed not to make a fuss. But there was no spare money around to pay off Charles' debts. So I offered him all that I could . . . comfort and advice."

"Advice?"

"I advised him to be honest with his father and sort it out before things got even further out of hand. Some people, I understand, were threatening to have Charles arrested. My son didn't like the advice, but he obviously took it, as Armand did settle his debts for him."

"That couldn't have been easy for him . . . your son."

"No, I'm certain that it wasn't. I'm sure that it was difficult for both of them."

She stopped and looked out across to the sea for a moment. The waves were low and broke very gently on the beach. Big gray and white seabirds were swooping along the surf, dipping, here and there, into the foam. Nearer, people were lying on the sand or splashing about at the water's edge. Further out, one or two better swimmers were cutting the water with ease. In the air, you could smell the distinctive tang of a big ocean.

"But then," the countess added, "both of them can be quite cowardly when it comes to facing up to unpalatable truths. It must have been an interesting—and noisy— meeting I'd say!"

They walked on without speaking for a few more moments. In the stifling heat, local housewives and their daughters, scattered amongst the tourists, managed somehow to stay both cool and elegant.

The countess stopped again and with that little bird- like movement—it looked to Lauriant as if she were about to peck birdseed with her nose—she looked hard at him.

"The Bergman girl is arranging the funeral I hear," she said.

"Your son will, I guess, help her now that . . . he is able," Lauriant replied, and he hesitated before adding, "By now the body will be back at Crissay."

"Crissay . . . it's a long time since I have been there."

The countess once more had that sad, pained expres- sion.

"I'm sorry," Lauriant said inadequately and then, angry with himself and his companion, he added, "Anyway, what choice did I have? Amelie Bergman was his wife."

The drive back that afternoon from St. Jean de Monts was marred by an irksome sensation.

Lauriant was aware that there were some things—some things said or some things seen—that he knew, subconsciously, were wrong, out of place, but which he could not positively identify.

He knew that these things may be—were—important, even though, of themselves, they were small. It was this apparent insignificance that had allowed them to evade his once sharp observation.

In his mind, he went over his talks with Count Charles and with his mother, with the Sarrazins and with Jacquot, with the colonel and with Countess Amelie. He even thought about pretty little Josette Letellier and what she had been able to tell him about the Cressons.

For most of the journey, these little pieces in the puzzle continued to escape him.

He edged around the Marais de Marchecoul and reached Chateauneuf before, from somewhere deep in the recesses of his thinking, he finally identified the first of these missing little pieces. After that the second and the third were not long in coming into place.

Suddenly, the sunshine was more pleasing; the countryside was more beautiful; life was more agreeable.

Lauriant smiled.

It was just possible that, at last, he was thinking on

the right lines. Finally, he began to believe, he was getting a feel for the case.

"We could try using the dogs," Duverger suggested. "As long as the Cressons stick to the story that she has gone away, I don't see that we can do much else."

Lauriant moved a pile of papers so that he could perch on the edge of the inspector's desk.

"Are they still sticking to it then?" he asked.

"Oh, yes. And if their hanging together over the mother's death is anything to go by, they will go on sticking to it."

Duverger looked glum and rubbed his plastered forehead with his usable hand. He had spent more than three hours with the two Cresson men that morning. And he had got precisely nowhere.

"We could use the dogs to search the fields and the woods around the Cresson farm," he explained. "I know the dogs would be no good in the marshes and around the canals and waterways, but we don't have the manpower for a proper search. The dogs might just sniff something out."

"Something? Like a corpse?" said Lauriant, lighting another Chesterfield.

"Well, the girl, alive or dead, has to be somewhere," Duverger said.

"That's true enough. But you'll be wasting your time hacking around the woods with a bunch of hounds."

"So, you think that she's still alive."

"I do."

A thought struck the little inspector.

"Wait a minute! Try this! Monique sees Count Armand and tells him that she's pregnant and that his son is the father."

"Go on," the superintendent encouraged his colleague.

"She makes demands. Money or marriage, something like that, and the old count tells her in no uncertain terms that he's not interested. She gets really enraged, shoots him in a fit of temper and then makes off."

Duverger looked at his boss.

"It's a possibility," Lauriant observed.

"There . . . not much, maybe—but, it's somewhere to start!" Duverger exclaimed, a note of excitement creeping into his voice.

"You'll start your head aching again. Okay. Where did she get the gun?"

"Plenty in the farmhouse. She just pinched it."

"All right. But when did she make off?" Lauriant asked. "If she killed the man, why did she not put as much distance as possible between herself and the crime right away?"

"Waiting for something? Or someone?" Duverger tried.

"Like Count Charles? Lot's of people who could have killed the old count seemed to have decided to hang around after the murder waiting for something. His son for one. He might have killed for money and from hatred.

I know now that he was not getting along with Count Armand lately—even his mother admits that they were at each other's throats most of the time. And Monique Cresson, who might have killed for money or marriage, she, on this analysis at least, hung about too."

"Perhaps she and Count Charles were waiting for each other. It was all arranged to get away together and, somehow, they missed the rendezvous."

"Not Charles! He had no intention of marrying the girl. At least, he says so."

Lauriant picked up a chair, spun it around and sat astride it.

"Anyway, Monique was still at the Cressons' next morning," Duverger went on, "Jacquot saw her."

Lauriant brought his hand down on to the chair back—not hard, but enough to startle Duverger.

"No he didn't!" the superintendent exclaimed. "Jacquot just got the impression that she was there from Max and from Michel. He just heard them call to her or refer to her as if she was in the house. It's an old trick that! But he didn't actually see her!"

"There you are!" Duverger now had a note of positive triumph in his voice.

"No! Wait a minute! And how did she make off? Tell me that. She can't drive and a boat across the marais wouldn't help much. What would she do on the other side?"

"Maybe get a lift," the inspector suggested. "There's a main road there. But that's a bit risky, though. What if no one willing to give her a lift came along?" Duverger continued, "She could have been there for hours, and she would be very likely to be seen, and recognized by someone rowing down the marais or driving or walking into L'Ile Bois Aubrand. Mind you, she would have been in a hell of a panic. She could have risked it. What was there for her to lose?"

"Sorry, it's no good," Lauriant apologized. "I've just remembered both of the Cressons' boats are still at the farm."

"She could have stolen one from somewhere."

"We'd have heard about it."

"Yes. That's true."

"So, maybe," Lauriant mused, "she really was at the Cressons' place the next day. Jacquot, who was sober at the time, got the strong impression that she was—it convinced him—and perhaps she was just waiting for a lift."

"From whom?" Duverger said.

"Who had a car?" Lauriant asked.

"Or a truck!" the inspector added. "Do you think that she jumped into the back of Jacquot's truck under the sheet and he, unwittingly, drove her off to Normandy?"

"Why not?"

Lauriant fell silent for a while.

"No, I don't like that," he said eventually. "Michel helped load the truck. He'd have seen her for sure. Also, what would she have done for money when she got to Normandy? Pregnant and with only the clothes she stood up in—her own clothes are still in her room at the farm remember—no it doesn't work, I think. Even if Monique murdered the count in anger, she'd have had enough time and sense to pack a bag by the time Jacquot got underway."

It was Duverger's turn to fall silent.

"Okay. The cars. Let's list them," he said after a moment or two.

"Well, we only need to consider those cars that were or could have been at the Cresson farm the morning after the murder. Count Charles left his car near there all night and all next morning. That's one."

"He might have taken her."

"What, the killer of his own father? Because that's what you're saying if this theory has any truth in it."

Lauriant did not appear to think that that was likely.

"And mother of his own child," Duverger pointed out. "Anyway, perhaps he didn't know that she'd committed the murder. Another thing, he might not have known that she was in the car. She could have hidden in the trunk."

"And in this heat, she'd have fried if Sarrazin had not turned up to drive the car back to Paris. The car could have been there for days. Don't forget, if you believe Count Charles, it very nearly was."

"Sarrazin! Could she have gone back to Paris in the Vedette?" Duverger asked.

Lauriant shrugged.

"And there's always André Letellier," he said.

Duverger looked puzzled.

"Why him?"

"His car, or one very like it, according to Jacquot, was at Pinocheau that morning. And Pinocheau is very near to Crissay and to the Cressons' farm."

Duverger was doubtful.

"D'you think that Letellier would have the stomach to take on the two Cressons and succeed in driving off with Monique? He'd be more likely to end up in hospital like me. I don't see him driving up to Max and Michel and saying 'Good morning, gentlemen. Can I have the girl please?' and them saying, 'Certainly, André, dear chap, here she is. Off you go now,' and then helping her into the car and waving the two of them goodbye. Do you? Also, what motive would Letellier have for doing any such thing?"

"I don't know," Lauriant said honestly. "It's just another possibility. All the same, check out that company in Paris he works for. Have a word with them. See what you can find out."

He lit a cigarette, offering the pack to Duverger.

"Also," he continued, his face surrounded by blue smoke, "we do know of one other vehicle, apart from Jacquot's old Berliet, which was definitely at the Cressons that morning. Fouquet's van."

10

THE BUTCHER WITH MUSCLES

———————————

Fouquet and Lauriant had, once more, lifted their faces to the sun. They were outside the shop leaning on the rear doors of the butcher's van in the late afternoon. Their talk had been desultory, punctuated by long silences as they enjoyed the coolest part of the day.

"I do the farms around Crissay twice a week," Fouquet had said. "That was one of my days."

The butcher with the bulging muscles was at least a head taller than Lauriant and much broader. He was a man used to physical activity and exercise and a man who enjoyed it.

"Okay," said Lauriant, "but why did you change your routine that day—the day we discovered Count Armand's body?"

"How do you mean? Like I said, it was my normal day for delivering in that area."

"Yes, but why do the round in the morning and not in the afternoon as usual? Surely some of your customers wouldn't be around for you then, if they were used to your calling on them later in the day."

Fouquet thought it over during another pause to enjoy the late afternoon sun.

"Busy, I think," he replied eventually, "I must have had

extra customers that day and needed to start earlier to fit them all in."

There was another silence, which was eventually broken by the policeman.

"Did you see Monique Cresson that day?" he asked.

The butcher seemed to be trying to remember.

"No, I didn't. But I spoke to her father, Max. And her brother was around somewhere—helping old Jacquot load some apples into his truck, I think."

"Okay. And, what meat did you sell them?"

"As it happens, none," said Fouquet.

"But you called there anyway?"

"I always keep an extra supply on the van in case someone has forgotten to order."

The butcher thrust his hands into his apron pockets as Lauriant considered this for a few seconds.

"So," he said eventually, "even on this busier than usual day, with more than the usual number of customers waiting for delivery, you took up precious time to make a speculative call at the Cressons' just in case they might want to buy."

"That's right."

"Do they normally order meat ahead of delivery with you . . . say, over the telephone or through Monique, when she pays a visit to L'Ile Bois Aubrand every few days?"

"Yes."

"But not this time?"

"No."

The sun had dropped lower in the sky and, by unspoken mutual consent, they moved around to the side of the van, so that they could continue to enjoy its more gentle warmth.

"What else were you carrying to the Cressons apart from meat that they had not ordered and did not want?" Lauriant began again.

"Something else?"

"Yes. Come on. You and I both know this meat story is a blind! Something else . . . like a message, perhaps." The superintendent paused. "Maybe even a warning."

"Look, I sell meat—it's how I make my living. I'm not a mailman and I'm not a messenger boy."

Lauriant thought that he had, at last, hit on something. The butcher's composure had slipped for a moment.

There was another silence as the men, both with closed eyes, continued to enjoy the evening sun.

"Let's try again," Lauriant, smoking diligently on a Chesterfield, interrupted their silence and decided on a calculated ploy. "What did Colonel de Troquer ask you to tell the Cressons?"

"The colonel?"

"Look, Monsieur Fouquet, you've got army written all over you. Your build, your walk, your physical condition. It all fits."

The butcher closed his eyes and did not reply, so the detective continued.

"Also, from the investigations of a friend, I know that it has always been the colonel's practice to keep a couple of bodyguards, for want of a better word, around him. Roland, at the house in Pinocheau, is one and I'm pretty sure that you are the other."

Fouquet shrugged and opened his eyes. He saw no point in denying it. Instead, the butcher said, "The colonel told me that it was all right to talk to you—within certain limits."

He sounded, nevertheless, as if he did not like it.

"What do you want to ask?" he said finally.

"Did the colonel, for example, want you to tell the Cressons about the count's death?" Lauriant asked. "After all, the body had not yet been found and it was not common knowledge at that point."

"How could I have done that? If I didn't know about it?"

"The colonel seems to me to have ways of knowing things before most of us. And, you were with him in the army and . . . afterwards," the policeman prompted.

"True. He helped me to buy the shop. He was my commanding officer in the army."

"And afterwards?"

"As you seem to think that I am some sort of body-guard for him, I would think that that question doesn't need an answer."

"What do you do in return for this help in buying the shop?" Lauriant inquired, without appearing to show too much interest. The sun was making them both a little drowsy.

"I pay him interest on the loan."

"And?"

"And," said Fouquet, "I help him out when he needs it."

"As a protector?"

"You can call it that if you like." There was a slight hes-itation before the butcher continued. "The colonel has many friends, but, also, he has not a few enemies. I'm sure that you have learned that."

Lauriant nodded.

"What about André Letellier?" he asked.

"We have a little arrangement: he doesn't sell meat and I don't sell drinks."

"You know that's not what I meant."

There was silence again between them. And, again, it was Lauriant who broke it.

"Letellier is supposed to work for a company in Paris which supplies medicines to vets and farmers. I've checked and the company doesn't exist—not apart from a door plaque, that is."

"Ah!"

"And also there's the car."

"What car?"

"Letellier's car, which is supposed to be the company's but has local plates and not Paris plates. I knew that there were some things that were odd in this case," Lauriant explained truthfully, "and I couldn't put my finger on them until the other day on my way back from St. Jean de Monts. The plates on André's car were one of these little oddities."

"On your way back from St. Jean de Monts. When you saw the old countess," Fouquet stated rather than asked.

"There, you see, you and the colonel do have ways of knowing things! So, at least, let's agree that André owns his own car. . . ."

"No. He doesn't."

"Who owns it then? The colonel?"

"No, the colonel wouldn't want his name on anything . . . he's too careful. I might as well tell you because you'll look it up anyway. The car belongs to Roland."

"The colonel's other man?"

"Yes."

"Do I assume then that André's wages—if that's the right word—are paid by the colonel? The so called company doesn't pay him, but Josette still gets her money every month."

"You're right. We pay him."

"We?"

"You know who I mean."

"And what does young André Letellier do for his money?" Lauriant asked. "He's not big enough, or powerful enough to be a third protector."

Fouquet smiled. "André would have a job to protect himself!" he said.

"I do have the impression," Lauriant replied slowly, "that he is not a violent man. But is he also something of a coward?"

"He can be—both morally and physically, I think. Put it like this: he will dodge trouble whenever he can."

The butcher shook his head, apparently disappointed in his fellow men.

"He was hopeless in the army," Fouquet concluded.

"Did you know him in the army?"

"Good God, no! He was the sort that they made into clerks. The kind who couldn't even keep their own rifle clean. Some good drill sergeant probably made his life hell when he was called up as a conscript—and quite right

too. André Letellier would've been no use for real sol-
diering, his type never are. Different from Roland and
from me. Now, we were true soldiers. . . ."

There was a pride in his voice and he seemed, without
moving his back from the side panels of the van, to snap
more upright, stiffen to attention. Lauriant was sure that
he was remembering other days in the sun—the burning
sun of Algeria and the Sahara. Perhaps his mind was back
for a moment in Sidi-bel-Abbès behind the ochre colored walls of an immaculate Quartier Viénot. Or was he
sitting once more under the trees in the town square
drinking wine or beer with his mistress on his sun-tanned
and muscular arm and listening to the army band playing
from the stand with its white painted latticed ironwork?
The mood was short lived.

"It's all over now," he added sadly.

"You still haven't told me what André Letellier did."

"You called me a messenger boy just now. Effectively
that's what André did for us. He was a courier. He traveled
around, using the job as cover, to collect and deliver for us."

"Collect and deliver what for you?"

"Messages, as I said, and money. Those two things
mostly. Also orders and instructions for . . . operations."

Fouquet stopped abruptly and looked pensive once more.

"Look, superintendent, I'll be honest with you. The
way things are now, a lot of our supporters need a morale
boost now and then. A visit helps. Additionally, once in a
while, André might take or bring back other things,
including weapons."

"Speaking of weapons, do you have a nine millimeter pistol?"

"Yes, I do." The butcher eyed the policeman and added quickly, "But I didn't use it to kill Count Armand. Strangely enough," he said, "I quite liked him. I met him a couple of times with the colonel—he was always very polite."

"He would be. But he changed sides. Didn't you think of that as desertion?"

"He did what he thought best," Fouquet replied.

Lauriant was surprised by this rather reflective and detached attitude. The surprise must have shown.

"Oh! I would have killed him if I'd been ordered to," Fouquet explained.

"By the colonel?"

"Yes. Or by another superior officer."

"But you weren't?" Lauriant asked.

"No. I wasn't. As far as I know, nobody in the OAS ordered it at all."

"Is there any point in us examining your gun?"

"None at all. But you can if you like. You'd only see that it hasn't been fired in some time."

Lauriant nearly said that the bodyguard business must have been slow lately, but he quickly changed his mind.

Instead he said, "You see, I have a case of murder to solve. And, that gives me problems—legally, philosophically and personally."

"I don't understand," Fouquet said.

"No. You wouldn't. But that's because you are a true soldier."

11

A TIME FOR A LITTLE TRUTH & SOME HELP

The slow walk from the butcher's shop across to the Letelliers' café was a lot less pleasant than usual for Lauriant that evening.

Normally, around now, he would be calling into the café for a beer or two and an enjoyable conversation with Josette and with any regulars whose habits included an evening aperitif before taking to their bicycles and boats.

This evening, it would be different.

"You're looking a bit out of sorts," Josette greeted him. "Do you want a beer? You'll need it after standing out there all this time with Fouquet."

There was no suspicion or fear in her voice. She was, as usual, just fishing for gossip with which she could keep her customers entertained whilst they bought that extra drink.

"Not just now."

"You really can't be feeling yourself then," Josette joked, the ready smile on her pretty face.

Lauriant glanced around the shop and the bar. There was nobody within earshot.

"Do you know where André is?" he asked.

"What do you want him for? I know! You need information about medicine for the cows you're going to buy. You've finally convinced yourself that you should take up farming, have you?"

"I'm serious, Josette. Do you know where he is?"

The smile vanished from her face.

"You really mean it? No, you don't . . . you're not really being serious."

The look on Lauriant's face meant that she knew that she was wrong even as she spoke the words.

"What do you think he's done? André wouldn't do anything that would interest you."

"It may be nothing," the detective said, immediately regretting that he had lied to her. He decided to be more honest and continued, "But it would help a lot, if I could talk to him before I'm forced to put out a warrant for his arrest."

Josette's arm reached behind her and she rested her hand on the shelf of bottles and glasses to steady herself. Her legs had become weak beneath her and she was finding it difficult to stand.

Lauriant slipped behind the bar, put his arm around her waist and eased her on to her stool.

"Arrest?" she whispered in disbelief. "He hasn't done anything—he can't have done anything. Not my André. He's too good, too kind-hearted." She stopped for a second. "And he's too gentle," she finished in an earnest whisper.

"Not all crimes are violent, Josette." Lauriant was also whispering now. He found himself trying very hard to be kind to her, but he did not regret it. "André's in bad company. He's out of his depth and in over his head. Some crimes," he added quietly, "are committed for good motives . . . sometimes even for the best motives. If I guess right, André would like to get out of the mess he's gotten into. I don't want to see him or you hurt. I'd like to help."

He listened to himself, and it sounded all too incongruous.

"But that must sound funny coming from a policeman," he said. "Whatever André has done, he will have done it for what he thought was the best—and he will have done it for you."

He waited before adding, "That's important, Josette. Remember it."

"But," she repeated, "Why do you want him?"

There were no tears as he had more than half expected. There was just shock and disbelief.

"There's no veterinary medicine company in Paris," Lauriant said quietly. "André has been working for quite another sort of organization. He carries messages for the OAS—that's what his rounds consist of. The stock of medicines and things in the car, which, incidentally, belongs to Roland, is just a bluff."

"Roland? Roland?"

She had never heard the name.

"He is another one of Colonel de Troquer's men. It's the colonel who pays André's wages."

She lowered her head into her hands. As she did so, the door to the shop opened.

It was one of the old women, one of the lunchtime red wine drinkers. She must have had bad eyesight, as she asked for two small tins of petit pois and a few hundred grams of ham without apparently noticing Josette's distress.

Lauriant clumsily sliced the ham with the large, razor sharp knife from below the counter, wrapped the meat in paper and handed it to the woman. Josette reached up for the tins. Her reaction had been automatic, the product of years of doing exactly that.

"Are you all right, Madame Letellier?" the old woman asked, finally realizing that there was something amiss, as Josette gave the peas to her and took the money with a shaking hand.

Lauriant answered for the little shopkeeper.

"Madame Letellier has had a bit of a shock. Nothing to worry about though."

The woman screwed up her eyes, trying to get a good, clear look at him. "The policeman!" she said in complete amazement. "Do they pay you boys so badly these days that you have to work in the shop as well?"

"Something like that."

Clutching tightly to her shopping bag, the woman, tottered out shaking her head.

"Whatever will it be next? Policemen working in shops!"

Despite everything, there was just the ghost of a return of that wonderful smile on Josette's lips.

"You wait till she sees the state of that ham," Lauriant said.

"I hacked at it. She'll be back tomorrow asking you to fire me."

Josette sat heavily back on her stool.

"Promise me something," she said very softly.

"You don't need to ask," he said, placing his arm around her shoulders, "I'll help André just as much as I can."

A little smile, weak and dispirited, broke through again.

"He's not a bad man. He wouldn't hurt anyone—André is just a bit weak that's all."

"He needs you, Josette . . . you know it and," the detective added, "maybe he knows it even more than you do."

Lauriant took a bottle of calvados from the shelf and poured them both a glass.

"Thank you," Josette said simply. "Not for this, but for saying that you'll help us."

The calvados was welcome. It burned in his throat.

"I'm not really interested in what André does for the colonel and the rest of his kind," Lauriant told her. "I'm not at all interested in counter-terrorism. . . ."

"Terrorism! My good God! Not André!"

There were a few tears now, quickly wiped away with the back of Josette's hand. She was making a mighty effort to hold herself together.

"Don't worry—that's what the government calls it. It's a title, a phrase, no more," Lauriant explained soothingly, although, truthfully, he was no longer sure himself about how seriously the politicians and judges would treat a minor member of the OAS who lacked high level contacts and the protection of old comrades.

He searched his pockets, found his handkerchief and

gave it to her. She patted her eyes and then she gulped at the calvados.

"I'm much more interested in something else André carried with him two trips ago."

"Something else?" she asked.

"Yes. Something else he took with him that was not from the colonel."

Josette looked confused.

"But you said that he worked for the colonel."

"Nevertheless! Now tell me where André's been this week."

"The Southwest."

"Where exactly, Josette?"

"I don't always remember," Josette confessed. "After a while the places all seem the same—the names are all different, but they don't mean much, if you see what I mean."

"Try," he encouraged her.

"Well, okay," she replied bravely. "This week . . . let me see . . . Perigueux first, I know that. Then Bordeaux, then Agen, again . . . he goes there a lot," she paused, thinking, "Could that mean anything?"

"Nothing that I am interested in, I don't think."

"After that," she continued, "Sarcelles sur Murs, Pau and Montauban. He wouldn't have been to all those places yet, of course."

"And," the detective asked, "what about two weeks ago? Can you try to remember for me where he went then?"

Josette frowned. "The Rhone and then on down to

Marseilles, I think . . . he goes there a lot too."

"Okay." Lauriant nodded. "Now, will you talk to him before gets home? Does he telephone you?"

"Always. He will telephone tonight."

"You must let me speak to him," Lauriant said. "It might be his only chance."

"Only chance?"

She looked frightened now.

"It's possible, probable even that when he gets back and Colonel de Troquer learns what I have guessed—worked out, really—and that I've been questioning André, he might be . . . upset enough . . . to want to deal with André in his own way."

There was no color left in Josette's face. By now, she was ready to believe anything. She had more than enough imagination to conjure up an adequate picture of what the colonel's own way might involve. She shuddered.

"André knows nothing about your murder—he didn't kill Count Armand. He wouldn't!" she said. "No, wait a minute, he couldn't. He was away."

She was very sure. André had said so and he never lied to her. But then the reality sunk in . . . he had lied to her—for months.

"I don't think that he was away," Lauriant said gently. "His—sorry, *Roland's* car was at Pinocheau, Colonel de Troquer's house, the morning the body was discovered. Jacquot saw it."

"My good God," she repeated. "But, you can't think that he did it!"

"I need to make a telephone call before André rings," the detective told her without answering her question.

"It's in the back," Josette said limply, pulling back the curtain behind the bar with one hand.

"Come on, I want you to listen to this," Lauriant said. "The bar and the shop can wait just this once."

Far away in Saint Sauveur, Mimi's telephone rang. For her, it was an odd time for a call—early evening. Her telephone did not ring often anyway, rarely more than two or three times a day. She picked up the receiver.

"Hello . . . it's me. How are you?" asked Lauriant.

"Better for hearing you," Mimi replied with relief. "I was wondering who it could possibly be."

There was a softness in her voice these days even over the telephone. Lauriant was getting used to it and he liked it, very much.

"Have you seen Colonel de Troquer?" Mimi asked. A little tautness had crept into her gentle tone now.

"Yes. I've seen him."

"And you are all right? Please tell me that there are no problems."

"Not for me, I don't think," he said. He was happy to be able to put her anxiety to rest. "The colonel was most hospitable—and helpful," Lauriant added to quell any final doubts.

"I was worried about you," Mimi said truthfully.

"I'm pleased," he replied, like a schoolboy happy that

a girlfriend had missed his company. "But there is trouble," Lauriant continued, "potential at least . . . for the husband of a friend of mine."

"Oh. What friend?"

Was there suspicion creeping into that lovely soft voice? Lauriant thought that he could imagine a flash, he would like to think, of jealousy in her violet blue eyes.

"No one you know," he replied. "It's a friend from here in L'Ile Bois Aubrand."

"Oh," she repeated.

"It's in connection with our colonel. I need a favor, badly. Can you help?"

"Tell me what it is."

It was not yes, but it was not no either.

"My friend's husband has crossed the colonel. I want a place to hide him far from here. I can't be sure that with the colonel's information network I can trust any place around L'Ile Bois Aubrand. I'm beginning to wonder whether anyone around here can be trusted at all. Will you hide him for me?"

There was a long pause.

"Is this dangerous?" Mimi asked. "I've got Alain to think of."

Josette had her ear close to Lauriant's face, listening to the conversation as he spoke into the mouthpiece. He turned his head to look into her eyes. He was sure that she saw something there that resembled anguish as dispirited, discreetly she moved her face away from his. Even in her own torment, pretty, clever

Josette felt for him. And his stomach churned.

Lauriant, for his part, realized that he and Mimi had reached an important crossroads in their relationship. For the first time, he had placed her into a position where, in her own eyes, Mimi had to make a choice—a choice between Alain and Lauriant.

He waited before replying. He tried very hard to keep the tension and emotion out of his voice, but he knew, in the end, Mimi would sense it. They understood each other too well; had known each other too long. They had grown too close as friends for her not to feel his anxiety.

"Yes, it might be dangerous," he said eventually and then stopped abruptly.

The hesitation at the other end of the line seemed agonizingly long. Lauriant thought that he could hear his own breathing. There was a slight tremble in his fingers as he held the receiver a little more tightly. Josette saw it and took his other hand in both of hers. She started to sob quietly.

Then, down the telephone line came seven simple words and the bridge was crossed.

"What do you want me to do?"

12

A TIME FOR A LITTLE CARING
& SOME SAFETY

A second telephone conversation behind the curtain in the Letelliers' bar that warm evening was more tearful, but equally tense.

At the end, Josette, her eyes red, handed the receiver to Lauriant.

"You know then?" André's first words were redolent with resignation. "I knew that it couldn't last," he added. "I've been trying to find a way out, a way to end it for weeks . . . Josette says that you might help."

"First tell me if you have been to Sarcelles sur Murs yet?" Lauriant asked.

"I'm due there tomorrow."

"Don't go there," the detective said crisply. "Avoid the town."

He waited. Would Letellier take his advice?

"Okay."

Lauriant heard a kind of muffled croak down the line and, then, André asked, "But are they going to try to get me or not?"

Like his wife, André was afraid.

"I don't know. But I—and particularly, you—can't afford to take any chances."

Fouquet had been right about him. It appeared that André was going to do as he was told without argument.

"What do you want me to do?" Letellier asked, a little too meekly for Lauriant's taste.

"South of Sarcelles sur Murs, there's a small town called Saint Sauveur. . . ."

"I know where it is, but how do you—"

"Go there. Go there tonight," Lauriant instructed him.

"But what do I do . . . where do I go when I get there?"

"There's a house in the Rue Voltaire off the Rue de la République. . . ." Lauriant gave André the number. ". . . go there and see a lady named Mimi. She is expecting you. She will hide you and she will find a place to keep the car out of sight. Stay there. Don't answer the telephone. Don't use the car. Don't even go out. When they realize that you are not making the rest of this week's calls on their supporters, they are bound to react in some way."

"Does this woman know that I'm coming?" André asked.

Something deep inside Lauriant revolted at hearing Mimi, Mimi of all people, being spoken of in this way. He beat the feeling back.

"I've told her," he said. "Remember this *woman*, as you call her, is putting herself in considerable danger for you. And only because I asked her to. You make a mess of this and I'll—" Lauriant stopped himself. "Anyway, the quicker you get to Saint Sauveur and out of sight the better."

"I'll book out of this hotel and start right now." André's

voice reflected the shock with which the detective's outburst had hit him. "It'll be very late, and very dark by the time I get there. That'll help. How do you know this Mimi?"

Lauriant ignored the question.

"André, what was it that you took to Count Armand in Nice two weeks ago?"

"So you know about that too."

He sounded very resigned. André Letellier was clearly a man who had accepted the inevitable. Lauriant suspected that he was probably very good at that. There was no fight in him.

"Come on André, I need to know. Frankly, apart from Josette, who deserves a lot better, it's the only reason I'm helping you at all."

There was another tinge of anger in Lauriant's voice. There was also worry and, certainly, a little belated regret. He was having second thoughts—thinking that he had been wrong to involve Mimi in this. After all, he thought, for this man I am putting Mimi at risk. The feeling was making him annoyed.

"A letter," Letellier admitted.

"A letter? Who from?"

"Michel gave it to me. But Max Cresson was there too. I'm always uneasy when he's around."

"There?"

"At the farm . . . the Cressons' farm."

"Was Monique there too when this letter was handed over?"

"No. Only the men. I heard her upstairs,

though," André replied.

"Why did you go to the farm to collect this letter? Did Max or Michel threaten you in some way?"

Lauriant could imagine that it would not take much to scare André Letellier into doing anything.

"No. Max didn't need to threaten me and Michel wouldn't. I took the envelope to the old count because Michel asked me to. No more."

"Were you and Michel Cresson friends then?" the detective asked, and he felt Josette tense beside him. Lauriant remembered her dislike for the younger Cresson.

"We were at school together—Josette too. Michel looked out for me when there might be trouble with the bigger boys. Anyway, later, I didn't believe what everyone said about his killing his mother. I told him so before he left the village. It was a time when things were very bad for him. I think he appreciated that." There was a slight hesitation. "He likes me," Letellier concluded, rather pathetically.

"Did you open the letter?" Lauriant asked.

"Of course not," André said very quickly—too quickly? He was trying to sound as if Lauriant was responsible for some affront.

"Pity!"

Lauriant thought for a moment.

"André, this is important. Do you remember if the letter was sealed, when you picked it up or did one of them—Max or Michel—seal it in front of you?"

"Max sealed it. He half turned his back when he was

doing it, like he wanted to make sure that I didn't see what was inside."

"And this was not Organization business?"

"Most definitely not. I did it as a favor . . . for Michel," André answered.

"Was Michel the one who suggested to the OAS in the first place that you might make a good courier? You were only a conscript in the army so the colonel wouldn't normally have chosen you."

"I needed a job. The shop doesn't make enough for both of us. Michel arranged things with that colonel at Pinocheau—the car and the cover story. Like I said, I needed the job, so I took it. I knew it meant lying to Josette, but I did what I thought was for the best."

"I thought so. That's what I've just told Josette."

"Thank you." André sounded sincere.

"So you felt that you owed Michel a favor in return," Lauriant went on, "and because of that, you took the letter to Nice."

"That's about it."

"What were you doing at Pinocheau on the morning following Count Armand's murder?" Lauriant asked.

"Getting my list of contacts for the next trip and destroying the list from the last one. They always insisted that I scrap the previous list in front of them."

"When you got to Nice, was the Count surprised to see you?"

"He was. I drove over from Marseilles—that was one of my regular stops. I hoped it would be quick, but I had to wait in the hotel lobby for him for nearly an hour, and I had to dodge the new countess into the bargain. She came in before him."

"Did Michel or Max tell you to do that—avoid the countess?" the detective queried.

"No. I just thought that if they were being that secretive about the whole thing, I should see the count alone."

"And eventually you did."

"Yes, as I said, after nearly an hour. He came into the hotel lobby and I said hello and gave him the envelope."

"How did he look when he read what was inside?" Lauriant asked.

"His face got very drawn. He went, well, a bit white. Then he said, very simply, "Thank you, André. You have done me a great service, but I need now to get home.' I don't know what he meant."

"That was all?"

"Yes. He thanked me again and said for me to give his regards to everyone in the village. Simple as that. And I just left."

"André, how did you know which hotel to go to?"

"Everyone in L'Ile Bois Aubrand, and at Crissay, too, knows it. Count Armand has been going there for years. He takes his wife to the same hotel every season."

"Thanks, André. Now get off to Saint Sauveur and remember what I've told you," Lauriant said.

"Thanks."

The detective sighed.

"I hope so."

Josette and Lauriant shared another calvados as the long evening faded into night.

All the customers had been gone for over an hour.

But Josette was reluctant to let him go.

He, in turn, was thinking about his landlady, Nicole Simon, and he was surely in no hurry to leave.

They sat together at one of the tables in the rear of the café, away from the street.

Josette's tears were gone now and her face was on the way back to its normal prettiness.

Once in a while she even managed her smile. But there was something missing from it now. The totality of its happiness was no more.

Poor Josette had, later than most, been introduced to the harsh realities of a life without daydreams.

Lauriant held his cigarette in one hand and his other arm curled around Josette's shoulders, as her head rested against his chest. She looked up at him. Their faces were very close.

"Will André be all right?" she asked.

He could taste the hint of calvados on her breath.

Lauriant squeezed her and smiled at her, but he could not give her the answer that she wanted.

13

THE FUNERAL & THE CON MAN'S WIFE

Next morning, the morning of Count Armand's funeral, Duverger found Lauriant in the main street of L'Ile Bois Aubrand.

The superintendent was leaning on the churchyard wall enjoying a tiny breeze which had come with the dawn to gently relieve the continuous, almost repressive heat of the last weeks.

He was gazing out across the marais, imagining Monique Cresson, skirt hitched and makeup applied, rowing her little skiff slowly through the water to the bottom of the main street. Would she, he wondered, have been savoring that instant of freedom away from her father and her brother? Would she be thinking about the moments of gossip she could enjoy by visiting the shop for some deliberately forgotten groceries? Did she have a sly drink at the bar as well? Lauriant had forgotten to ask Josette that. Or, perhaps, she was more concerned with anticipating a furtive meeting with Count Charles somewhere on her way back up the marais—a meeting at which they would make love and, eventually, conceive a baby?

"Where were you last night?" Duverger asked him. "I tried to get you three times on the telephone. I gave up then. Your landlady wasn't happy with me . . . or you either I think."

"How's the head?" Lauriant said.

Duverger touched his forehead with his good hand. The plaster was smaller now, but the inspector was in no mood to belittle the extent of his injuries in the line of duty.

"Bad," he replied, "very bad and the arm . . ." He looked down mournfully at his sling. "The doctor reckons that will take months before it's any good again and—"

To stop a long recital Lauriant asked, "What time do you think the cortege will get here from Crissay?"

"Another half an hour at least."

Inside the Letelliers' café, long lines of sparkling empty glasses were already lined up on the counter and over a hundred bottles of white wine had been put into the big square wooden lead-lined coolers and covered with ice. A mass of jugs containing red wine were stashed on the shelves behind the bar ready for instant use. Next to them came the cognac and the calvados—there to satisfy those who needed to be more melancholy or who merely wished to spend more money than most to send Count Armand decently to his restful fate.

Lauriant knew all this because he had helped Josette with the heavy work that morning. It gave him an idea.

"Time for a dry white wine then," Lauriant said.

Fittingly, Josette Letellier was dressed in black. Lauriant thought that it suited her. She poured them each a large glass of the cold wine and refused payment.

Duverger, from his previous visits to the café over the years, was surprised. He looked from Josette to Lauriant and then back again, but wisely said nothing.

"The whole village has gone up to Crissay to follow the coffin," Josette explained.

"Not you though?"

Duverger's question was irrelevant.

"Too much to do."

She turned away from the little inspector, looked affectionately at Lauriant and vigorously polished one or two glasses that did not need it.

"Everyone will be in here afterwards, except the count's family of course," she added by way of explanation as she turned back to Duverger.

"What about de Troquer?" the superintendent asked, lighting a cigarette and watching Josette carefully. "If he comes in, what then?"

"He'll get his glass of wine or cognac like everyone else."

The point of this conversation completely eluded poor Duverger.

"Anyway, where were you last night when I was trying to reach you?" the inspector repeated.

"Taking out an insurance policy."

Little Duverger looked lost again.

"Well, what was it that you wanted, chasing me around like that?"

"Mayor Rocard wanted to know when the Cressons would be out of the cells. The mayor's left Jacquot up at the farm, but he's been spending most of his time drinking his way through the stock of cider. The old crook is accepting the money Rocard is giving him and doing less and less work by the day."

"I think that Rocard might have to wait on the Cressons for a little while yet," Lauriant said dryly.

"I thought that you'd say that . . . and . . ." The inspector blew out his cheeks, ". . . it leads me to Rocard's other point. Who's going to pay him back the wages that he's been giving Jacquot?"

"He'll have to sort it out with the Cressons."

"He won't like that!"

"You pay Rocard then," the superintendent said abruptly.

Duverger gave Lauriant a quick glance.

"Something worrying you?" he asked.

"Yes."

"The case?"

Lauriant suddenly looked depressed. He finished his wine quickly and looked at his watch.

"Sort of. Come on. The procession will be here in a minute."

The hearse was the old fashioned type with tall wheels and a fringe above its glazed side panels. Inside, the coffin lay surrounded with white lilies. On the roof a coronet had been tied with a suitable ribbon. The four dark colored horses had black plumes on the heads and the driver was wearing a top hat and a somber expression.

The cortege made its way gradually up the street. Beyond it the marais, covered at its boundary by floating green growth, glinted in the sunshine, incongruously cheerful and lively, the little breeze rocking the weeds and making wavelets along the water's edge.

Following the hearse, Count Charles walked slowly with his mother on one arm and Amelie Bergman on the other. All three were, finally, in mourning clothes and both the women wore black veils. Lauriant looked closely. It was not possible to make out the detail of their faces.

So, the detective thought, those two have met at last. He wondered how that meeting—or was it confrontation?—had developed.

The rest of the neighborhood followed behind them, a complete sea of black.

Amongst them were George Rocard, prominent in his official role as the mayor, and the colonel, head uncovered, with his wife. Within a meter of de Troquer was Roland. A little further behind, tall above all of the others in the crowd, Lauriant had no problem in spotting the butcher Fouquet. Like Roland's, his eyes moved constantly. All their training told them that in large crowds the greatest danger lay.

A little further back, but still set apart from most of the local villagers, a gray haired man walked slowly—de Bonvalet. Duverger raised an eyebrow, wondering if the examining magistrate was there officially or personally to pay his respects to the dead man.

As the hearse passed and stopped in front of the

church, Josette appeared on her doorstep and crossed herself before bowing her head.

The church at L'Ile Bois Aubrand was, like many others in rural France, much bigger than the size of the community seemed to merit—a leftover from the Middle Ages when France was the power in the world. Everyone went inside the great stone cavern except Josette, who slipped back into the shop, and the two policemen, who found a shady place in the churchyard between the vast arched door and the open grave already prepared in the family plot.

Lauriant idly examined the headstones and the monuments. The count's family had been in L'Ile Bois Aubrand for nearly four hundred years and at Crissay for over two hundred of them. They had survived war, plague, revolt, rebellion and revolution. One ancestor had gone to the guillotine at the hands of the sans-culottes.

Now the current chapter in the story was one of murder and of a new, younger count, who thought his place was with people like the Sarrazins.

The Sarrazins—a couple living on their wits and, Lauriant did not doubt it, funding their lifestyle by betting on the horses with stolen money and negotiating shady deals. A couple constantly on the lookout for the weak and the gullible.

The superintendent shook his head.

The old count had been right to worry about the future. The old countess had been equally right to worry about her son. In the end, they were the same thing.

If any good was to come out of all this, the two women, the two countesses were going to have to struggle hard and they would need, somehow, to learn to like each other.

The shiny, ebony colored coffin was carried from the church to the graveside by six men in black, one of whom was Pinay, the gardener, and another was Paul Sarrazin, the swindler and the friend of Count Charles.

In the procession to the grave, Lauriant fell in next to Madeleine Sarrazin.

"You didn't come in," she said to him.

"I want to talk to you," he replied. "Something's been worrying me since we last met."

"Met? Is that what you call it?"

Lauriant dropped back, his hand on her arm.

"Let's go over there away from all these people."

They walked back down the path towards the church-yard gate. Across the street, outside on the pavement again, Josette watched them.

"Something's been worrying me," he repeated.

"So you said."

Her voice was flat. She was doing her best to appear completely disinterested.

"I didn't bring it up in front of your husband," Lauriant continued, "in case he didn't know about it, but you were arrested once by the vice squad."

"And released without charge," Madeleine said quickly and added, "Paul knows about it."

"You didn't make a complaint, though—about false arrest, I mean. You could have."

"No point. It wouldn't have got me anything except an apology."

The detective thought about offering her a cigarette, but they were still in the churchyard and he decided against it.

"I couldn't spend an apology, you see," she explained, "and I needed money at the time."

"What were you doing alone in a known area for prostitutes? You were certain to get accosted by men looking for professional girls, if not worse."

"I don't really remember."

"Well, let me tell you why I think you were there."

"You're welcome to try."

Again there was that air of feigned disinterest.

"You were there in one kind of professional capacity. I'm certain of that," he began.

"Are you saying that I was a working girl? Because, if you are, I'll tell now that—"

"No. You were there because you were a nurse," he explained.

"How do you mean?"

The superintendent detected more interest now.

"Did you specialize at all as a nurse?" he asked.

"Yes . . . obstetrics and gynecology."

"Do you want me to spell it out then, Madeleine?"

She shrugged her shoulders.

"You do? Very well! You, Madeleine, were there to

perform an abortion for one of the girls when you were caught up. Tell me that I'm not right."

She said nothing.

"You said that you were without money right then," he went on. "It was easy money for you."

Still, she was silent, but Lauriant could sense that she was thinking furiously. She looked around for her husband, but he, at that precise moment, was engaged with the others in lowering the heavy coffin into the dark, deep maw cut into the earth.

Little Duverger, off to one side, was dividing his time between watching the crowd and then watching the superintendent and the woman with him.

"And, also, that's why you came down here the morning after the old count's murder," Lauriant continued. "Count Charles had already arranged it with you. You were going to abort Monique Cresson's baby."

She found her voice.

"That, of course, is pure speculation."

"I wondered why Count Charles waited for you so long there, next to his father's body, and I wondered why it took you and Paul so long to get down from Paris. The reason? It was because he didn't call for you to rescue him. All Count Charles had to do was wait—he knew you were coming. Am I right? The only thing that added to his tension was that you got lost."

"How did you know that?"

"I saw you."

She shrugged.

"Just our luck! There's never a policeman around when you want one and always one when you don't."

"So Charles didn't send for you after the murder and you didn't rush down from Paris. There was no need. All the arrangements had been made. You two were coming anyway. Charles, dead drunk, on your own admission, only had to wait for you. He's a stupid man. . . ."

Madeleine did not protest this.

"He waited for you and your husband to come and sort out his mess for him because he was too brainless and too drunk to sort it out for himself. And, in a way, you did kind of sort things out for him. You moved him and his car off to Paris."

Madeleine looked at him for a moment.

"If that was to be true, what would happen to us—to Paul and to . . . me?" she asked.

"The examining magistrate is over there." Lauriant pointed out de Bonvalet in the crowd around the graveside.

"I've met him," she admitted.

"Well it's up to him."

They stepped out on to the pavement. This time, he offered her the cigarette and lit one for himself. They smoked the Chesterfields silently for a few moments.

"But," Lauriant assured her, "you didn't actually carry out the abortion."

"No," she said reluctantly. "You could say that . . . events overtook us."

"But you did fail to report the crime," he added, "and you both did leave the scene. You're as guilty on those matters as much as is Count Charles himself. He, of course, also might be guilty of the murder."

"Not Charles!" Madeleine exclaimed.

"Why not?"

Lauriant leaned back against the churchyard wall. He was tired. It had been a long night.

"He inherits the major part of his father's wealth . . . my guess is that it's an amount worth killing for," he said.

Madeleine was unconvinced.

"But he'd get that soon enough anyway. Count Armand was getting old. Charles reckoned that he was failing fast. And don't forget, his father had cleared his debts before the murder, so he wasn't really in need of money right now."

"Yes . . . that's true," Lauriant said thoughtfully. "They disliked each other, though," he added, "or do you think hated would be a better word?"

"Yes, it is—but surely not enough to kill."

Madeleine leaned her back against the wall next to him.

"Charles, very drunk, his father returning home unexpectedly in the night," Lauriant thought aloud. "He could have lost control. Don't forget, you were arriving next morning to . . . deal with the Cresson girl . . . to take away another of Charles's self-generated problems, so to speak."

He watched the smoke from their cigarettes carry lazily away in the breeze for a moment.

"The old count turning up like that would have finished your plans for Monique and her child. Charles could have murdered Count Armand in a drunken temper.

That's possible. Yes? Or maybe his father knew about the Cresson girl and, on top of clearing his debts, this was the last straw for the old count. Perhaps, Count Armand told his son that he would disinherit him. That would be a strong motive for murder—and it stands up," Lauriant finished.

Madeleine Sarrazin was silent for a long time. She was considering every option—including whether she was any longer quite so sure that Charles had not killed his father. Lauriant was certain of that. He watched her come to a decision.

"Okay. I confess that I was here to do the Cresson girl the . . . favor you talked about," she began. She turned to face the detective and looked him straight in the eyes. "But that's all," she added firmly. "Paul and I were shocked when we found out about the murder."

Madeleine stopped for a moment, smoking quietly, before rubbing her long fingers against her forehead.

"Paul's good in difficult situations," she continued, "so he took over. What else was there to do anyway? Charles could hardly stand and there was a body with a hole in its back lying around. I stayed in the car—not because I'm squeamish, as you suggested, but because Paul told me to. He said the less people in the house, the less clues we were likely to leave. He was right, of course."

Lauriant waited, giving her time to collect her thoughts.

"I was all for getting out of there straight away and leaving Charles to face the music, but Paul wouldn't hear of it."

The superintendent stubbed out his cigarette.

"He's a fast thinker, your Paul. He knew Charles was either going to be arrested or come into a lot of money—

perhaps both. Paul stayed because he wanted a chance to get his hands on some of the money and, Charles being the kind of man he is, your husband would have succeeded."

Madeleine sighed.

"That's about it," she said.

Lauriant eased himself upright, threw away his cigarette and walked back into the churchyard to the examining magistrate.

The two men shook hands. De Bonvalet looked embarrassed.

The examining magistrate released the Sarrazins from the restrictions on their movements the next day—at Lauriant's request and with his full approval.

"You're sure that you don't wish me to file charges?"

"What would be the point?" the detective asked.

De Bonvalet's only other comment concerned the distress of having, as a part of his office, to come into contact with such people, let alone having to communicate with them.

"They packed the Vedette and went back to Paris without going over to Crissay," Duverger told Lauriant.

"They're biding their time," the superintendent replied. "If Count Charles gets away with it, they'll be back—and he'll welcome them with open arms, if he's allowed to."

"Allowed to?"

"That's what I said."

Duverger closed his eyes. He was finding it more and more difficult to understand his superintendent these days.

14

THE COLONEL COOPERATES

"I appear to have underestimated you. It's a mistake that I don't often make."

Colonel de Troquer sat in the same room at Pinocheau in which he and Lauriant had first met.

"You are responsible in some way for the disappearance of André Letellier," he paused before adding, "my courier."

"It's possible." Lauriant was trying to be non-committal.

The detective watched the ex-soldier, who was making an effort to control his anger.

"I don't like being crossed!" de Troquer said coldly. Recovering himself, he explained in a quieter voice, "I wasn't untruthful with you about Letellier, when we spoke before. I just answered the wrong questions."

He suddenly smiled the disconcerting smile which had made Lauriant so uncomfortable during their previous conversation. It still had the same effect.

"Fouquet told you about him, I know that," the colonel continued. "I had good reasons to authorize cooperation, but that was somewhat excessive."

"That, too, is possible."

"And what do you intend to do with Letellier—assuming, as I do, that you have him hidden away somewhere?" de Troquer asked.

"Pursuing your assumption," Lauriant replied, "I intend to do nothing with him, apart from protect him."

"What is this Letellier to you?"

The colonel, for a moment, looked doubtful.

"He is a witness in my murder case," Lauriant explained and then added, perhaps a little too quickly, "I have no further brief for him."

The ex-soldier gave the detective a quizzical look before continuing.

"Are you really saying that you think that I, for some reason, might wish to . . . make him unavailable as a witness?"

"Yes."

"Why?"

"Because he used his connection with you—just once, I think—to do a little message delivering of his own."

"Ah! I see. That wasn't very sensible of him."

The colonel, thinking this over, spun a small paper knife in his fingers.

"This little bit of freelancing by André," he said, "has, then, an impact on your investigations into Count Armand's murder?"

"I think," Lauriant admitted, "that it was vital. If that message had not been sent, I don't think that the old count would have been murdered. Not then at least, and probably not at all."

The smallest hint of resignation crept into the colonel's voice. "Are you now looking for some further cooperation from me? If you are, I am about to render it to you."

"I want your help. But I also want it on conditions."

"Conditions? I am not used to being subject to conditions, Monsieur Lauriant."

The paper knife spun more rapidly in de Troquer's fingers for a moment or two.

"You realize," the colonel began again, speaking slowly, "I know that you realize—I believe you to be a clever man—that André Letellier's knowledge would be a great embarrassment, indeed danger to many people, if it were to become known in certain quarters."

"Or was made public," Lauriant added, turning the screw.

"That too, naturally," de Troquer admitted. "I see that we understand each other very well, superintendent."

He looked down intently studying the handle of the paper knife and was silent for a while. Then, briskly, he said, "Let's start with things a little more important than André Letellier."

"Agreed."

"You still have Michel in custody—which is no good for him and," the colonel added with emphasis, "a difficulty for me. Also, you still have not located Monique—alive or dead."

"I think that she's alive," the detective said.

"Why?"

"Count Charles would not have the stomach for

killing her, nor would his friend Paul Sarrazin—"

"But—"

"But weak men do kill when frightened or provoked beyond endurance? That's what you were about to say, I think, and it's true of course."

"But you don't think that we are dealing with that situation here?" the colonel prompted.

"No. I don't."

"If that is true—"

"It's true. Those two fine fellows were too busy arranging to get her baby aborted."

The colonel's eyebrows rose.

"If they were in that dirty game, then they were not in the business of killing her. So," de Troquer added thoughtfully, "we are left with Max and Michel."

"Unless Count Charles had a change of mind about how to deal with Monique, we are left only with Max and Michel."

"And, if she is dead, one of them murdered his own daughter or his own sister," the colonel mused. "Well, of course, the mother died in circumstances that could only be described as curious. Michel has never spoken about it—not to me, which he would be unlikely to do anyway—or to his friends in . . . the ranks."

This time it was Lauriant who adopted a quizzical look.

"I would have heard. You can be sure of it," de Troquer explained.

"But even so, I think that Monique is still alive," the superintendent concluded.

"From what you've said, I'm inclined to agree with you."

"Still," Lauriant said in a dispirited voice, "None of this gives us a reason, a motive for Count Armand's death."

"I agree with you."

They sat quietly for a while. Abruptly, de Troquer went across to the side table with its row of regimented bottles and shot glasses. Without asking he poured two large shots of whisky and gave one to the detective.

"You lent money to Fouquet to buy his business, didn't you?" Lauriant asked.

"Fouquet has, once more I see, been disarmingly honest," de Troquer said dryly.

"Did you also lend money to Max?"

The ex-soldier sipped his whisky, but did not answer. So Lauriant continued, "He has been investing very heavily in his farm. The money, I reasoned, must have come from somewhere and I frankly could think of no other source than you."

"I knew that you would reach that conclusion at some stage," the colonel said, "but you are wrong."

Anna de Troquer, taller than her husband and looking very cool despite the heat, came into the room. She placed a small tray of hors d'oeuvre on the side table, pushing aside the neat lines of bottles and glasses. Lauriant thought that the disruption of his bottle and glass parade annoyed the colonel.

"It's getting late," Anna said simply, "I thought you would like a little something."

She smiled warmly at Lauriant and shook his hand before leaving the room.

"It's a pleasure, as always, to have you with us, superintendent," she said.

Lauriant heard himself saying formally and politely, "Thank you, Madame," as he sat back into his chair.

De Troquer moved a few small pieces from the tray to his plate and added some olives. The detective sheepishly followed suit.

This mixture of Spartan room, suppressed violence and almost banal domesticity was still so difficult to assimilate. Somehow Lauriant just could not get comfortable with it.

"I said that I would render cooperation," de Troquer repeated, wiping his mouth with a napkin. "This might help. I have lent no money to Max Cresson. None at all. Not a franc."

"Then, if that is the case, my thinking has been wrong and I have not been making any sense of this case up until now after all."

Lauriant looked both puzzled and depressed at the same moment. He had built up an idea in his mind of why and how the crime had been committed. De Troquer in a simple, single sentence had destroyed it.

The colonel smiled again. "De Bonvalet will be disappointed in us both," he said. "Still. No, you have not been entirely wrong . . ." There was a little glint of mischief in his normally torpid eyes. ". . . as I have, however, lent considerable sums to Michel Cresson."

"So that's it! I was right! Well, in a way!" Lauriant exclaimed, very relieved indeed.

"Take this how you will," the colonel added, "and for what it's worth. You see," he smiled once more, "I don't intend to underestimate you again."

Lauriant got a strong impression that he was being played with. He tried to trust de Troquer—everything in him wanted to—but he just could not suspend his professional mind long enough to enable him to do it.

The ex-soldier clasped his hands together and lowered them very slowly into his lap.

"The truth is," he said, "that the farm, thanks to my lending some money to Michel and to my giving him much more, is now effectively his."

"That," Lauriant observed, "is very generous indeed!"

"Not as generous as it may sound. Look, the money is, was, OAS money."

"I understand that . . . but, nevertheless—"

The colonel sighed.

"I have learned in this life how to accommodate certain mistakes," he said with an almost theatrical wave of the white napkin.

Suddenly, an intangible link had somehow established itself between them. Neither man had intended it, but there it unquestionably was. The detective felt it and responded to the invisible bond.

"Me too," Lauriant said quietly, his thoughts creeping back through dark passages in his own history and mainly his broken marriage. "It isn't easy," he added.

"No. It's not easy at all."

In that moment, it was as if de Troquer could see through him and as if he could see through the colonel. It was a sad feeling for both of them. The spell needed to be broken. The colonel's hand made a sweeping gesture—to swipe away, it seemed, the painful memories both were enduring, before he continued and the moment had passed.

"Also, I have learned that it is often best to cut one's losses. You and I have chosen to do that. Or, perhaps . . ." The ex-soldier looked hard at the superintendent. ". . . it was forced on you?"

"Forced is closer to reality," Lauriant admitted.

He took a long drink of the whisky. Without hesitation, de Troquer refilled both of their glasses.

"You and I, after all," the colonel went on, "are not fools. Putting aside our own troubles, we both know that the OAS is finished. Oh, there are the hot heads who will never give up. There are always men like that. But I need to look beyond the OAS now. I have to make a future—for me and for Anna. I do not intend going down in flames in some French version of the twilight of the gods."

"And to help you do this, you have a part of the Organization's treasure chest?" the superintendent asked.

The colonel smiled his disconcerting smile.

"I have, and I'm . . . investing it."

"Like a good businessman?" Lauriant asked. "In Fouquet's shop and in the Cresson farm?"

"Amongst other things."

"I see."

The policeman sat quietly sipping his refreshed whisky for a time.

"I also see why you need to keep Fouquet and Michel in your debt. They desert you or you get . . . eliminated . . . and others in the OAS will come looking for their money. That would be extremely bad for you and for them. No doubt," Lauriant added, "you have a similar arrangement with Roland?"

"I do. We, all of us are, as I put it, looking to the future. André Letellier, I'm afraid, isn't the only one who has been doing a bit of freelancing."

It took a little while for Lauriant to put this new information into his thinking about the old count's murder. Eventually, he nodded, ready with another question.

"How has Max reacted to this—this purchase of the farm by his son? And why did he agree to it?"

"He agreed because he would have lost the farm without the money. Max is an oaf with no head for business. Strong, of course, good for the manual side of farming, but that's all. How did he react, you ask? Well, sullen and resentful would describe it less than adequately, I think. All of it, the whole situation, wasn't helped by their . . . already difficult . . . relationship, or by the shooting of Mother Cresson."

Lauriant thought this over.

"Getting back to Letellier—"

"Before we do," de Troquer interrupted, "you'll need to know that Max has been making more trouble lately about Michel's hold over the farm. He's been threatening to buy back the farm."

"Would Michel let that happen?"

"Max, like many of his sort, can be stubborn—even mulish. He's pigheaded enough to get his own way most of the time. He has every right to buy back the farm within two years of the original agreement, according to the contract by which he handed over control of the farm to Michel in exchange for the money. I saw no harm in it at the time. It wasn't worth arguing about. Max needed the payment for the farm to pay off his debts. He would never raise that sort of money twice."

"But now things could be different. Is that it? Where could Max possibly get the money?"

"I don't know," de Troquer admitted. "It may be that it is just bravado—only talk. Max is fond of that cider they make up there. It may only have been the alcohol talking. But how can you be sure? And, this might be important, the two year period is up in the next few weeks."

"Are you saying that Max is running out of time?"

"Precisely. If there was anything in his threats, he would have to come through in a very short time. Also, he is afraid that Michel will throw him off the farm as soon as the time does come."

"Well, that leaves us with the question of does Max have

the money and, if so, where did he get it from."

"You must have guessed that I sent Fouquet to the Cressons' farm on the morning following the count's murder," the colonel said.

Lauriant shrugged.

"I sent him to warn Max not to contemplate anything violent. Michel can't stay awake every hour of the day and night, can he? Also there was Monique to consider. With the deadline approaching, the cauldron of relationships in that house must have been, was getting close to an explosion."

The detective sipped his whisky and leaned toward the colonel.

"But, and this is getting back to Letellier, they were close enough to work together in sending André with his message to Count Armand in Nice."

The surprise showed on de Troquer's face.

"So that was little André's bit of freelancing! He took a message from the Cressons—both of them—to Count Armand!"

"Yes."

"I don't understand that," the colonel said honestly. "Why would those two do that? They were constantly at each other's throats."

"It is true, nevertheless."

Lauriant paused and looked the colonel straight in the eyes.

"What do you intend to do about André?" he asked.

"Personally, nothing," de Troquer answered. "The

time for killing is over, as far as I'm concerned."

"What about the others in the OAS? They are bound to realize how badly he can compromise them."

"Those that I can control will do nothing as well."

"And, what about the rest?" the detective pressed.

"He's going to have to take his chances," the colonel replied, his face set firm. "And I can't do anything about it."

"I think that you can," Lauriant said quietly, laying aside his napkin and placing his plate carefully on the little side table.

"What are you suggesting?"

"André carried a lot of messages to a lot of people. He knows names and he knows addresses."

"Yes. And that's exactly why others will be very tempted to insure that he will never share that knowledge."

"Colonel," Lauriant's voice had become grave, "tell everyone that you can in the Organization that Letellier has listed every one of them—every name, every address and every message carried—and that he did it before he destroyed each week's schedule in front of your men. If anything . . . untoward . . . should happen to him, you can add, for their information, that there are arrangements in place to make that list available to the authorities and to the newspapers."

"Did he do that? Make a list?" de Troquer asked.

"They," Lauriant concluded, as he made for the door, "and you . . . can never be sure one way or the other. Can you?"

15

A TIME FOR THINKING & REFLECTION

In most cases there comes a time when the investigation reaches a crossroads; a point where the solution becomes obtainable or, alternatively, the crime becomes one of the many added to the list of the unsolved, to be filed away and collect dust on some archive shelf. At that point the criminal gets away with it. Or does he?

Lauriant, although hard put to give a logical explanation for his beliefs, knew instinctively that every murderer, whether brought to justice in a court or not, ultimately paid a price for his crime. It was not a religious belief, not in the conventional sense. Everything in life has its price. Success in one area is paid for by failure in some other.

Murderers who, as they saw it, got away with their crime might spend the rest of their lives looking over their shoulders, never sure of safety. He had heard of murderers giving themselves up decades after the original crime had been forgotten, because they could no longer live with the strain of uncertainty.

Lauriant was convinced that the crucial point had now been reached in the case of the murder of Count Armand. He was certain that he had the information he needed or that it was close to hand. Now, he had to clear his mind and organize his thoughts. Of course he wanted to appease de Bonvalet, but most importantly he needed to satisfy himself.

He pulled the big Citroen off the road at the point which was becoming usual to him on his drives back from Crissay or the Cressons' farm or Pinocheau. This time, after the dust had settled, he got out of the car, leaving the radio playing softly. His hands in his trouser pockets, he walked over the lay-by, turned abruptly, kicked at an errant stone and retraced his steps. His mind was made up. Arms folded belligerently, he sat heavily on the bank.

The flowers had lost some of their color in the last week. Even the poppies had paled from bright crimson to a more somber burgundy and their leaves had been scorched at the edges by the sun.

Lauriant decided in the quiet of this, his private place, that it was time to—he must—look at the facts once more. Maybe, whatever the outcome, to look at them for the last time.

In his thoughts he lined up the suspects, the potential murderers of the old count. It was an old ploy of his: to look each of them in their imaginary face as he reconsidered what they had said and guessed what they had withheld.

It was time for a cigarette.

Of course, if he could not solve the case it would be the innocent who would suffer most. It was always that way. They would constantly be under suspicion, neither guilty nor yet innocent beyond doubt either. What effect could, would that have upon their lives? The villagers would watch them down the years—never sure, making their choices repeatedly: guilty yes, then later, guilty no, then later again, guilty yes. It meant a lifetime of uncertainty and mistrust which was the sort of suspicion that can destroy friendships, families and communities. And Lauriant was rather fond now of this particular community.

With eyes half closed, Lauriant looked across the still waters. Nearby they were dark green, but further out into the main expanse, they appeared pale, cool and inviting. In the drowsy heat, he struggled to keep his thoughts on the case and away from the marais.

As he had just left him, Lauriant decided to begin with Colonel Pierre Alexandre de Troquer.

The colonel was a man who resisted having conditions placed upon his actions. He had said so. But, Lauriant, and life, had imposed conditions. The colonel in the end was no more immune than other men.

From whatever motives, the colonel had made some bad decisions. His days of military and political ambitions—ambitions which, according to Mimi and her contacts, he undoubtedly once had—were over.

But it was somehow hard ever to imagine Colonel Pierre Alexandre de Troquer ever being one of life's losers.

These days, de Troquer was a man looking for a way back from the edge. He was a man looking for a return to the mainstream. His preferred options of the army and government were, however, firmly closed to him. So, he had chosen business . . . investments. Dangerously, it was the OAS's money that he was investing.

Sooner or later, the superintendent was sure, someone would decide to deal with that issue, and that meant with the colonel himself. No matter how careful de Troquer was, guarded by Roland constantly and by Fouquet and Michel Cresson by turns, no man is completely safe.

Lauriant lay back on the bank. He watched the blue cigarette smoke curl away above his head for a moment and then closed his eyes. The sun was warm upon his face.

This planned return to a more normal existence for the colonel, he wondered, was it spoiled, threatened in some way by Count Armand? The ex-soldier had made it perfectly obvious that he strongly disliked the man he called a Fascist. Lauriant had to recognize that fact and fit it into its proper place in the puzzle.

True, de Troquer had specifically said that he did not order the old count's death, but he had also been careful to tell the truth about André Letellier, whilst actually conveying the opposite.

Did the words "I did not order the murder" only mean that "I did it myself"? It was the same form of truth telling as the colonel had practiced before when he said, "I didn't give Max Cresson the money."

Lauriant's second cigarette burned down and he lit a third.

If, after all, the colonel did not order the killing, even

on his peculiar basis of truthfulness, it absolved Roland and Fouquet and it might also absolve Michel—at least as far as the colonel and the OAS controlled him.

But Michel had other motivations, family causes, beyond any that the Organization or the colonel might recognize.

This reasoning brought Lauriant to thinking about Monique Cresson—the girl he had never met and the girl who, it seemed, was a feature at every turn and, yet, still invisible.

Her absence was a worry. That was true. But it was not proof positive of an involvement in the murder. Assuming that she was alive (and the superintendent did assume just that) she may have run from fear or she may have had no choice.

It was a strong possibility that she was taken away, rather than went alone. After all, pretty Josette had said that the girl could not drive and there was a limit on how far she could row in a boat that was still at the farm!

No, Lauriant concluded, to get away, Monique needed help and someone had given it to her.

The real question the detective had to deal with was why she wanted to get away. What was she trying to escape from? The murder scene or at least the area of the murder of Count Armand, which she had previously committed was a strong possibility. If she was not the murderer, what was she trying to escape from?

Duverger's motives of money and marriage were not to be lightly dismissed.

Did Monique see marriage to Count Charles as a viable option? Did she see it as a possible escape from the domination of her father and of her brother? Had Max mistreated her as he had, according to the colonel, mistreated Michel? Was it, more prosaically for Monique, a way to exchange elegant dresses for hitched-up skirts and to substitute expensive perfumes for cheap hastily applied makeup?

The superintendent got up and strolled across the dusty lay-by once more. He shook his head quickly, as if to clear his mind.

On reflection, Monique might have decided on action—been forced into it, perhaps—when she learned of the plans Charles had made with the Sarrazins to abort her baby.

Did she feel that, in the end, she would not have the courage to resist their demands and supplications? Did she think that a talk with the old count would be her best chance of a brighter future . . . and the best chance of survival for her baby?

Did her father and brother, knowing that an abortion would end any possible hold they might have over the old count, make her write the note to Count Armand in Nice, and did the note demand his return to settle the matter—by money or by marriage?

Lauriant wondered whether the Cresson men were incensed that the young count had made the girl pregnant and that he was trying to get out of his responsibilities. It was also possible, of course, that they saw only an opportunity for blackmail. But they did know Charles well enough to guess that he would avoid his responsibilities to Monique given a ghost of a chance. Otherwise, why did they get him to sign that paper promising marriage at gunpoint?

Michel, at least, would have known that the document signed in those circumstances would not stand up in a court, but perhaps they thought it might be enough to trap the old count—a man with an exaggerated sense of family obligations.

Did they want Count Armand's return to right a wrong or did they want him back so that they could broker a deal?

And that led Lauriant to the message and the messenger—the note carrier. For André Letellier, the man who was physically and mentally unable to stand up for himself, was a pivot point in the murder.

He was around Pinocheau on the morning of the day on which the old count's body was discovered. But where had he been during the night before? Not with Josette. André had set off on Sunday evening as usual. Lauriant would need to know where he had been. It was a loose end.

So that was Colonel de Troquer and Monique Cresson.

And what of childlike, empty-headed Amelie Bergman?

The young countess who was, on her own admission and in her own words, devoted to feelings, whatever that could mean. What was her place in this problem?

More broadly, how did this essentially superficial woman fit in with the myriad enthusiasms invented by her own generation, a generation to whom, in many cases, ideals were psychologically vital? A generation which was capable of taking those ideals to the streets in spates of violence and also capable of producing beautiful songs of protest in their frustration and their optimism that they could offer a truly civilized existence to all mankind.

Sadly, it appeared to the detective that she did not fit in at all.

All this had passed Amelie Bergman by. Whilst Nathalie Sarraute and Michel Butor struggled to bring forth the New Novel and Sagan began her svelte explorations of human relationships, Amelie Bergman sat in twilight, a dreamy, fluffy world engendered by the unrealities of romantic fiction, where love always triumphed, bills never arrived and everyone lived happily ever after.

Had the young countess decided at some stage to live out the plot of one of her little novels? If she had done so, what could have been the consequences?

Count Armand, it appeared, was infatuated with her and her essentially undemanding nature. Lauriant thought that it also told him something more, something fundamental about the old count that he should be attracted to a vapid creature like Amelie Bergman—that this inherently self-centered man should even turn his whole life over for her.

So who was this Amelie Bergman, the woman who had

destroyed the comfortable world of the bird-like old countess? A world bordered by the great house at Crissay and by her friends and by L'Ile Bois Aubrand and by its villagers. . . . Like having a part of you—your own past—removed, she had admitted, like a bereavement.

Amelie was from a comfortable and privileged background. She was used to taking holidays in fashionable resorts and living in the grand manner. Her father was a rich industrialist and her mother who had left her and her father for the company of a mediocre actor was an object of loathing. It was Amelie, like the deserted heroine of one of her novels, who swore that her lover would never wrong her.

Amelie Bergman was also the woman who was the object of the puerile affections of Count Charles, another innately weak man with a constant need for buttressing and approval. He had found that in the Sarrazins, who gave it for their own selfish reasons, and, Lauriant was sure, he sensed it in his stepmother. After all, she had admitted that they supported each other in difficult moments.

That consideration added weight to Georges Rocard's theory. The mayor had been right after all: old, rich man and young, attractive wife—it had caused trouble.

Had there been more to it than the old countess thought? Had two essentially banal people found physical attraction in each other? If so, where did that leave Count Armand? In addition, where did it leave the all too obviously intimate relationship between Count Charles and Monique Cresson?

Count Charles and Monique—Monique Cresson! The Cressons: Max and Michel—a father and a son who hated each other. The parallels with Count Armand and his son did not escape Lauriant.

Worse, in both cases money or lack of it was an added element poisoning the relationships.

Had the colonel been right? Was Max not really able to regain control of his much-improved farm simply for lack of money? It was possible that he had found an alternative source of funds. Or, was it only when he was drunk that his brain could fantasize about buying out his son? Was he really worried that in a few weeks he would be without a home, that he would lose the house he had grown up in?

If all or any of that were true, what actions would a man like Max Cresson take?

It was likely to be violent, Lauriant was sure of that. He even felt that it might be indiscriminate violence. But, on balance, the detective thought, Max would have attacked his son—his mind, direct and unsubtle, worked that way. He would not have shot the count, would he? The count had no part in the financial arrangements over the farm. He was not an obvious target on which Max Cresson would take out his frustrations.

Also where, if at all, did the death of Max's own wife fit in? Michel, it seemed, had killed his mother by accident, although almost nobody around L'Ile Bois Aubrand believed that. Except, perhaps, André Letellier, who found it difficult to believe anything bad of a man who liked him.

Also Max and Monique had taken Michel back into the home on his return to the Vendeé. So it was possible that his version of his mother's death was the truth.

Lauriant shook his head. It did not appear to him, as he lit another Chesterfield, that that could be right.

The detective sat quietly on the bank, looking out over the marais, or walking the lay-by and smoking his cigarettes for another hour before he got back into the Citroen and drove off to La Roche sur Yon.

He had decided that his confrontation with the two Cressons and with Count Charles could be put off no longer.

It was time for a proper interrogation.

16

A TIME FOR QUESTIONS & ANSWERS

Lauriant telephoned Mimi, while he waited for little Duverger to return from Crissay with Count Charles.

The inspector, smiling, pleased with life, had been driven off in one of the little Renaults with a feeling that his chief might, at last, be on the right track.

"How is your prisoner?" Lauriant asked Mimi.

"He hasn't been out. He's done everything you asked. Amiable sort of young man really," she replied. "He's restless, though, and not a little frightened."

"You will need to keep him a while longer I'm afraid."

"You haven't found the murderer yet, then?"

"No."

"Are you going to tell me that you are any closer?" she asked.

"I think so."

"Does poor André really have grounds to be frightened?"

Lauriant thought that she sounded very concerned for the young man.

"I've done my best for him, but there are no guarantees," he answered a bit irritably, sensing that Mimi was dissatisfied with his reply. Disappointed in him.

"Do you think that it will take much longer?" she asked.

There was, again, he thought, that slight note of disappointment or disapproval in her voice.

"No. I think it will be over today."

Mimi was relieved. "I worry about you, you know," she said quietly.

"I worry about you too."

"Please, call me when you can."

"As soon as I can."

"I want your word," Lauriant said to the Cresson men, "that if we remove the handcuffs, there will be no violence."

The two men, big and imposing, eyed each other.

"All right," Michel said reluctantly.

Bosquet, who had brought them up from the cells, unlocked the cuffs.

"Well, Max?" the superintendent asked.

Max Cresson held out his hands without answering and, on a nod from Lauriant, the *gendarme* removed his cuffs too, before moving away to stand at the door.

Duverger sat in one corner of the office, looking uncomfortable. Lauriant was sure that, in his position, the little inspector would have made sure that the Cressons could do no more damage. For Duverger, removing their handcuffs would not be an option.

Count Charles, sitting on a third chair opposite the superintendent, looked as uncomfortable as Duverger. His proximity to the Cressons made him likely to be the first object of any violence which might erupt.

Lauriant stood up and slowly paced the room. Now and then there was a flash of unease on his face. It was not that he was worried about the Cressons' fists, his anxiety ran more deeply. He lit a cigarette and threw the pack on the desk in front of the prisoners.

"Help yourselves, boys."

This time the count shook his head, although the superintendent guessed that he must be desperate for a cigarette.

Both Cressons took a Chesterfield and used the lighter from the desktop.

Michel leaned back in his chair like a man content with the world and his lot within it. Lauriant thought it a good attempt at composure.

Max, next to his son, leaned forward, tense and taut, waiting. His dark head, his eyes narrowed and the face still bruised, moved from side to side taking in everything in the room.

"You two sent for Count Armand to return from Nice," Lauriant said to the Cressons.

"That little Letellier talked!" Max scowled at his son. "I told you that he was useless—no guts."

"Why did you send for him?"

Neither man answered.

"Okay. Let me tell you why," Lauriant said. "You wanted him to deal with his son," the superintendent pointed at an increasingly uncomfortable Count Charles. "You wanted him to sort out the problem with Monique."

The detective watched his cigarette smoke for a moment.

"How did you want him to solve it?" he asked.

"We wanted him to make this . . . " Michel gave the young count a look of disgust. ". . . marry her!"

"How did Monique feel about that?"

It was Michel who answered again.

"Oddly enough, she was not too keen," he said, casting another malevolent glance at Charles.

"But you went ahead anyway," Lauriant prompted.

"Yes. I thought that it was the only real option. We even got him to sign a paper promising to marry her."

"But she didn't want to do it. Is that why she ran away?"

Max growled. "She didn't run away," he said firmly, his voice gritty with malice.

Michel added, "He's right. She just went . . . there's a difference."

"Neither of you tried to stop her?"

"No."

"Why?"

Michel shrugged and Max looked at the floor.

"You know that Count Charles planned an abortion for her?" the superintendent asked.

Max looked ready to kill the young count there and then.

"She told me," Michel said simply.

"And did you get her away before that could happen? After all, it would have been the end of your hold over Count Armand, wouldn't it? Or," Lauriant added quietly, "would it have been the beginning?"

"What do you mean?" Michel asked.

"The beginning of blackmail. Count Armand wouldn't want that known around the place."

The superintendent turned to face Count Charles.

"Did you fall in love with your stepmother before or after you began this affair with Monique?"

The superintendent had put the question bluntly, but the abruptness appeared to have no effect on Charles at least. Max Cresson looked startled and Michel murmured, "There! I knew it!"

"Before," the count replied.

"And so, Monique was a kind of substitute for Amelie Bergman."

"It wasn't as straightforward as that," Charles explained inadequately.

"Both women were blonde with good figures!" Lauriant continued. "Were both undemanding too? Perhaps, both were equally . . . compliant, when it came down to it."

Real anger showed in Charles' face.

"You have no right to imply such a thing of Amelie!"

"But every right to say it of Monique," Lauriant said very quietly.

The superintendent looked angry and Michel violently pushed his fist into his palm.

"You worked out some kind of selfish mental juxtaposition between the two women, didn't you?" the detective said, his finger pointed straight at the count's eyes.

The count, instantly calmer now, shrugged as if all

this, although self evident, was of no concern to him.

"Monique was only an object as far as you were concerned—just a compilation of flesh and blood. There was no feeling in it for you, was there?" Lauriant lowered his voice. "It was about as far from love as it's possible to imagine!"

"She didn't complain," the young count replied with a touch of that defiance he had shown on his return from Paris. It did not last long. He cringed away as Michel half rose to his feet. The superintendent was quick to place a restraining hand on his shoulder.

"Did she agree to the abortion?" Lauriant asked.

"She'd have come round to it," Charles said flatly.

"And now, with your father dead and his money—and, perhaps, his wife too—coming to you, you would want a complication like Monique Cresson even less."

"That goes without saying."

Lauriant could feel Michel's anger rising.

"Easy! Easy!" he warned him. "It's also obvious that you would be an even more attractive proposition for the Cressons as a husband for Monique. I say this because, although you two dislike each other," Lauriant turned to the Cressons, "you cooperated when it suited you. You both wanted Count Armand back from Nice! It suited both your purposes!"

"I told you," Michel said, "we wanted him to make sure that his son married my sister."

"Even against her will?"

"Yes! No! Well, not against her will. But I didn't know that then, did I?" Michel added.

"Monique told you that she wasn't willing to marry him," a thumb jerked in the general direction of Charles, "only after you sent for Count Armand to come home. Is that what you are telling me?"

"That's right," Michel said, and Max nodded slowly.

Monique's father was clearly mystified as to why his daughter should refuse to marry all that money.

"It never occurred to you that Count Charles might be genuinely in love with Monique?" the detective suggested.

"Not once!" Michel replied. "He proved me right too—him and his abortion!"

"What about you, Max? Did it occur to you at all that this relationship might just have involved love?"

"What did that have to do with anything?" Max replied irritably.

Once, when his back was turned to them all, Lauriant allowed his face to register the depression that he felt. He was scouting around the edges of the problem, looking for stimulation and finding it only momentarily. One quick question, one short answer and all inspiration slipped away from him once more.

He was getting annoyed with himself—he felt that he was failing, that he should have been more direct, more incisive, more sure of his ground.

Worse, this squalid little relationship between Count Charles and the Cresson girl was beginning to dishearten him. The whole business seemed unspeakably tawdry. He changed the subject.

"What happened when your mother died?"

He stood over Michel, who waited a long time before replying.

"It's time for the truth about that, I suppose."

He sounded resigned.

"Shut up, you swine!" Max shouted.

Michel, breathing heavily, ignored him.

"I took the blame," he said. "It wasn't me, of course, not even accidentally."

"Shut up, damn you!" Max repeated.

"My father was drunk. Something happened, my mother may have said something, I don't know. And he lost his temper—it was always like that. He loaded the gun slowly. Monique was there. She told me. He took deliberate aim and pushed Monique to the floor when she tried to stop him."

"It's a lie! He's a damned liar!" Max hissed. His grip tightened on the arms of the chair. Lauriant saw the blood drain away from his knuckles.

Michel ignored him.

"My mother started laughing. She sounded hysterical. I heard her and ran into the room just in time to see him shoot her."

"So, it was a deliberate act?"

"Yes." Michel turned to his father. Their faces were inches apart. "Yes," he repeated. "It was very deliberate."

Lauriant thought for an instant that Max would strike or at least spit at his son, but the moment passed as Michel slumped back into his chair and stubbed out his cigarette.

The older Cresson was beside himself with anger.

"He did it! And it was no accident," Max snorted, "and it was me who covered up for him, not the other way around. I only pretended it was bad luck—that the gun just went off—but he did it, not me!"

"I took the blame," Michel continued, ignoring his father, "because he would have beaten me, and worse Monique . . . into submission regardless and . . . because I couldn't let people know that my father had killed my mother."

"I see. And that's why you hate him so much, is it?" Lauriant asked, adding, "It's a good reason."

"It's partly that, mostly that . . . but he was no proper father to us when we were children. He would hit us and hit our mother too. I'm ashamed of it. Especially now that I have been away from the village and seen how real men behave. But, at least I did get out. Poor Monique stayed. She had no choice."

"Do you think that this relationship between her and Charles was a way for her to get out—in her mind at least?"

Michel considered this for a moment.

"Maybe. She's probably not thought of it like that, but instinct is a strong thing. She wanted to escape our father."

"And now she has."

"Something like that."

"Where did you take her, Michel?" Lauriant asked calmly.

"I didn't take her," he replied.

Inside, Lauriant cursed himself. He had missed the target again!

"When you left L'Ile Bois Aubrand, you got involved with Colonel de Troquer," the superintendent said.

"He helped me when I needed it," Michel replied.

"And you helped him in return?"

"It was not entirely a one way street."

"Did the colonel come here at your suggestion?" Lauriant prompted.

"He was finished with the army and they were finished with him. He was looking for somewhere with certain . . . characteristics, so I suggested Pinocheau."

"Which fitted the bill," the superintendent nodded. "Simple to watch, not easy to approach unseen, near a village where strangers stand out and are readily spotted . . . those kind of characteristics?"

"Yes. He liked it, so he bought it."

"Using OAS money?"

Michel shrugged. "Probably."

"And he's also been using Organization money to fund Fouquet and to fund you and your improvements at your farm."

"I wouldn't know where his money comes from," Michel said firmly.

Max moved in his seat. "It's not his farm—not yet!" he snarled.

"And Max, where are you going to get the money to stop Michel from kicking you off the farm?" the superintendent asked. "Looking at him, and listening to what he's been saying, Michel's not going to keep you around a minute longer than he has to!"

"I've got plans," Max said darkly, and Lauriant's thoughts went back to the colonel's idea that it might be all bravado.

"Doesn't matter now, in any event," the superintendent said.

Max screwed up his features, trying to work it out.

"Hasn't it sunk into your brain yet, Max? You're not going home at all. You're going back to the cells to await trial for the murder of your wife."

"He did it!" Max sneered at his big son. "You want to arrest him, the swine! Not me!"

"And," Lauriant continued, as if Max had not spoken, "when we find Monique, as soon as she knows that Michel has finally told the truth, she will confirm it. Then, she, at last, will truly have got away from you."

Realization had come to Max now.

"You can't do it! It was him!" he repeated loudly.

He looked furious, then a little short of wild. Like a cornered animal, he resorted to the final argument of violence. His hands clenched into fists and he jumped up to face his son. His right arm shot out, but Michel, still in his chair, moved his head like an expert. The blow met nothing but air, the spent power of it causing Max to stumble clumsily. Before he could recover Lauriant and Bosquet had pushed him back into the chair.

Then Max smiled—a wicked smile. "Anyway, Monique won't talk. She knows better."

17

A TIME FOR DECISIONS & SOLUTIONS

"You were a great frustration to your father."

Lauriant spoke the words quietly to Count Charles. It was a simple statement of fact.

"Really . . . is that sort of comment actually necessary?"

"He knew that you weren't much of a man, all those childish ways you used to get back at him. For what? Was it because he had the woman you wanted or does it go back much further than that?"

Charles turned his head away.

"I'm sure that Amelie Bergman was only another factor. The old count tried to groom you to take over from him and somewhere along the way, pretty early on, I'd guess, he realized that you were going to fail him. Did he tell you to your face? Or, as you hardly were close, did he only show you by his sense of anger?"

"Look, this is family business and nothing to do with you."

"Towards the end, Count Armand must have been difficult for you to live with—to tolerate. You lost your money on the horses. . . ."

Charles looked about to protest, but Lauriant waved him away.

"Let's not have all that nonsense about stocks! Even your own mother knew that it was lost in bad bets! You're so stupid, you couldn't even fool her—the one woman in the world who would have been glad to be fooled for your sake. And you got mixed up with people like the Sarrazins. Your father would have hated that! Did he hate it to the point where he threatened to disinherit you? That would have frightened you. You're too useless to manage on your own, what would you have done?"

"My father would never have cut me out of his will," Charles said.

"Family honor, you think? Passing on the responsibility to the next generation. Maybe he would have decided that in the end he had a higher duty than to throw the work of generations away on you. Perhaps he decided that he would keep the control of the family assets away from you. That's a strong motive for you to kill him, before he carried out his threat!"

"I didn't kill him."

"But you were there in the house!"

"I was dead drunk . . . I didn't do anything . . . I didn't hear anything."

"I think you were drunk, and I also think that you lacked the courage to go to your father's help, that was much more important. You must have heard something. Raised voices or the shot."

"I've told you . . ."

"You only got, as you put it, dead drunk after your father was killed. You drank because you were ashamed—

because you hid upstairs like the coward you are, while your own father was being murdered!"

Lauriant discarded his cigarette.

"I hope, for the peace of his soul, that Count Armand didn't know you were there. After all there was no sign of your car. Now, you detestable little swine, come clean with me, because I've had enough of you and enough of this whole case."

The detective stood in front of the count looking down on him.

"I've got the three of you here. One is already going back to the cells to stand trial for murder and it would make me happy to send you down there with him! You were in the house! You hated your father and you wanted his wife! That sounds good enough for me and it will be good enough for the examining magistrate."

Lauriant went back to his desk and sat down heavily.

"Now the truth!"

"All right! All right!" Charles' voice was raised. "I did hear him come home. I thought he was in Nice. Thought the house would be empty for the abortion! I avoided him by staying in my bedroom. I didn't want to have to face him and another of his harangues about everything I should be and everything that he thinks, thought, I'm not."

"And about Amelie Bergman?"

"That too . . . yes!"

"So, whilst you were playing this little game of hide and seek, what did you hear?"

"I heard voices."

Lauriant looked exasperated.

"Don't make me drag this from you!" he said. It was all he could do to stop himself from shaking his fist at the count.

"Men's voices. Low, not angry. It sounded more like a discussion than an argument. It was a strange time for visitors, but . . . I decided that it was none of my business—"

"So you stayed hidden. Did you recognize the voices?"

"I told you. They were speaking low, almost in whispers. I knew it was my father, but that's all. I couldn't hear what was said. Then, I heard the shot."

"And . . ."

"And I heard my father's dog barking . . . then the damn thing began to whine."

"And?"

Charles was rigid. His eyes were blinking quickly. He swallowed hard.

"And . . . I stayed in my room."

"That was the first time that you'd heard the dog?"

"Yes. My father must have let whoever it was in himself, otherwise the dog would have barked right off . . . he always does."

"That's probable," the detective said. "There was no sign of a forced entry."

Lauriant moved about the room for a few minutes. He slowly rubbed his cheek and then his forehead like a man seeking inspiration.

"So," he said finally, "Count Armand knew his visitor, at least he let him in. At that hour, it must have been an appointment. It had been arranged."

The detective faced Charles.

"How long did you wait before you got up enough courage to come out?"

"About half an hour. I wanted to make sure whoever it was had gone."

"You didn't see or hear a car?"

"No."

"I'd have been surprised if you had."

Charles and the two Cresson men looked at him.

"If I'm right," Lauriant said, "there would have been no need for a car."

"When you finally came down, you saw your father's body."

"Yes."

"What did you do?"

"I knew that he was dead. I sat there for a bit, on the stairs with the dog, and then went and got the cognac from the cabinet. . . ."

"And began drinking yourself almost senseless."

"If you want to put it that way," Charles said. "I was scared. I thought that, as I was the only one left in the house, I'd be arrested . . . everyone would blame me."

"And by the time Paul and Madeleine arrived, you were hardly able to stand."

"Yes. Paul decided that the best thing to do was to clear off."

"And you did, leaving Count Armand's corpse to be discovered by the servants."

Charles' head dropped lower. "We thought . . . Paul thought . . . that I could buy some time that way. To sober up and to get my story straight."

"Sarrazin was too clever a man to let a prize like you slip from his grasp too easily." Lauriant paused and then asked the young count, "Why did you set fire to the carpet?"

Charles looked as if he was about to protest, but he quickly thought better of it.

"I'm not exactly sure now. I was very drunk. I had some idea of a Viking funeral, I think."

"And for this futile, childish gesture you were willing to risk burning down your own home. More importantly, a large part of your own inheritance?"

"I was very drunk," Charles repeated inadequately.

"Are you sure that it was not, as my friend Duverger here believes, a clumsy attempt to cover up the evidence of your crime?"

The little inspector gave a start, apparently not sure that he believed any such thing.

"I did not kill my father," Count Charles replied, trying, but not succeeding in making his voice sound steady and firm.

Lauriant turned back to Max and Michel. Both took the cigarette that he offered to them.

As he lit his Chesterfield for him, the detective noticed that the back of Michel's giant hand was covered in pale ginger hairs. Were they the hands of a killer?

The younger Cresson sat back once more, his blond head tilted towards the ceiling.

Max took his cigarette gratefully, cupping it in an equally massive palm.

Lauriant did not offer a smoke to the count. He had had enough of Count Charles. The detective, seeing his twitching fingers, decided to let the count suffer.

"Two things only need to be cleared up now," Lauriant said to the Cressons. "First, the appointment which led to Count Armand's death—it must have been arranged by you in the note André delivered to Nice. There was no other way. Which one of you wrote the letter?"

"I did," Michel said.

"So you arranged to meet the old count!"

Michel immediately realized the implications of his admission.

"No! I didn't!" he said quickly. "I just wrote down the situation for him . . . about Monique and said that we, the three of us—him, me and Max—would have to decide what to do. About how to get Charles to marry my sister, and pretty quick too! It's not Paris down here, you know. In Paris these days, anything will do! People are having sex all over the place. . . ." Lauriant was surprised at the note of old fashioned disgust in his voice. "And sleeping around. Well, here it's not like that—rock and roll music and girls in short skirts throwing themselves at any man who passes by!"

Lauriant recalled Josette's depiction of Monique's trips down the marais, of her quickly applied amateur makeup and her hitched-up skirts. He felt sorry for the girl.

"This is good Catholic country!" Michel went on. "We needed Monique married off before, well, before things showed too obviously," he finished.

"Except that she didn't agree," Lauriant said. "That must have been a problem. She knew our count here a bit too well by the look of things! He may not have wanted, as he told me, to be stuck with Monique for the rest of his life and she, with much more reason, I think, didn't want any further part of him."

There was a stifled protest from Charles.

"Shut up!" Lauriant said brutally. "Look, Michel, you had to have made the appointment. There's no other alternative."

The younger Cresson looked confused. He struggled, but could find no answer.

"I don't know how it was done," he said quietly, "but, believe me, I didn't have any part in it."

"Where's the gun, Michel?"

Michel lowered his head.

"Come on," the detective continued, "everyone involved with de Troquer had a nine millimeter gun. It was standard issue in his army. Are you going to tell me that you were the only one of his . . . helpers, who didn't have one?"

"It's missing," Michel said.

"So you got rid of it after the murder! It would damn you if it were found. We would know that it was the murder weapon—and it's damned you too because it's missing. Unless you killed Count Armand, you would have no reason to dispose of the gun!"

"I didn't dispose of it! It's just missing!"

"Like Monique!"

Lauriant sat down again. This was getting on his nerves. He knew that he was close, but he also knew that he was getting something wrong. It was another of those little irksome things, like Madeleine Sarrazin's vice squad arrest and André Letellier's number plates . . . but what was it?

It was thinking about André, safe for the moment with Mimi in Saint Sauveur, that cleared his thoughts. Lauriant knew that he was, at last, on the right track.

"What else did you put in the envelope for Count Armand?"

The detective asked the question of Max Cresson.

"I've nothing to say. You've got the killer," Max said looking at Michel, "There he is. If he could kill his own mother, murdering the count would have been child's play. Working for that colonel, he's probably done it before!"

Lauriant stood in front of Max.

"André said that when you sealed the envelope, you turned your back on him. He thought that you wanted to make sure that he couldn't see what was inside."

"So what?"

"That wasn't it, though. You really didn't want your son to see you put a second note in the envelope . . . the note where you arranged your fatal meeting with Count Armand!"

Lauriant was very quiet for a few seconds.

"You wanted money to buy back your farm, and to keep Michel from throwing you out. You couldn't get it from any normal source and hardly from the colonel. That only left Count Armand. You probably thought about putting pressure on Count Charles first, but that fool had lost any money you could have squeezed out of him. Blackmailing Charles over Monique would have been a waste of time, but his father, with that enlarged sense of family honor, that was much more promising!"

"Michel did it!" Max growled.

"You met Count Armand as arranged at Crissay in the middle of the night, at a time when no one else would be around. Charles turning up was unfortunate, but in the end it didn't matter. He was too scared to get in the way. You showed the old count the paper promising to marry Monique that his son had signed. He laughed at the idea and probably told you that the paper would not be accepted by a court. But that wasn't your game. You didn't care about your daughter, you only thought of yourself."

"Prove it! Any of it!" Max spat out.

"Your idea, Max, was better than that. By now, you might have realized that Monique wasn't going to marry him after all. She'd seen in the magazines that there were girls who were mothers without husbands these days. She was brave enough to want to be a part of that new world, not stuck on the farm or buried at Crissay, while her husband made drooling eyes at his stepmother and ignored her completely."

"I don't know what you're talking about."

"Yes you do! You were going to blackmail the old count using the paper. Not into having Charles's marry your daughter, but into giving you the money to buy out your son. And, like Michel, you were running out of time. Michel wanted his sister married off in short order and you needed to beat the deadline in the contract of sale!"

"You have no proof!" Max repeated.

"But it didn't work. The count told you, no doubt in no uncertain terms, that he was not going to pay up. I think that he pocketed the paper Charles had signed, turned his back on you, and walked down the stairs to open the door. Then you got really angry. The farm was slipping away, your last hope was vanishing, and you shot Count Armand in the back like the coward you are!"

"Where's the proof? No one can even give evidence that I was at Crissay!"

"But, Max, you were not so angry that you didn't keep your wits about you. You went through the dead man's pockets and took everything, including the incriminating paper."

"Prove it!" Max demanded.

"On the way back to the farm, you disposed of Michel's gun. You had to take his gun, as the old count would hardly carry on a late night conversation with you, if you turned up with your own shotgun, which was too big to conceal. If you didn't intend to kill, why take Michel's gun at all? What did you do with it, Max? Threw it in the marais, is my guess."

"I've nothing to say."

"Let me have him for ten minutes," Michel said calmly, "I'll make him talk."

The heat had suddenly become even more oppressive. Lauriant wiped his forehead. "No need," he said. "We'll find the gun or the note he scribbled to Count Armand. Either would do."

Max looked triumphant.

"No you won't!"

"Why are you so sure, Max? Because you took it from the dead man's pockets with the rest of the stuff?"

Max Cresson shrugged and laughed. As his head went back and his mouth opened, Michel's fist caught him full in the face. He jerked backwards. This time Lauriant and Bosquet, the *gendarme*, were not quite fast enough. Max slipped unconscious to the floor. Lauriant tried to get between father and son, but was too late again. Michel kicked the prostrate form.

"That's enough!" Lauriant ordered.

Bosquet pulled Michel back with almost no difficulty. His anger was spent now.

After a moment or two, Michel turned to the detective.

"Can you prove it?" he asked Lauriant.

"Only if André Letellier tells the truth about opening the envelope," the detective replied. "He's lied to me about it once already."

"He'll tell me, if I ask him," Michel said.

18

A TIME FOR CHANGES

André Letellier returned to L'Ile Bois Aubrand in the Peugeot 204 a few days later.

Lauriant did not inquire about his reception by Josette.

Afterwards, Michel Cresson met Lauriant at the little bistro opposite police headquarters in La Roche sur Yon. They sat at one of the pavement tables, elbows resting on the checkered cloth.

With Michel came an unexpected partner. The old countess.

This day, Cresson had with him another paper—one which had not needed a shotgun to obtain the signature. It was properly witnessed and signed by André.

"He did open it," Michel began, his huge hand wrapped around his beer.

"I knew it!" Lauriant said.

"But," Cresson continued, "he was too frightened to admit to it and, of course, he didn't think of removing the second letter. How was he to know what it implied or what it would lead to?"

Lauriant closed his eyes and put his hand to his face, fingertips rubbing his forehead. André, it seemed, would continue to disappoint him.

"And afterwards," Michel added, "André kept quiet, because he was worried, perhaps even certain that I did it."

The superintendent lit a cigarette as the countess sipped at her aperitif with her habitual bird-like movements, looking from one man to the other.

"Have you spoken to Colonel de Troquer, yet?" Lauriant asked Cresson.

"He's taken things very well, I think. I don't believe that he will be bothered about André."

Michel shook his head slowly and Lauriant wondered what could have triggered the movement.

"He can be a strange man, the colonel," Cresson added. "For some reason, he told Roland to give André the Peugeot. Now, why on earth would he do that?"

The detective smiled a little, but ignored the question.

"So, with a new car and a new cover story, someone else is doing the rounds now," Lauriant said.

"I wouldn't know," Michel responded quickly, closing down that line of conversation immediately.

After another drink of his beer, he added, "The colonel says that you're all right, but . . . you are a policeman after all."

"Can't help that!" the superintendent said. "Often I feel a bit stuck with it. It's hard to forget the job. But ignore that for now."

Michel relaxed as he drank down the rest of his beer.

"Has Max . . . my father . . . said anything? You know, admitted it?" he asked.

"No. But, he doesn't need to now."

Lauriant leaned back in his chair and let the sunshine warm his face.

"Tell me," he said almost lazily, "where did André take Monique? I know that that's what he was doing during the night of the murder."

Michel remained silent.

"Oh! Come on! It had to be him," Lauriant continued. "Monique wasn't in the back of Jacquot's Berliet and by the time the colonel had sent Fouquet to the farm to warn off Max, she was already gone."

Michel turned to the little countess, who replied for him.

"André brought her to me, of course, in St. Jean de Monts." After a tiny sip of her drink, she asked simply, "Where else would the mother of my future grandchild go?"

Lauriant, remembering his meeting with her added, "And that's why you kept me out of the house and why we went strolling around St. Jean de Monts like tourists." Lauriant looked at his drink and observed ruefully. "Families, secret worlds and closed societies. We all have them, live in them somehow, do we not?"

They drank in sunny silence for a few minutes.

"Are you staying on at Crissay?" the detective asked the countess eventually.

"Yes, for the moment at least. Amelie and I have come to an understanding."

"Oh?"

"We think that it will take both of us to do the job."

"I see."

"I'm sure that you do," the countess said to Lauriant, ignoring the puzzled Michel, who clearly did not see.

The countess laughed loudly and Lauriant found himself joining in, whilst Michel, still mystified, looked uncomfortably around at the occupants of the other tables.

"For this generation," the countess said, recovering herself a little and wiping a laughter tear from her eye, "the continuance of the family's history will, for once, reside in the hands of a woman—two women to be absolutely precise. We thought that it would be safer that way."

"I'm sure that you're right."

"It really seems that it is a time for changes," the countess concluded.

"Changes? Yes, but what about Count Charles?" Lauriant asked.

"He is somewhat . . . chastened now. Monique, naturally, won't have him, I won't let him near the money and Amelie seems to have more sense than I gave her credit for. She won't marry him either!"

The countess took another, larger, sip at her drink.

"Also, I have dealt with the Sarrazins," she added, as if they were an irritation easily mastered.

The superintendent was even more impressed.

"A friend, her name is Mimi, recently told me something about really interesting men," Lauriant observed dryly and then added, "but, you, countess, are a quite remarkable woman."

She gave him a quick smile.

"We both have something to thank you for," she said thoughtfully. "I am back at Crissay where I belong, and Michel has his farm and the suspicion that he killed his own mother lifted from his shoulders."

Lauriant, for once in his life almost contented with his own performance, smiled back at her, raised his hands and opened his palms upwards.

Judge de Bonvalet came as close as he ever did these days to a smile.

Lauriant sat opposite him in his opulent office on one of the Second Empire chairs. The detective looked uncomfortable and out of place.

"I congratulate you," de Bonvalet said.

"Thank you, *Monsieur le juge*."

The superintendent tried hard not to look embarrassed.

"You've done a good job . . . from all points of view," the examining magistrate informed him.

Lauriant hesitated. "I was only interested in one point of view," he said.

"Of course. But you can't block out reality, any more than de Troquer can! From his conduct, it appears that even he has at last recognized the way the world is going. After all, from my own careful observations," he paused before adding quickly, "and, naturally, from your own report," a manicured hand nudged at the dossier on his desk, "it seems that the colonel has done almost everything we could have wanted from him."

"We?" Lauriant asked.

"You must realize that his behavior—particularly towards you and your activities—was of the greatest importance for his future, and also significant to those of us interested in such things."

"Those of us?"

It was de Bonvalet's turn to look uncomfortable. He coughed.

"Of course, your efforts and your conduct have not gone unnoticed, you know."

He had twice emphasized the "your".

"Thank you again, *Monsieur le juge*."

De Bonvalet momentarily had the uncomfortable feeling that this interview was not to go entirely as he had planned.

"There are those who would be pleased to see you back at police headquarters in Paris, back where you belong," he continued.

"Are they the same people who were pleased to send me to the Vendeé last year?" Lauriant asked spitefully.

"That attitude is not helpful."

"I know. I'm sorry."

De Bonvalet took a deep breath.

"I am authorized to offer you your old position in Paris once more," he said.

"I'm grateful for the offer."

De Bonvalet frowned. It was not quite the answer that he had expected.

"When would they want me to leave here?" Lauriant asked.

"As soon as you're ready."

"I'll think it over."

"I don't understand," the examining magistrate said flatly.

"I know," Lauriant repeated, standing up and offering his hand to the judge. "Maybe I don't really understand myself. But I will think it over."

Mimi telephoned again that evening.

Lauriant was with Duverger in the Letellier's bar leaning on the counter with a second cold beer.

Josette had been particularly attentive all night, and André had tried to avoid talking to him at all.

That, the detective consoled himself, was entirely the right way around.

Nevertheless Lauriant had a sort of strange foreboding when Josette called him to take the call. It was almost a premonition. Perhaps, it was something in her pretty face—a warning or. . . .

"Hello?"

There was a pause and, when Mimi began to speak, there was a terrible break in her voice.

"Thank God I've found you," she said.

Lauriant was sure that she was crying.

"What's wrong?" he asked her quickly.

"Alain," she sobbed, "he's died."

Her voice faded and he asked anxiously, "Are you still there?"

"Died," she repeated. "In his sleep. One second he was alive and another second. . . ."

Her cracked voice trailed away again.

"I'm coming," he said simply.

Lauriant, hand trembling, put down the telephone.

"Have another?" a surprised Duverger called after him, as he walked past the inspector and out of the bar.

Josette looked at his hunched back. He almost tumbled into the street.

Outside, Lauriant straightened himself up in an effort, which she knew instinctively was massive, and walked on into the darkness.

Pretty, clever Josette Letellier was somehow sure that it was the last time that she would ever see him.